RESCUE SHE

A NOVEL

KARA LIANE

Cover design by Alyne Hart. Cover images by Lindee Robinson Photography. Cover models Jeremy Moser and Rashontae Wawrzyniak.
Clipart chapter images by Pixabay.com.
Author logo designed by the author through Canva.com.
Edited by Mountains Wanted Indie Author Services.

ISBN-13: 978-0-578-21408-5

Disclaimer: This book is intended for an adult audience. This work of fiction contains strong language and explicit sexual scenes, with mature content, that may not be appropriate for anyone under the age of eighteen.

Also By Kara Liane

***

A Tryst of Fate Series:

Playing Heart to Get—Book 1
Every Heart Inch—Novella 1
A Force of Nature—Book 2
Heart to Follow—Novella 2
Nursing Myself Back—Book 3

***

Standalones:

Combat Boots & Candy Canes

***

Stay connected with Kara Liane by visiting her web site:
www.karaliane.com

Dedication

To all the heroes out there who are first responders: this one's for you! Thanks for keeping us safe and for rescuing us when duty calls. Know that you're appreciated.

Once again, another book was inspired by my husband. Not only is he serving on active duty in the military, but he's also a volunteer firefighter and EMT.

Matt, you continue to amaze me. You're my hero. You're my everything!

Table of Contents

Epigraph

If love is like fire, then I'll get burned.
My body will be consumed, my soul engulfed.
If love is like a key, then I'll be turned.
My heart will be locked up, my innocence devoured.
If love is like fire, then I'll be ash.
—K. L.

Prologue

Olivia

Spring 2002

"Will you be going to the senior prom?" I ask my crush.

Trying not to be obvious about inhaling his masculine cologne, I stand before him with wide, pleading eyes, shivering with anticipation as I await his answer. My heart is beating erratically—it's also calling out to him to say *yes*. I don't think he's invited anyone else, so there's hope.

Prom is only two weeks away. I've waited until the end of the school day to work up the courage to ask, but the clock is ticking and time is running out.

"Uh, no, sorry, I don't like to dance," he simply states.

That's it?

He suddenly white-knuckles the hell out of the bookbag strap slung over his shoulder.

Acting nonchalant, I pretend to be unaffected by his answer, but of course, I'm disappointed. I decide to play it off anyway.

"Well, you don't have to dance, silly. You can just come and hang out…with me."

Swallowing my nerves, I had to go for it. I had to ask. Once and for all, I had to know if he felt *something* for me—friendship or attraction; I'd take either. The organ in my chest still flutters frantically, and my belly tightens, willing him to put me out of my misery.

His face puckers as if he's eaten something sour, and I realize I have my answer in *that* look. This was my last-ditch effort to get him to notice me before school ends. He moved here last year, and I've been waiting for him to ask me out. There are times I've felt his stare across the room and thought, *this is it, he's finally going to ask me!* Only to be let down.

Crush is too tame of a word. *Infatuation* fits the bill. However, it's not some mindless fantasy I've built up in my head. I feel something for him as a person—there's an unspoken connection we share, or so I thought. And I don't care if no one else would understand it. I don't care if everyone thinks I'm a stupid girl for wanting a boy who clearly doesn't want me. My feelings are the ones on the line here.

"Okay, well, that's a shame you're not going," I convey, running my fingers through my wavy hair to distract myself from the tears forming at the backs of my eyes.

My heart is retreating back to its cave to hibernate. I'm a glutton for punishment at this point as I try one more tactic to get close to him.

"I decided I'm going to start volunteering at that animal shelter you're always at." I attempt to smile, and hope fills my veins once again.

It's not a selfish motivation to volunteer at the shelter. I genuinely want to give back to the community. The perk would be seeing *him*. He winces, and I wonder if he doesn't want to be anywhere near me and hates the idea I just proposed.

I'm not a pariah! I scream in my head. This gorgeous boy probably thinks I'm a stalker.

"Uh, I had to stop working there. I'm attending fire training to be a junior firefighter. When I turn eighteen, I can be fully certified." He looks deeply into my eyes, trying to communicate some sort of message—it's lost on me, though.

He has a big heart—volunteering whenever he can. A selfless individual. It's one of the many things I adore him for. I will not sniff the air again to breathe in his cologne because it will destroy me. Although, that scent is forever burned into my brain anyway.

"Oh, that's cool," I try to sound upbeat because it is cool what he's doing. I just wish I'd see him.

He readjusts the strap and rubs the back of his neck. As his arm comes up, I notice a large, angry, purple-bluish bruise. I don't comment. *Poor guy, it looks painful.* He must do a lot of chores or something around the house to get bruises like that. It's not the first one I've seen on him, and I know he doesn't play sports—believe me, if he did, I would be the first to know and cheer him on from the sidelines.

"Listen, I need to get home or I'll…," he trails off then squares his shoulders. "I gotta go. I'll see you around," he says firmly.

God, it's not *that* big of a campus. I see him every school day, but he makes it seem like we should be total strangers.

"Okay," is all I reply.

At that, he walks away. I have this sinking feeling I'm going to have to put thoughts of Weston Thorpe out of my mind—lock them up and throw away the key.

We're not meant to be together in this lifetime.

Chapter 1: When Duty Calls

Weston

August 2018

"Hell yeah, another call in the bag, brother," my best friend—or, for all intents and purposes, brother—Grant Denton remarks and gives me a high five.

"What're we up to this week? Like five or six saves, I think, right?" I wipe my brow from the humidity as we're on decontamination duty, cleaning the ambulance.

It's like one-hundred degrees in this box. After we pulled back into the fire station, the first thing we were obligated to do is decon the apparatus. Our fleet of vehicles—whether it be an ambulance, a water tender truck, or firetruck—are all referred to as an *apparatus*.

Grant hops out of the back to retrieve more cleaning supplies while our probie Ethan helps me to continue to wipe everything down. Ethan's a good kid. Young, wet behind the ears, but he may get there the harder he trains, and through observation.

He cocks his head and stops cleaning the wall to ask me, "Is it always gonna to be like this with patients?"

My lips twitch because this rookie has no idea what he's in for, so I apprise him of the situation. "Yeah, pretty much. You'll see some shit as time goes on. Lately, we've had to revive patients left and right with naloxone spray, hence why we dub them our latest *saves*."

The opioid epidemic has hit our town of Pineville, New Jersey, severely. Ethan can't assist during a medical call, but he can drive the ambulance for us so Grant and I can perform our duties.

He nods his head contemplating my words, "So, how long have you been doing this?"

"I've been a firefighter for seventeen years, and an EMT for fifteen—I'm dual-certified, which is a requirement by our chief. Now that you're done the fire academy, I'm sure he'll be hounding you to go to EMT school if you want a future here."

Rubbing at a stubborn spot on the floor from remnants of vomit, I further explain, "Calls these days tend to be more medical-related; otherwise, we don't see a lot of action. There are occasions when the pager goes off, and you're surprised it's a fire call. I do prefer firefighting duties, but if that's your preference too, you'll need to move to a bigger city if you want more action."

He shakes his head indicating he has no intention of seeing more action.

At our firehouse, we're Pineville Task Force 21. When we man the station, we can either answer calls going out on the ambulance or the firetruck; it depends on what the situation entails. Central Dispatch has one of the hardest jobs since they guarantee all grids have coverage. Hell, we've even had to pull in crews from Pennsylvania, or we've been called into that state since all companies sometimes need to be in service—this happened during September 11th.

Exciting times always await us, with emergencies coming from a plethora of sources. There are motor vehicle accidents involving extrications, car fires, structure fires, downed wires, forest fires, and the list goes on. It's what we call *Jobtown*. When that term is thrown around, it means we have a good call, or a lot of calls in one day. However, sometimes we get *recalled* if we're not needed to respond.

Grant jumps up in the back to join us as if he never left, and chimes in. "Yeah, man, I think we're at six saves with this last one. Let's hope that's it for this week. Fuck, let's hope that's it even for today," he replies, his frustration mirroring my own.

Blowing out an exasperated breath is relaxing—it's intense on an assignment. I know we both live for helping people, but it sucks ass when some individuals won't help themselves—like with this current heroin problem.

Ethan gets that look again wanting answers to his burning questions. With the number of trainees who have come through our station since I joined, I'm used to this.

"Why'd you want to become a firefighter?" Ethan eyes both of us when he asks.

"Ah, shit Probie, don't go making this into a bonding moment," Grant teases and then starts taking inventory of the supplies.

Feeling compelled to answer the kid, I offer him my honest response. "I've always liked helping people—it's in my nature. With my shitty upbringing—which is putting it mildly—I've felt driven to do some right in the world. By shining some light out there even when there's so much darkness and things seem bleak, it tends to keep bad things at bay; there still needs to be some good deeds no matter what. At seventeen, I went to the academy and never looked back. I didn't find firefighting, it found me."

Grant turns slowly toward me and raises his brows. It's because my best friend is surprised I'm getting personal in this conversation—to someone I barely know, and to a rookie no less.

The tables need to be turned on the kid, so I ask Ethan, "Why'd you sign up?"

"Well, my dad's a retired NYFD member, and I'm a legacy—so I'm told. I guess I'll see how it goes."

He doesn't appear to be confident. This is one of those moments I want to take him under my wing, but I also want to make him realize if it's not for him, then he shouldn't venture down this road.

"Just because it's in your blood doesn't mean it's in your veins," I remind him.

"That's some deep, philosophical shit right there, man," Grant comments.

"I admit I'm a little scared to go into a structural fire. I guess I'm being a pussy," Ethan says sheepishly.

Grant and I look at one another because as much as we joke around, give everyone hell, and banter back and forth, we're still a team here and a family. This rookie better settle in for story time.

"No one's a pussy in fighting a fire. It's natural to have reservations. For me, I've wanted to make a difference in this world since a young age. Working at this firehouse, I found my calling. But that doesn't mean I don't get scared at times—for myself, my team, and for the victims involved."

"It just seems like you guys are tight knit, and that's hard to come into, ya know?" Ethan grimaces.

"Having a brotherhood here is important. Grant and I met during EMT school. We were in the same study group. We ended up getting hired here even though he lived forty minutes away at the time."

Pausing for a moment, I set the canister of wipes down and sit on the hard metal of the ambulance floor, wishing it was cool to the touch—no such luck. I don't know if Ethan's going to cut it in this field or not—time will tell. Yet, I'll make the effort to help him decide if it's right or wrong.

"Look Probie, we all have different purposes. However, here it's a family unit on our squad. My family situation wasn't ideal, and my goal was to move out of my parents' house as soon as I could. I got an apartment with Grant. We lived together up until about five years ago when we both realized we needed our own space because he's a damn slob, and I'm not."

"Hey!" Grant yells in protest.

"All joking aside, Grant's my brother. He literally saved my life before, but I have yet to return the favor; maybe one day I will."

"How'd he save your life?" Ethan wonders, evidently astonished by this news.

"It was about two years ago in a neighboring town. We were called in to fight a three-story house fire. I fell through the roof. I should've known better, but hey, we all make mistakes. The crew working below us thought they had the flames contained. There was miscommunication from Command. Grant and I were venting up top. They had to evacuate below us when the solar panels started falling through, and consequently, the fire got out of hand. We were still on the roof, and it all happened so fast."

"It was a bad scene," Grant whispers and stares off into space as if reliving it.

"All I can tell you Ethan is you might think you're protected by your turnout gear, but you never know how unprotected and vulnerable you are until you're about to be barbequed. I was hanging by a rafter when my air pack got snagged by the strap. The strap and Grant were my saving grace—I have that strap mounted to my locker door to remind me not to repeat past mistakes."

I run my hand over my head to remove more sweat and finish my story. "Luckily, Grant was able to pull me up using his pickhead axe, and he had a secure anchoring to the structure. We immediately hauled ass off the roof as the fire raged out of control; there was no fighting it at that point. None of us were able to save the dwelling."

I walked away with no injuries, except a bruised ego. We can laugh about it now, and I make sure any probies coming to the station know the story for the express purpose of learning to ensure it's secure below before you go up top—words of wisdom to live by. Rookie errors are made—it's practically a rite of passage. Probies pack hoses wrong, accidentally strap their air packs into the seatbelt and get hung up, forget a piece of equipment or their gear, and get cocky, thinking they're invincible.

So I can resume my duties, I pick up the wipes and finish scrubbing. After a few minutes, Ethan talks once more.

"Ya know, my girlfriend Olivia is just worried this isn't the career for me, but I gotta make my dad happy I guess."

I grip the bottle of wipes—so hard the plastic is cracking beneath my hands. "What'd you say your girlfriend's name is?" *Did I hear him right?*

"Lydia. Her name's Lydia." *Oh, I thought… Never mind,* I tell myself.

Two things hit me at once: the shock over the misheard name, and knowing how Ethan is trying to make his dad happy. I swallow, my mouth suddenly dry, and loosen my grip on the plastic container.

"You'll make it here if you want to make it, Ethan," I tell him in a serious tone.

He gulps and then nods. Suddenly, the wall has become very interesting to him as he turns and focuses on scouring the surface vigorously. I'll let him digest all the information I've imparted this afternoon.

"Pick up the pace, man; I'm almost done with my side," Grant rubs it in.

"Yeah, yeah, yeah." I bump him in the shoulder with my fist to warn him to shut the fuck up. That's how it is with us two. Life would be boring if he weren't in it, though.

Jesus, I have tons of stories. We may not see a lot of action in Pineville, but there's enough to write a book about.

Chapter 2: Below the Surface

Weston

After we finished our decon duties, we had sent Ethan inside to do more cleaning—another rite of passage.

Grant and I decide to sit outside the station. We climb on top of the picnic table and plant our feet on the bench seat, then look out across the lake that's next to our facility. The water is beautiful. It's hot as balls, but it doesn't take away from the sparkling blue pool, the pine trees surrounding the sandy perimeter, or the mallards lazily dipping their beaks below the surface.

I never expected to move to this place in my junior year of high school and call it home. My dad got fired from his job as a truck driver. At the time, we were living in north Jersey. He moved us to the southern part of the state hoping there were more job opportunities and a lower cost of living; however, there wasn't anything available for someone like him. Shit got really bad after that. It was bad before, but that's when everything changed in my life once we moved here.

His depression led him down a dark path he couldn't come back from. My old man has a vicious temper and an unforgiving right hook—I would know, considering I've been on the receiving end of that hell more times than I care to recount. I endured the beatings myself so my mom and little sister wouldn't be subjected to them—I'm no hero, though.

"You okay, man? You seem kinda off today. It's not like you to be so talkative to a trainee."

My best friend doesn't miss a thing with my change in mood, so I tell him, "Yeah, just got a lot on my mind, I guess."

Somehow he knows I'm thinking about my family history and when I start dwelling on the past, it's hard to bring me back to the present.

"Get that shit outta your head, brother. It's not good to go there." *Boy, don't I know it.*

We stare out at the water again and stay silent for a bit.

How my father ever agreed to let me do the junior firefighting program I'll never know, especially since I was barely allowed to do anything while I was under his thumb. Doesn't matter how or why, I'm just grateful it worked out in that regard.

Retreating back in time again, I think of how sixteen years ago, there was one shining light in my life. Sighing, I can hardly bring myself— even to this day—to say *her* name. When I misunderstood the name Ethan said, it was a direct hit to my heart. It stings like a son of a bitch even now. Never would I have believed in love at first sight had I not experienced it at seventeen. That sort of thing is reserved for movies, yet she did exist, and thoughts of her got me through each damn day.

Back then, I admired the caramel-colored, wavy-haired goddess from across the way. My eyes and attention were always on her whenever we had lunch or class together. I'm lucky I managed to graduate because she penetrated every ridge of my brain with her eyes, smile, curves, and spunk. I pretended not to be interested, and fuck me, I tried to resist her! I almost had a moment of weakness and was going to ask her to prom. She actually ended up asking me, and I shot her down. Shit, it hurt to look into her eyes and refuse her.

There's no way I could bring her into my universe of pain and torment—everything to do with me was grossly infected by the hand of my father. If he had found out about *her*, he would've made it his life's mission to destroy her. He used everything I loved against me, and she would've been my biggest downfall. I couldn't let that happen.

His favorite thing to say to me repeatedly was, *You ruin everything in your path like a hurricane of destruction.* Saving her from the nightmarish world that consumed my life was imperative. So, I had to let her go…

"You're staring at the water like you wanna make out with it or something," Grant verbally jibes, trying to pull me from my broodiness. Leave it to him to always crack a joke.

Damn, my head isn't in the game. I shake it back and forth to clear it because our shift isn't quite over yet, and I still have a job to do. I can't go down this rabbit hole of darkness. Fuck, dredging up old memories does nothing but put me in a foul mood, and I don't ever want to act like my sperm-donor-asshole-father. *I need to get my head on straight.*

Ethan walks up to us providing a necessary interruption. He looks worse for the wear. "I'm all done mopping inside," he pants.

"Great, thanks. You did a good job today, Probie. We're proud of you." As I stand up from the table, I square my shoulders and look Ethan directly in the eye. "Can I give you one last tidbit of information while I'm at it?"

"Sure!" He says while shrugging his shoulders.

"Just so you know, I'd take that roof scenario any day over being subject to a flashover—you're automatic toast in that situation. One thing we try to educate the public about, in terms of fire safety, is to not further supply the fire. Oxygen feeds the beast, and those infernos are nasty motherfuckers when they've been fed to the point they devour everything. You probably heard this spiel in school, but I'm telling you now it's one of the single most important pieces of information: Don't feed the fire!"

"You got it, Lieutenant. I won't forget," he promises.

Satisfied with his response, we dismiss him for the day. The next shift should be coming on soon. Grant and I will have to go out for drinks tonight and unwind after this long-ass week. Revisiting the past takes its toll on my psyche, and I need a way to let loose and escape. Neither one of us are on duty this evening. We just pulled a twenty-four hour shift, so we have forty-eight hours off—we're in desperate need of a break. Blowing off some steam is on the menu, and it wouldn't hurt to have some female company to distract me.

It shouldn't be a surprise to anyone that ladies' panties drop pretty easily when you're a firefighter, especially when you take care of yourself. Grant and I hit the gym hard and keep in shape. There are lots of guys in the field who don't concern themselves with health, but those are usually the volunteer members. Heart attacks are a killer in this industry for those who don't suit-up enough.

"We're going out tonight, right?" Grant arches a brow my way as if reading my damn mind.

"You read my mind." I surreptitiously smile to myself—we're both on the same page for tonight.

Some good drinks and some pretty ladies will do the trick. I can get the reprieve I so urgently need from wondering once again where *she* is out there in the world today.

Chapter 3: Tunnel Vision

Weston

"Ever been in love, hero?" the buxom blonde standing before my bar stool asks.

Her eyes glisten as I return her gaze in challenge with my own predatory stare. She trails a manicured nail down the front of my black, fitted shirt, then casually rests her hand on my jean-clad thigh. She sought me out. As soon as Grant stepped away to dance with some twenty-something, she strutted right over here. This girl is ready to party.

"Mmm," she groans as her mouth vibrates with desire.

As I've said, I don't need the *hero* title she just gave me. But, there's no missing the fact that I'm a firefighter and EMT—even without the uniform. On the right bicep, I have a huge black, gray, and red tattoo of a kneeling firefighter in supplication with an axe in hand, wearing an oxygen mask. On the left bicep, I have the traditional EMT emblem in blue. It consists of the six-pointed star, and in the middle is a serpent wrapped around the rod, which denotes the medical field and derives from a story of a Greek deity.

This chick plays the flirting game well as she runs that long, pink fingernail around the outline of my tats. She lowers her lashes and bites her lip. In true contemplation, I begin rubbing at the scruff on my chin, which boasts only a slight shadow from stubble. Since I never know when I'll get a call during duty hours, my face must be clean-shaven in order for my mask to fit properly.

The blonde continues to look me up and down while licking her lips. My colorful tattoos make it easy for women to know what I'm about—

of course, that's not why I have them. The tats effectively cover up old bruises, scars, and memories that were left in my father's wake. Grant knows about my past; however, it's not something I share with the ladies who occupy my bed from time to time.

It's been fourteen years since Grant helped me console two of the women I treasure most in the world—my mother and sister. My best friend showed up after I had fought tooth and nail with my old man; it was the last time I ever laid eyes on Dallas Thorpe. The piece of shit went to prison for going after me, my mom, and my sister Malory—Mal was nine at the time.

The devil himself was paroled for good behavior, though, after serving only four years of his ten-year sentence. Thank the Almighty, none of us have heard from him since—I plan to keep it that way. His sentence wasn't long enough. The attempted murder charges didn't stick, and they could only get him on some felony charges like assault and battery. Although, in our state, it's aggravated assault, which is a second degree crime. What happens in actual court is never how it's portrayed on those popular TV crime shows, so we were shocked at the way everything went down.

"I like this one the most. So, *yes* or *no* to love?" The woman murmurs while still touching my bicep of the kneeling firefighter.

She chuckles at my apparent state. Then, she goes on to massage the area, clearly unperturbed by my lack of response and trying anything to get my attention—this girl is determined; I'll give her that. It's like I'm in a trance. I'm here physically, but subconsciously...I'm somewhere else. I can't give her a reply yet.

Lost in thinking about how if the authorities didn't make it on time that night to stop me from pummeling him, I don't know if I would've stopped. I'm not a violent person. I'm not a confrontational person. It's the first and only time I ever stood up to him. Prior to the incident, never before had I even *thought* of challenging my dad. It wasn't because I was afraid of him or because I didn't have the muscles. My dad and I were equally matched in size. What stopped me and paralyzed me with fear was the idea of him wanting revenge on Malory and my mom when I wasn't around.

He used to reserve his anger *only* for me. Until that one day, he finally snapped. And I lost it just as much as he did. The need to protect drove me. Instinct took over. I came home to find my mom and sister huddled in a corner, and my dad had a fist raised to their skulls. I saw red and rage...nothing else—I pounced!

Once the dust settled, no one could tell whose blood was whose between us men. Mom sobbed the entire time and just held Mal. When Grant arrived, he and my mom were able to convince the cops it was in self-defense and cited I was protecting my family.

My mom never experienced my dad's wrath—he and I were both good actors around the two women. I'd pretend everything was okay and take the hits, and my father acted like the model husband. It was a sick game he and I played. In hindsight, I let it go on far too long and should've stood up to him sooner. I deluded myself into thinking he'd never go after Mom and Mal if I remained his loyal punching bag.

My mother—Judy is her name—is a good woman and didn't deserve what happened. Her life was shattered that night too. Everything she thought she knew was a sham. Obviously, she took it incredibly hard when I had to sit down and break the news to her that her life was not what she thought it was. She didn't know my old man was beating me. As I said, I hid it well from her. I was good at concealing the evidence, like bruises— well, except for when there were *distractions*, namely a certain goddess who made me almost reveal things I didn't want to, and why I fought so desperately to avoid said goddess.

Damn…why did I drift off to recounting hellish times? My dad wasn't what the blonde asked about. *What was her question?* I don't know why thoughts of the asshole have popped into my head all day—maybe because of my discussion with Ethan.

Then, I remembered she asked if I'd ever been in love. Fuck, that's a complicated question to answer. What makes it more painful is I had experienced love but never got to act on it.

"If I say *yes?*" I play coy with her as I finally respond.

Taking a swig of my beer, I stare into blue eyes shimmering with curiosity—they're not the right color, though. I love violet ones.

"Then I'd wonder who and where she is," she practically purrs and fluffs her hair.

She's effectively drawing my attention to her perky tits as her arms come up. She thrusts the creamy skin forward for emphasis. I can't help but admire the beautiful body on display. Her skimpy sky-blue dress leaves little to the imagination—*good thing I don't have much of an imagination.*

I tilt my head as I regard her response and reply, "And if I say *no?*"

"Then I'd say it's my lucky night. I've never been in love either, hero." Her pouty lips are inches from my face.

It's quite loud in the bar area, but she's managed to get as close as she can to easily be heard. I'm skeptical that she's never been in love. Something tells me she's not the type of woman who can easily move on from someone. Personally, I don't want commitment. I don't want complications and entanglements. Fun, simplicity, and a clear conscience at the end of the night in which we both know the drill is what I'm after.

I'm not going to tell her the truth that I was in love once. Swallowing hard, I finally say *her* name in my head.

Olivia Watson...

She's not a girl anyone forgets. Fuck, she's a woman now! Out there somewhere in the world. *Probably happily married with a bunch of kids,* I grumble to myself. I've done my best to forget about her over the years, but even my seventeen-year-old self knew back then how special she was. I knew she's the type of person who comes along once in a lifetime—I missed my chance.

I didn't love her on accident; I loved her on purpose.

After graduation, I never looked Liv up. I'm sure she knew what happened with my dad. It was in all the local papers, but I never heard from her either. After giving her the brush-off all those years ago, what did I expect?

Internally, I sigh again as all those old feelings of longing and regret creep up on me and threaten to swallow me whole. I take another sip to do something—anything—and plunk the bottle down on the bar top.

Distract me, blondie! I implore with my eyes.

She moves her hand to my beer and glides her fingers up and down the neck of the bottle, mimicking the action of rubbing a cock.

Bingo! Distraction.

"What's your name, princess?" I grin mischievously at her. *I can't say the endearment "baby"—that name has always been reserved for someone else.*

She gives me a dazzling smile and says, "Della. And you are?"

"Wes. Nice to meet you. Wanna dance?" I take her hand in mine to shake it in greeting.

"Of course. Lead the way, handsome." She licks her lips again.

After easing myself off the stool, I fully stand up and begin to pull her along to the dance floor. A memory assaults me while a wave of guilt bulldozes me over. It's fleeting, but it's still there. Each time I'm in a bar or club, I think of the one regret regarding a dance I never got to have with the one girl who stole my heart.

Shaking off the memory, I scan the floor to locate my best friend. Grant is already grinding his dick against some girl's ass. We both easily draw women wherever we go. Where I'm the broody, don't-give-a-fuck type who keeps to myself until the girls come my way, Grant's the manwhore flirt. He pushes his floppy dark hair off his face, and the girls fall at his feet.

We've been told we could be twins at times, but his skin is a shade tanner than mine—the tawny color that beckons for attention like he's a surfer or whatever. But when we go to the Jersey shore, surfing is not something we do. His eyes are lighter in color than mine, not quite gray, but not quite blue either. We're trouble on the town and own that shit because it works to our advantage.

Della and I linger near them, and my friend nods in my direction.

He's with a svelte, dark-haired girl with incredible legs. We both did good with our companions for the evening.

My nights off-duty aren't spent fucking girls, but there are those times when it's necessary. I'm not careless or reckless. I always take precautions when I'm having sex. Whether it's fair or not, I don't do relationships because my work comes first. My heart has never been in it because no woman has ever compared to *her.*

"So, Della," I start by saying, holding her hips while we move to the beat reverberating throughout the club. "You looking for some company tonight?"

She giggles, "Isn't it obvious? I'm surprised you didn't ask how I take my eggs in the morning, or some line like that."

"Nah, not my style. I'm just looking for a good time and nothing more. You're beautiful and sexy, princess, but I hope you realize this is a one-time thing. And I don't do the sleepover-breakfast thing." I lay it on the line; she can choose to bite the hook or swim away.

I'm a straight-shooter when it comes to these things. I don't think it's assholish of me. I'd rather a chick not get her hopes up in thinking she can *change me,* or she's the *exception* to my no-commitment rule.

Della adjusts the grip she has on my neck and pulls me in for a kiss. Sometimes it's just that easy to be with a woman. After our lips part, she whispers close to my ear, "I get it, hero. I like my eggs over hard, by the way, even if we don't get to eat them." She nibbles my ear lobe and adds a little bite at the end to make her point about the *hard* part—*duly noted!*

We dance for a bit longer and then have a round of drinks with Grant and the woman, Kelly, he's cozying up to for the evening—and whom I imagine he's taking home. After about an hour, we all decide to call it a night, and Della comes home with me, while Kelly goes with my boy.

Going down the rabbit hole of darkness is the last thing on my mind now. I've got a date between the sheets with Della. There's only one place I want to tunnel into—and it's not revisiting the past.

Chapter 4: It's About Time

Olivia

Time has always been my enemy.

It's never *the right time*. There's never *enough time*. It's always *perhaps another time*.

Or maybe it's not just a *matter of time*; it could also be a matter of *timing*.

At thirty-four, I thought I'd be happily married, have a few kids, and live in a big house. Things don't always work out the way you dreamed. After high school, I went away to college in Florida and became an environmental engineer. Upon finishing grad school, I moved back to New Jersey and bought a small house to be near my dad. He was lonely for years, and it was just time to come home.

I've been back here a few years, and Dad seems happy to have me in the area, but sadly, life isn't fulfilling…for me. All those years ago, I needed to get away from this place after high school and spread my wings. I had to find something that was my own and separate from the life I left behind.

I haven't decided if I want to stay here or go again…for good. It depends on what transpires in my personal and professional lives. Currently, I commute to north Jersey for work. It's a little bit of a hike, but I'm lucky my boss lets me work from home most days. Usually, I only go into the office to coordinate with the other disciplines on my project team or to meet with the architects and other professionals who hired my firm. I'm employed by Kellan & Associates, and we heavily compete with Philadelphia-based firms to obtain projects. We also offer consulting services, and our help is enlisted by other companies for our collective expertise.

Headhunters are constantly trying to convince me to move to the big cities like Chicago, Detroit, and San Diego to work on developments. Most organizations these days are going green with their developments. With me being LEED certified, I'm highly sought after. The big push is to promote sustainable practices in the planning and design phases. There's a point system for certain aspects of a project in which a building can receive the illustrious title of *green*.

Today, I'm in the office looking over some as-builts to close out my one file. There's a creative buzz in the air, and it's mainly because I love being in my office building; our firm designed it long before I came on board. It's classic in design with all the sleek upgrades in energy efficiency and sustainability.

My personal workspace is small, but I don't need a sprawling office. Some design firms only offer workers cubicles, so I feel fortunate to have the space I do. It's a basic room with a landscape view, a desk and chairs, drafting table, and, of course, my computer with three monitors. Most of the Computer-Aided Drawing (CAD) work is done in the other corridor by the CAD drafters.

A planter is in the corner for some greenery, and I always bring a fresh arrangement of flowers on the days I come into work. Today I placed a bouquet of daisies in a purple vase on my desk. I wholeheartedly believe fresh flowers are a friendly reminder to *appreciate the little things*—my mom believed in that as well.

Being nose-deep in my drawings, I can easily lose myself. So when my current boyfriend of six months, Jarrod Donovan, startles me, I immediately bristle. He holds on to the door frame and sticks his head in. "Hey sweetheart. Are we still on for lunch today?"

I look up from my drafting table with my hands firmly planted on the surface and lean forward. My lips are clamped shut, and I'm desperately trying to hold back an annoyed sigh.

"Uh, yeah, sure. That sounds good." I plaster on a smile for his benefit.

"Alrighty. I'll be back to collect you at noon then, sweetheart," he promises and blows a kiss at me.

Acting like I catch it in my hand, I transfer the invisible kiss from my fingertips to my lips. He walks off, and I expel my breath rather obnoxiously. I don't know what's with me lately, but it's not working with him. *A monster is what I am for dragging this out!* I don't know why I just won't end things. He's such a nice guy, but he doesn't *do it* for me.

I've sabotaged every relationship I've ever had. I really like Jarrod, but he's not my type. He's a dork and corny, and not like the knight-in-shining-armor type guy I always pictured myself ending up with. Jarrod is also going too fast for my taste in terms of our relationship. He's itching to move elsewhere and continuously pressures me to make a change and take a leap of faith with him.

We're employed by the same firm, and he works as a construction consultant. He mostly goes out in the field visiting the jobsites, conducting walk-throughs, and drafting punch lists for projects near completion.

Jarrod hasn't professed his love to me...yet, *thank God*; the blowing of kisses is the closest we've come to that. But I know it's coming. And if I'm being honest with myself, I pray that next step never comes. Again, I care a great deal for him, but I'm not *in love* with him. I get the feeling he's putting his plans on hold for me regarding moving in the hopes I'll want to get more serious—I've tried not to think about it.

There's some type of connection we don't have. But I haven't had that type of connection with anyone except for...

Nope, I won't say it.

It's been sixteen freaking years, and I still can't bring myself to utter *his* name. He came into my life at a time when I thought he'd break through to me on a level no guy could. I seemed to have this innate sense that he needed someone the way I did. My mother had just died of cervical cancer when he moved to our town—it was uncanny timing. I was so lost and broken back then, but *he* was the one bright spot in my life. I lived for those furtive glances across the way in the cafeteria.

A feminine voice clears her throat. I look up, and there's no sign of annoyance this time on my end because of who's now standing in my doorway.

"Knock, knock, Liv. I need those plans by four o'clock for my meeting. Will you have them looked over by then to see if the new HVAC lines will suffice?" my fellow co-worker Samantha Ford asks.

I'd been lost in thought again until she walked in. I lick my lips and shake my head to clear the cobwebs.

Sammy, I call her, is a mechanical engineer and one of the most talented I've ever had the privilege of working with. We've been best friends since I started working here. She and I are like two peas in a pod, and I'm grateful to have found someone who understands me even though our personalities don't parallel one another. She happens to be married, so she's constantly giving me advice on how to land the opposite sex—unsolicited, I might add, but I appreciate her efforts.

Sammy has expensive taste and dresses as such. Her least expensive designer outfit rivals the most expensive outfit in my closet, but she'd give someone the shirt off her back if need be despite the price tag that once hung from it. The sex appeal she exudes has men salivating and serves her well when dealing with clients. There's no mistaking her brains as they speak for themselves; her looks are a bonus, along with stunning auburn hair, long limbs, and the taut body of every man's dreams.

"Absolutely. I'm going out to lunch with Jarrod, so as soon as I get back, that'll be the first thing I tackle," I explain and tuck my long light brown hair behind my ear. As is habit, I also tug at my earring.

She starts chuckling. She always chuckles at the mere mention of my boyfriend. We've talked about him in great detail—after all, that's what girlfriends do. Sammy's not on board with me keeping up this farce of a relationship. The sex isn't even that good. I'm not a callous person or some man-eater who strings guys along, *so why I am doing this?*

She raises a sculpted brow with a tsk tsk expression on that Cover Girl face of hers.

"I know, I know. There's no need to say it. I'll tell him soon," I vow, holding up my hands in surrender then letting out a heavy sigh.

She walks over to me, puts her arm around my shoulders and squeezes me to her side. "You know I only want what's best for you. I know he's not *the one*. Good Lord, girl, *you* know he's not the one. We'll have to expand our circle of friends and find someone for you who doesn't work here," she replies, shrugging her shoulders.

"Yeah…" I take a deep breath.

"You okay? You know what I say comes from a loving place and not a bitchy one, even if it comes out that way sometimes." She winces as if she's expecting me to say she's being bitchy.

"I know. It's not you; it's definitely me. I got myself into this situation with Jarrod. I guess I just thought as time went on, I'd somehow grow more attached to him."

And there's that pesky *time* thing again.

She shakes her head in understanding and responds with, "Hmm, yeah, I can see that. It makes sense."

Not sure why I feel compelled to tell her this next part, but I do. "Before you walked in here, I was thinking about my mom." My tone holds a melancholy note.

"I figured as much when I saw you tugging at your earring." She smiles affectionately at me. Sammy knows about my mom's death, of course.

"You know me too well. It's scary sometimes. I swear if I didn't prefer men, and you weren't already married, we'd end up together. My life would be a whole lot less complicated without men in it anyway. I think that's why I miss her so much. She had a way of dissecting a situation and helping me rearrange the pieces so it made sense." I get choked up toward the end as tears threaten to fall.

I was aiming for funny with the comment about us being more than girlfriends, but I failed miserably on the delivery. My sorrow overwhelms everything.

My mom always knew what to do. She was so put-together. Even at the end when death came for her, she didn't let on that *this was it*. I didn't believe she was really gone until the open casket at her viewing said otherwise.

Always assailed by heartbreak when I think of her, I swallow hard when I ask my dear friend, "Did I ever tell you why I wear these earrings so often?"

She shakes her head. As I lick my dry lips, one lone tear slips silently down my face.

"Mom always said there are two things you need in life. One is a good set of pearls. Now, our family could only afford cultured pearls. So, the ones I'm wearing are her most treasured set. They were handed down to me upon her passing."

Needing a second to collect myself as more tears fall, Sammy squeezes me again in comfort. All this talk about my mom and my past has me riddled with anxiety. I proceed to roll up my sleeves on my white button-down top that I've tucked into my gray pencil skirt.

Sighing contemplatively, I go on, "She always told me to strive for a set of 'power pearls' one day. Saltwater pearls are more expensive, if you didn't already know—but knowing you, Miss Fashionista, I'm sure you're aware. Well, anyway, I have yet to buy a set. But one day, I will to honor her memory. It probably seems ridiculous." I shoot a watery smile my friend's way.

"It's not ridiculous at all. Your mom sounds like she was a very special woman. You've only ever shared a few things about her, so it's nice to hear this. I'm just so sorry, Liv. I can't imagine the pain you still feel and always will. I don't know what I'd do without my mom. What's the second thing?" she questions with genuine curiosity.

Oh wow, I'd almost forgotten to impart the second piece of advice. My mother's wisdom is something that can live on through me. I'm happy to share about her. I *should* talk about her more frequently. If I close my eyes tightly enough and concentrate, I can still hear her voice singing a bedtime lullaby to me. Listening to "Edelweiss" without crying isn't possible.

"And the second thing she said is to 'always be the lead in your own movie—not a supporting cast member.' Mom was a bit on the dramatic side of things." I grin at the warm memories rolling through my mind.

Then, I tug at my earring again. It's almost my nod to my mom up above, letting her know I'm thinking of her. Half the time, I don't even realize I'm doing it.

My mother, Beatrice Kay Watson, was a witty, vivacious, and

captivating woman. She'd never leave the house without her face on; I swear, you'd never catch her without a lick of makeup. We couldn't afford the finer things as we were a middle-class working family, but she'd dress as if we could. There was no stitch out of place on her ensemble. There was no hair out of place on her head. Her resourcefulness and zest for life knew no bounds. *God, I miss her more than is humanly possible to convey.*

"I love that, Liv! She sounds like she was sassy in all the right ways. I wish I could've met her. You certainly are making her proud. Wherever she is up there, I know she must be beaming with pride, girl. I love and adore you."

She hugs me one last time then starts to move away. We both have to get back to work because, as always, we have deadlines and can't just stand around for a therapy session on our employer's dime.

Before she leaves my office, she turns back around, "Oh yeah, before I forget, when are you going to the animal shelter again to volunteer? I want to come with you this time." She claps her hands together for emphasis that she means business.

My expression becomes even softer over the fact that Sammy wants to help me out. Well, it's not really helping *me*; it's helping the animals. I've been volunteering at least once or twice a month at Pawsome Place Animal Shelter since moving back.

"It's funny you ask because I'll be there tomorrow. Are you seriously coming?" I squeal in excitement.

She nods. "Count me in. I'll see you later when you've looked over the plans."

Sammy waves goodbye and makes her departure. I'm thrilled she'll be going. The animals need all the help they can get. There are never enough volunteers, and the poor creatures need affection and attention in the worst way.

My love for animals is because of *him*. After volunteering at an animal shelter for a few months in my senior year, I fell in love with the selfless deed. I was hoping to work alongside him back then, but he ended up becoming a junior firefighter. Unfortunately, I stopped volunteering when I moved away for school.

Now, the animals help me cope with everything with my mom even after all these years. They also help me cope with the stress and mess that is my love life. If I could take all the fur balls home, I would. I've been tossing around the idea of adopting one of the pets as my own, so maybe this weekend will be the perfect time. My issue is, I have no clue how I'm going to choose! It's going to rip me apart giving a home to only one when they're all in need.

Stop it, Olivia!

I can't be sad any longer today. Work is calling. Deadlines are knocking. And lunch is imminent with Jarrod. *Ugh.*

So, I put on my big girl panties and dive back in to the as-builts. As I study the top drawing of the children's hospital we just assisted in rebuilding, I glance to the left of the structure and remember it's situated next to one of the chain hotels, The Westin.

God, I didn't want to say his name, let alone think it. Sucking in a sharp breath, all the feelings for him come flooding back like I'm a teenage girl again.

His name is on my tongue even though it shatters me. I go to bite my lip to stop the quivering, but it's too late. Looking to the flowers on my desk, they're of no help with my current mood.

"Weston Thorpe…" I flinch at the sound of my own voice. I will not cry, though. Too many tears have been spilled because of that guy over the course of *time.*

Chapter 5: Ashes to Ashes

Olivia

Arriving home later that night, I'm still thinking about Wes—even during my uneventful lunch date with Jarrod.

Lord, it's been an arduous task to sidestep thoughts of him since my teens. I was running away when I went to Florida; it doesn't take a genius or shrink to figure that one out. It was silly, childish, and stupid of me, but when he shot me down for prom, it was the final blow to my psyche. I wasn't able to deal with everything since it was practically on the heels of losing my mom. When I lost Wes, it was too much!

You never had him, my subconscious reminds me. I tell her to *shove it!*

The day he refused me and never looked at me again is the day I closed my heart off. It was like turning off the flow in a faucet; not even a drip would leak out thereafter.

Some people you just never get over, no matter how hard you try—he's *that* for me. Unbeknownst to him, Wes buried himself so deeply and completely within my very existence, no amount of incantations and séances to dispel the spirit would remove him, not even if I tried to cut him out with a serrated knife.

When I decided as a teenage girl I had to let him go, when I finally admitted it wouldn't work out in this lifetime between us, I knew it wasn't the end of our story. For he'll remain with me for eternity. We're inexplicably intertwined. Somehow our paths are interwoven, and we've fashioned this quilt that spans over a millennia, it would seem. My secrets about him are locked behind a closed door, not to be shared with anyone. I've been harboring these feelings for years but sharing it with anyone would've been too painful—even sharing it with my dad or best friend would've been too much.

Thoughts of him continue to plague me and rattle around in my head. God, Wes had the most alluring gray eyes I'd ever seen. I can only imagine what he'd look like today—my deepest, darkest desires have a wild imagination and paint a vivid picture. Those eyes were gorgeous and turbulent, smoldering whenever he met my gaze. I always thought I could see a storm brewing in his irises, and I always wanted to be the one to clear those clouds away.

A shiver rolls through my body remembering the way I used to feel when I looked at him. His eyes have haunted me for years. His voice has driven me crazy, taunting me in my sleep—hell, taunting me when I'm awake. The sound, the timbre that washed over me like a warm blanket caressing my soul. The feral scent that emanated from him, conjuring up every teenage girl's fantasy in my mind will never be forgotten. And his body…I can't go there. His hands were strong, and he had the type of arms I wanted to envelop me in a hold that said, *I'll never let go of you no matter what*.

No one, not even Sammy, has any idea as to how hard it was to come back to Jersey. My father knew to avoid talking about anything Jersey-related when I was away at college—he assumed it was because of my mom, but that was only part of the reason. Hearing anything pertaining to Wes would've thrown me off track in my studies and in life. My dad didn't know I was in love with Wes anyway, and I resented any reminder of the boy—now man—I once pined for with every fiber of my being.

Dad would've understood, though. He wouldn't have treated me like I was some dumb kid with an unrealistic crush. Dad—ever the romantic—would've helped me through it and been a source of comfort. However, I wanted to deal with it on my own terms. *Emotionally unavailable* is most often associated with men, yet my dad is the polar opposite—he's emotionally available.

Currently feeling my way through the darkness and fumbling for the light switch in my living room is something I do each night. During the day, the natural light in here is breathtaking. At night, it's a different story. This old house seems to talk, and I wonder what the walls are saying.

"Ouch!" I cry out as I stub my toe on the leg of the end table.

Living in the Borough of Pineview, which is nestled right next to Pineville, is convenient; my dad is only a ten-minute drive. It was love at first sight—for the house. This historic Victorian structure called to me, and I didn't think twice about buying it. Lots of character and personality greet me each day when I pull in my driveway, but lots of repairs and TLC are required—which I never get around to doing. When I first saw her faded and chipped yellow-painted exterior, I just knew she was beautiful underneath the neglect.

Finally, I manage to turn on the tableside lamp and place my purse on the couch. I'm taking off my high heels while my cell phone rings away. I rummage through my bag to get to my chirping phone. I don't have a landline and it drives my dad nuts. Speaking of Dad, it's him calling.

"Hey, Dad! What's up?" I say in greeting.

"Hi, honey. Nothing much, just wanted to see how you're doing?" he replies with such love and affection in his tone. It always causes my face to split in two.

I laugh at his comment, though. "The same as I was yesterday when I talked to you."

"I know, I know. I'm sorry. I probably smother you, don't I?" he questions.

"No, you don't. Sorry, I don't feel like that, it's just nothing new ever happens to me. Although, I'm thinking of getting a pet this weekend when I go to the shelter," I explain, beaming.

"Really? That's great. Cat or dog?" My dad's a dog person, so I already know his preference.

"Actually, I don't know yet. Let's hope I don't come home with one of each because I don't see how that will work. I don't want to be *that* person who starts with one but then decides the animal needs a friend to keep him company. Then before you know it, you can open your own petting zoo!" I say in mock horror.

He chuckles. "Yeah, that's probably a slippery slope indeed. I never let your mom get you a pet growing up because a pet is like a gateway drug. You can't just have one species, it seems, because magically they multiply."

Discussing Mom with my dad makes my throat tighten. It's still hard for us to converse about old times, but on the rare occasions we do, it's both cathartic and painful. *Why is Mom the main topic today?* I tug at my earring—*I miss you!*

Swallowing hard, I clear my throat. "Remember when we'd be driving in the car with her, and whenever we'd try to make a turn onto a street, she'd yell 'we got a break'—in the traffic—and then we'd yell back 'hot dog' when we were finally able to turn? God, I miss that." I sniffle and bite my lip.

"Yeah, honey, I remember well. And I miss it too. It's the little things I yearn for the most," he practically whispers.

Blowing out a long breath temporarily calms me. I'm wishing things could be different for him and me. We both mourn her loss greatly even to this day.

"I can understand," I swallow again, "I still put flowers on my desk at work every time I go into the office."

Dad sniffles back. "Yeah, I loved when she had fresh flowers all around the house. I should start putting some out too. All I do is set out a cup of tea every morning as if she were still here. I just can't drink my coffee alone each morning."

"God, Dad, I didn't know you still do that." I'm overwhelmed with guilt and swamped with sadness for my father.

"Oh don't pity me, hon. When you've lost the greatest love of your life and you'll never get another, there are some things you'll never get over," he simply replies. *Don't I know it.*

My dad is only sixty-three years old. He *could* find someone this late in life to be happy with, it's more of a matter that he doesn't want to. He had his one, true, great love. And that's it for him. It makes me depressed, but it's his choice. I wish I had a husband and children to share with him so we were a family and he wasn't so lonely, but it hasn't been in the cards for me. That's why I wonder if I'm destined to remain alone like my dad because I already had my one, true, great love.

Wes...

"Dad, I gotta go. I have a deadline," I say in a rush. *Liar!*—having already met my deadline today.

"You work too hard, kid. Well, let me know when you're free so I can take you out to eat. And you're gonna have to tell me which pet you end up bringing home. If I hear a ruff or meow in the background, I guess I'll know," he laughs.

"Okay, Dad. Love you."

"Love you too, hon."

"Bye," I tell him.

Once I hit the button on my cell to end the call, I slump down on my couch. Raking my fingers through my hair, I decide after this long day of reminiscing about good and bad memories, I need a bath. I head up to my bedroom to undress and start the water.

A good soak will do the trick. I'm sure I'll be in there long after I prune because today warrants relaxation.

***

Olivia

This shelter is my happy place. Solace surrounds me when I'm here where the animals offer companionship and unconditional love, which is a different layer than that of human interaction, of course. Volunteering is something that fills me with purpose. Each time I walk through the huge brick building located twenty minutes from my house, I'm elated to be embarking on a mission that will help the community and my spirit.

"So, what's this breed again?" Sammy asks me while examining the pup.

Her face overtly showcases her bewilderment as she scrunches up her nose. Although, I think her wrinkling nose is partly due to curiosity over the breed, and partly because she's combating the odors she's not accustomed to.

I'll admit, the poor little guy at her feet, barking in that yipper-yapper way little dogs do, is somewhat ugly. However, he's got that ugly-cute thing going. The pup is all black with one white spot on his left ear that appears as if someone dripped a dab of paint on him.

Smiling down at the little guy in the dog run where he's currently playing, I reply to my bestie. "He's a chug."

"What the hell kind of dog is that?" Sammy looks horrified and is trying to sidestep the little piles of excrement I'll be cleaning up next.

I can't stop laughing at her reaction. "It's a Chihuahua-pug mix. His name is Ash. He was brought in two weeks ago to the shelter. Someone abandoned him on the side of a farm road near a burn pit. Do you believe that?" Of course, it's a rhetorical question.

"Didn't they, boy?" I baby-talk to the dog and scratch behind his ears, after which he wags his tail faster than a jet plane's engine fan—*I'm waiting for him to take off in the air.*

"*I* think he's cute," I announce and turn to Sammy, arching my brow her way, daring her to argue with me.

"If you say so," she giggles.

Rolling my eyes at her seems fitting. I know deep down she has a big heart, and she's a good person—if she wasn't, she wouldn't be here. She and her husband live in close proximity to New York, so the fact that she drove down here to spend her Saturday with me says it all.

We had different upbringings, and her privileged childhood was a far cry from my meager one. I'm glad she came today and made the effort to help. Sammy may be a person who doesn't like to get her hands dirty as far as cleaning the cages, but she's walking the animals and giving them the attention they crave. Sometimes that's more important than anything.

And to be fair, she hasn't complained all that much since we started making the rounds an hour ago. We're handling the dogs first, then we'll move on to the cat hallway. I haven't decided which animal I'm adopting, but it seems Ash is in the running. The best guess the on-site veterinarian could provide for his age is around ten months old. He's crate-trained at least.

"You never said how your lunch went with Jarrod when you dropped the plans off to me yesterday," she teases.

Sammy backs out of the cage and puts Ash on a leash so I can hose the area down now that I removed the waste. Thank God my rubber boots are tall because, inevitably, I'll get splashed. When I texted Sammy this morning, I reminded her to wear old clothes because nothing stays nice when you enter this place. Her version of old clothes and my version differ significantly. My denim cut-off shorts and well-worn T-shirt are proper attire, but to her, they're an abomination. Her nicely pressed khaki capris and chiffon cap-sleeved top are moments away from being soiled, I imagine.

"It was fine," I simply reply.

"*Fine?*" she scoffs.

"Umm, yeah. There's not much to tell. We went to lunch; nothing remarkable happened." I shrug my shoulder and chuckle because that's it to the story.

"Don't you ever just want something more than *fine?*" she basically whines.

She feels I'm settling—it's the same argument I've had with her and with myself. Even if it's just temporary, it's still settling. Hell, I've admitted this relationship is going nowhere. My hope is I'll get out of it before anyone gets hurt—namely Jarrod—or we continue this platonic thing we seem to have going.

"Jarrod's a good guy, and I like spending time with him—albeit in more of a platonic rather than romantic way, which I realize probably isn't reciprocal." Another sigh escapes my mouth, which she most likely can't hear over the stream of water.

Then I continue, "I know you worry about me, and I love you for it, but we can't all have fairytale romances like you and Tom are blessed with. That man is one of a kind when it comes to the passion you two share. I think they broke the mold when they made him, you lucky duck!"

The mold for my future husband probably exploded in the kiln and that's why he remains to be seen.

"I know, I'm lucky. I just want to see you come alive with someone the way it's meant to be." She waves her hand dismissively. "Enough of that. I'm gonna take this *chug…*," she says the word as if it's a vile taste in her mouth, and I start laughing, "…for a walk. I'll be right back."

My friend—in her pristine capris—disappears from view with Ash, and I start removing the water from the dog run by using a rubber scraper on a pole. My mind is invaded by thoughts of my boyfriend and what my dad said last night.

Taking stock of my love life is inevitable. Jarrod's hints—and not-so-subtle hints—of further committing to one another are forthcoming. Maybe I should admit to myself I downplayed to Sammy that yesterday's lunch was uneventful. Jarrod's and my conversation was a glimpse into a future I have to decide if I want or not.

"You look beautiful, sweetheart," Jarrod tells me and squeezes the hand I was resting on the table's surface.

Smiling warmly at him, I glance down at my attire for the office and can't believe how complimentary he always is—whether I'm in sweats or a button-up and pencil skirt. I know it's a rarity for some women to have an attentive man at their side.

"Thank you, you look nice as well. This place sure is fancy for a quick bite to eat."

"Well, I wanted it to be special. I have something important I want to talk to you about."

My heart is galloping, and immediately I become tense at his words. Oh no, is this the "next step" conversation he wants to broach?

Clearing my throat, I explain as congenially as I can—because it's true and not just some excuse: "I'm on a deadline! I'm sorry. Lunch probably wasn't the best idea today because I'm so swamped. Plans are due to Sammy for her meeting later, and I'm still reviewing some as-builts. Is it something that can wait?"

The hurt is written on his face, but he masks it. "No problem. I should've asked earlier about your schedule. When we have dinner on Sunday, I'll talk to you about it then."

"Okay. Thanks for understanding. You are truly one of the most understanding men I've ever met," I convey and squeeze his hand in return.

I'm abruptly brought back to the present because I stupidly left the hose on, and it's spraying water at my bare legs and running into my boots. Reaching to turn the knob and shut it off, I stand there for a beat, steadying myself by using the pole for balance. I feel the guilt taunting me. It's gnawing at me—I don't deserve Jarrod.

My heart is heavy as I return to cleaning the floors. He and I will have that serious talk on Sunday, and I won't chicken out.

Chapter 6: Sweatin' it Out

Weston

It's Sunday. My time off went too quickly, and I'm back on the rig. The reprieve was appreciated, though, and expending some energy and decompressing were two goals I achieved.

Grant and I went out on a report of a downed wire near a gas station about two hours ago and just pulled back in with the firetruck. We had to stay on-scene until the power company showed up, the worry always being that the transformer will blow or a line will arc—all was well when we left, and the situation was contained.

It's hot as shit in my turnout gear. I'm dripping with sweat from every pore on my body—my eyelids are perspiring; it's gross. It's the late afternoon and supposed to be a full moon tonight. Most overdose calls coincide with a full moon, but I'm sure there's no scientific backing to it. Nevertheless, we're prepared to take on whatever the evening may bring.

Next weekend, I promised Mal I would come over and help with the yardwork. She can't afford to pay someone at the moment. Offering to pay is something I would do, but for one, I don't want to insult her, and two, it gives me a chance to visit. She really took on a lot and had to grow up fast when Dad went to jail. Mom fell apart more and more as the years went on, and now she's a recluse. I was hoping Mal would've gone to college, but it wasn't a desire of hers.

My sis is working as a hairdresser. I'm extremely proud of her for putting herself through cosmetology school while she cashiered at our local supermarket. Even though she bounces around from salon to salon depending on who charges the least for renting a booth, she still makes enough to support her and my mom. They had to sell their house years ago, but at least Dad didn't benefit from that transaction.

They're currently renting a modest two-bedroom cottage on the far end of town. It is my hope that my sister, who is now twenty-three, will eventually find someone to start a life with and do the whole kids, pets, picket fence thing—I'll live vicariously through her since it's not my deal. She's still young, so I'm not encouraging her to do anything drastic anytime soon. But she needs to have a life of her own one day that's not marred by the past or the present due to her role as caretaker. Mom is the issue—I don't expect Mal to be saddled with her forever, especially if she doesn't get better. I do what I can for both of them and often worry it's not nearly enough.

After placing my helmet on the shelf in my cubby and hanging up my jacket, a long sigh escapes my mouth. I need to sit down on the bench for a second before I remove the rest of my gear. Exhaustion looms in the air.

"You're a pussy. It's not *that* hot!" Grant walks by and ribs me.

"Fuck you! It's hotter than balls out there."

Not only is it hot out there, but it's hot in here. We have the bay doors wide open to the non-existent breeze. They'll remain open until we finish our duties, so there's no break from the oppressive warmth. Grant doesn't know I feel the weight of the world, the pressure, and the heat for another reason. I can't fault him for his unawareness—he's not always in tune with every little thing going on with me, as no one person can rightfully be.

"Nah, you just don't work out enough. It's not the damn heat that makes you a pussy." He's laughing his ass off.

I shoot him the middle finger and explain, "We work out together and do practically the same routine, so how can you say that, dumbass?"

Christ, we bicker like an old married couple.

"Dude, that's exactly my point. You're pussying out. If you're this hot and tired after that call, then damn!" He smirks.

I'm not in the mood to play as if we're fucking kids teasing each other on the playground during recess. I gaze off to the side. I know he'll understand when I tell him, "I was just thinking about Mom and Mal." My friend knows this subject always puts me in a glum state of mind.

"Oh fuck. What's wrong now?" He's on high alert as if there's some threat he wants to help me eliminate.

I shake my head back and forth. "Nothing's wrong. I just…want something better for them, ya know? I talked to my sister the other day and promised I'd come over to cut the grass at least. I could hear it in her voice that Mom was having one of her bad depression episodes. Of course, Mal wouldn't tell me even if that was the case. I swear, sometimes I think she's more of a big sister than a little one the way she tries to protect me."

We both chuckle at the comment over her protectiveness. My baby sister is headstrong, intelligent, and too beautiful for her own good—her beauty on the inside is what makes her even more appealing. I've had to beat guys away with a stick over the years, and I'll continue to do so until the right one comes along.

Grant runs a hand through his hair looking sheepish. "Sorry for giving you shit. I know you worry about them. Listen, I'll come over and help you with the yard. Plus, I can keep Judy company while you spend time with Mal, or vice versa."

"Thanks, man. I'll probably take you up on it. Mal may be at the salon on Saturday anyway, but I'm sure she'll be home at some point. You know I won't be able to get Mom to leave the house for dinner, but maybe we can take Baby Girl out. That kid works too hard."

He clears his throat, "You know she's not a kid anymore, right? And the last time I checked, she's definitely an attractive woman."

It's habit for me to refer to anyone in their twenties as a kid.

"Don't even fucking think about it! I thought the last time I warned you off would be *the last time*," I practically growl. My hackles are up. All my big-brother instincts—mixed with some primitive behaviors—are on display for the world to see.

He holds his hands up in front of his torso in surrender and grins. "I know, I know she's off limits. I'm just stating fact. That *baby sister, kid* shit you spout is not going to be well-received as the years go on. You gotta back off and ease up a bit. Otherwise, she'll rebel just to spite you."

Damnit, he's right. I know he's right. It's difficult to stand down when it comes to her. And I'd be ecstatic if she found someone like Grant—just not *him*. He's my best friend, it'd be weird.

Shit, we have to get off this subject. I can feel my blood boiling. The thought of my ba-…*I mean grown sister*…in the arms of a man has me spitting nails. I'm fine with her being with a guy as long as my brain doesn't process what exactly that entails.

Grant can see I'm waging a war with myself, so he claps his hands together and rubs them as if to indicate the conversation is over. He proceeds to store his gear in dead silence. Then, out of the corner of my eye, I see him walk off toward the communal restrooms.

Long after he's walked away, I continue to sit there unmoving. I need to work. My sorry ass needs to get up and clean the firetruck. It's dirty from driving through some puddles on the way back. The smell of exhaust fumes also hangs in the air—it's especially bad on humid days, and you can almost see particles of heat floating all around. Today, the asthmatics will be hit hard; I imagine we'll be dispatched for those calls too.

Well, time to get moving.

***

Olivia

Ah, crap!

I take a tumble on the couch, faceplanting, as I practically fall out of my shoe. Bending down, trying to strap my sandal led to disastrous consequences when Ash jumped on my leg and scared me half to death. I perch on the edge and try to straighten out my hair and outfit.

It's going to take a while to get used to having a pet around my house. I'll have to constantly be on the lookout for the dark, one-spotted little thing so I don't step on him or trip—*I see a lot of tripping hazards in my future.* This will be the first time I've left him alone since bringing him home last night. He even went with me to the store so I could get the proper supplies for him: doggy bed, food, bowls, leash, collar, mats, toys, snacks, and puppy pee pads, just in case.

I hope the fella handles it well because Jarrod is supposed to be here any minute to pick me up for dinner. Ash may not have shared a kennel with other dogs at the shelter, but I'm sure he was used to the comforting sounds of people and other animals around him. *Maybe I should leave the TV on for some background noise?* Surely he'll be okay even without the TV—I'm probably fussing and worrying for no reason. Besides, he needs to get used to his surroundings.

Last night I had to block him off in the kitchen, and all throughout the night he made several escape attempts to get upstairs to my bedroom. His whimpering kept me tossing and turning as well. I'm very patient and understanding, so each time he Houdini'd it out, I'd tell him *no* and gently place him back in his doggy bed. It was pathetic to see the little sad face he made. Those big eyes of his that denote the classic pug look about did me in, and my determination was temporarily weakened. But I knew if I didn't put my foot down on the first night, I'd forever be catering to him—I don't want a spoiled chug on my hands.

My dad was thrilled by the news when I called him this morning. He said he'd be by sometime this week to meet my little man. Dad retired from his job as a school bus driver at fifty-five and works odd jobs here and there if he wants extra pocket change, so he has the time to spare. I'm surprised he retired because I thought he'd be lonelier, and it would be a reminder he doesn't have Mom to share his golden years with, but that doesn't seem to be the case. Dad even offered to come over when I go into the office to let Ash out to play and potty—I'll take him up on that.

A knock on my front door tells me Jarrod's arrived. I get my sandal strapped just in time and without falling over. Ash did his best to climb up on the couch to get to me, but thankfully he hasn't mastered getting up there yet.

"No, no, Ash," I gently reprimand and keep pushing his paws off the edge. "Okay, now you be my good boy while I go out." I rub his adorable soft head.

He trots along after me as I answer the door. I'm greeted by a toothy-grinned Jarrod. My boyfriend moves in to place a chaste kiss on my lips. He smells nice. *God, I love how men smell.* Even when they're sweaty, there's just something about it.

Jarrod notices my pup at my feet wagging his tail so fast, it's a black streak moving back and forth. "And who's this?" he asks as he kneels down and lets Ash attack his face with licks and sniffs.

I'm giggling at the sight before me. Jarrod is such a great guy. He'll make the perfect husband and father…*for someone else.*

"This is my new dog, Ash. I brought him home from the shelter yesterday. Come on in while I put him away."

"He's a cute little guy. Wow, I didn't know you were gonna get a dog," he says with a tinge of sadness laced in his words. Seems like the thing he's thinking—but not voicing—is *you got him without including me?*

I pick up Ash from jumping at my legs and tearing at the skin. After walking to my kitchen, I deposit him on the tiled floor. Immediately he whimpers, and I quirk an eyebrow at him. He stops right away and trots over to his bed to pout. *Good boy!* I have to block him off with a storage container so he can't escape. I mentally remind myself to get a baby gate the next time I'm shopping to make this easier.

As I'm sliding the container in place, I tell Jarrod, "Yeah, I've been thinking about getting a pet for a little while now. I couldn't decide between a dog or cat. But it just seems like this was meant to be. Ash just sorta happened." I shrug in explanation.

"Well, you think you'll ever want a brother or sister for him one day?" he asks while looking down at Ash instead of looking me in the eyes.

I hear the hope in his tone, the undercurrent of desire to join our lives in holy matrimony is there. I'm momentarily stunned. I don't want to have this conversation here. This isn't an innocent reply he's trying to pull out of me. He's doing the hinting thing again, trying to ease me into the idea of *more* with us. I won't even let him sleep overnight here, so getting a pet together is ludicrous.

Answering his question in an evasive manner, I claim, "Umm, I'll have to ask him when the time comes." Being flippant isn't my thing, but in this case it is.

He finally looks in my eyes. Those probing blue irises of his are trying to unearth a direct answer from me. I clamp my lips together tighter than a bank vault, and I'm sure he not only sees, but also senses my resolve.

So, he smiles and asks, "Ready to go then, sweetheart?"
Am I? I gulp in response.

Chapter 7: Dine or Dash

Olivia

Jarrod and I walk into the restaurant and are immediately ushered to our two-person, intimate table. We're heading to the corner near a beautiful stone divider that looks like something inspired by Portofino, Italy. He made reservations. Of course he did; the gentlemanly and chivalrous behaviors he exhibits are encoded in his genetic makeup. He's a planner, organizer, and a doer.

The Italian cuisine is decent at Bella Maria's, and this restaurant is situated a few towns over when heading toward the shoreline. I've only been here one time before and enjoyed the experience. Candlelight flickers on the tabletops, casting a sensual glow upon patrons. Couples happily eat, and my mouth waters as my tongue registers all the smells swirling in the atmosphere.

White tablecloths, dark furniture, and a long wall of wine invite us in. What beckons me to the table are the fresh flowers. I lean down and inhale the bouquet before Jarrod helps me into my seat and pushes in my chair.

I'm not dressed to the nines or anything, but I'm wearing a flirty sundress in a soft, pale blue color; it's perfect for a summer night out. My confidence ticks up when I wear something that makes me feel empowered. I love this dress because the shoulder straps are thick enough to provide coverage, and the hemline flirts with my lower legs just above the knee as if to say *I'm fun, classy yet sassy, and alluring.*

Normally, I straighten my hair or wear it up out of my face, but tonight I opted to wear it down and let my natural curls bounce at my shoulder blades and dance around my face. The strappy nude-colored sandals and my pearl earrings add to the overall appearance of self-assurance I was going for. I wanted to look good, but not too good—for Jarrod's sake. I'm going to have to let him down easy; the time has come.

Admittedly, he's quite handsome in his forest-green collared shirt that's snugly tucked into his pressed and belted khaki slacks. The green showcases his tan and toned arms nicely. He's got a great body, standing at six foot even. Jarrod's almond-shaped sapphire blue eyes complement his long nose, square chin, and oblong face.

His most handsome feature, however, is his hair—it's movie star quality. He styles it perfectly like the blonde, architecturally-crafted hairdo is waving at you to say *hello*. Even his manicured hands suggest he's a man who cares about exuding a certain persona. What drew me to him when we first met was his personality. The corny side of him I thought was a nice change of pace compared to the previous guys I'd dated. Jarrod's manners are over-the-top—so much so, you'd think he's fake.

When he reached to hold my hand in the car and knitted our fingers together, I knew telling him to move on from me would be the best course of action before he gets too attached. Maybe it's the week I've had; maybe it's something I knew all along since we started dating, or maybe it's the conversation I had with my dad—whatever the reason—it's abundantly clear I don't feel for him the way I should. He deserves to have a woman hang on his every word and adore him. And I deserve to feel that *zing* you're supposed to feel when you've found the one who fills your heart to the brim.

I want to remain friends, so I'll tell him as much. We just ordered our beverages and meals, so there's no better time than the present to have this conversation.

He's always one step ahead of me, though. While I'm licking my lips and sipping the water that was waiting for us on the table, he's already executing his plan of attack on my resoluteness.

"You know why I asked you here for dinner, right?"

Nearly choking on my water, I sputter to say, "I-I-I think so."

"I've been wanting to tell you for some time now that I'm hopelessly, deeply, and profoundly in love with you, Olivia."

A sharp breath races through my lungs—it's like ice shards are piercing the interior. That breath is lodged right in my airway, preventing me from exhaling or speaking. He continues persuading me, while I stare at his green shirt like a panicked deer stuck on a busy highway road.

"I know you're scared. But don't be. It's natural to have these feelings when you're in a relationship. I don't expect you to say it back yet, but I needed it to be out there. You know I'm an upstanding guy and want to be up front with you—I just couldn't hold it in any longer."

He reaches for my hand like he did in the car, and I flinch on instinct. God, I don't want him to be so wonderful because this will make it so much harder on both of us. I'm so undeserving of his patience, acceptance, and love. Not being able to reciprocate is excruciating.

I finally find my voice as I squeak out, "Jarrod, you're an amazing man." *Deep breath.* I begin to tack on, "But…"

"Please don't do that, Olivia," he interrupts.

Sighing, I try to forge ahead, "But you are! You're everything a woman could want in a boyfriend. You have all the qualities that women make a big list of and then try to check off as they go—all the check marks are there. You've made me feel very special in dating you, and I'm fortunate to know you. Believe me, any woman would be over the moon to hear the words you said."

"Yet, you don't want me," he softly accuses. He juts out his chin, and I see the pain flash in his eyes at my rebuff.

"Not in the same way you want me to. I wish to remain friends, though." I try to sound upbeat.

"I don't want to be *friends,* Olivia. Yeah, sure, you'll always have a friend in me, but I want more between us. We're so good together. Can't you see that? I feel like you're not giving us a chance."

His mood sours, and his eyes change like a dark, ominous cloud rolled in. Then, as if he remembers himself, he rubs my hand with his thumb in desperation. When his eyes change back, they're pleading—his pupils alone are begging me to continue this charade. *Why?*

Taken aback, I try to carefully choose my words, "I think we're good together *as friends.* I enjoy spending time with you. I'm sorry to say, but I'm not in love with you. Are you willing to remain in my life as a friend at least?"

The server comes over and delivers our salads and wine. I'm not a drinker by any means, but the wine is a welcomed resource to help steady my nerves.

We don't dig into our salads since this conversation is far from over. Jarrod looks at me lovingly, tenderly. *God, why couldn't I just love him back?* It would make my life so much easier and probably make his life easier too.

Then my subconscious reminds me, *because you love someone else—always have, always will.*

It's the worst form of torture loving someone who doesn't return your affections. Wes did it to me, and I'm doing it to Jarrod. It's sad because I still wanted Wes long after he dismissed me from his life, and Jarrod still wants me—an impossible situation because someone is always going to get hurt in this equation.

He stops rubbing my hand and straightens back in his chair,

looking off in the distance. "Ya know, sweetheart, if I'd met you in high school, I would've snatched you up right away. There was no need to date any other girls in high school and college. You would've been *it* from the start. I would've taken you to prom, and we would've been named Prom King and Queen."

Jolted and thrown off-kilter, my chest constricts. My lungs are starved of oxygen as I clench my fists at the mention of *prom*. As childish and juvenile as it may seem, it's a trigger for me because of what that word represents. No one has to remind me I'm a grown-ass woman and that I should be stronger. I can't help what my heart feels, nor can I help the zaps of hurt that are frying my insides as I sit here.

I never told Jarrod about the prom refusal, so he couldn't possibly know the feelings it stirs. It takes me back to the moment of Wes's rejection, the moment I was ripped in two and never found the other half of myself again. Tears prick the backs of my eyes, and the knife in my heart twists a quarter turn.

Jarrod's not looking at me, thankfully; instead, he's concentrating on his salad bowl and spearing a wayward crouton with his fork. He just speared my heart without realizing it. Of course, he didn't mean to.

My boyfriend is trying to squeeze through that door I shut and locked at seventeen years old—the one I threw away the key to. I locked myself away and didn't leave a crack, yet somehow he's managed to wedge his way through the keyhole and make my insides crumble. If he keeps going, I'll cave because I don't want to do what was done to me.

After he captures the crouton and chews it, he looks in my direction again. I'm sure my eyes give me away because the spark of determination comes back in full force.

"You can still be my Prom Queen, Olivia. Just give us more time. I know you can grow to love me. I'll take you any way I can get you." He runs his hand through his blonde hair. He's putting his heart on the line, and it's so reminiscent of what I did all those years ago.

After his momentary pause, he further explains, "You're an incredible woman. You're so smart, compassionate, and loyal. I watch you at work when you're not aware. I see the way you interact with clients and colleagues, see the way you are with your friends and dad. You're a keeper."

I'm flabbergasted by his assessment of me. It's difficult when you don't view yourself the same as others do. I always strive to be a good person with a big heart, but I'm not perfect. He's saying all the things a woman wants to hear.

Could I give this more time between us?

"Jarrod, I just don't want to hurt you," I whisper with so much truth and emotion behind my words.

"Then don't. Just give it some more time. No pressure. I won't even ask to come home with you tonight." He successfully delivers a boyish grin that's meant to break my resolve further and to remind me of my no sleepover rule.

Biting my lip in contemplation, I finally make my decision and hope I don't regret it for both our sakes. "Okay."

He stands up, comes to my side, and kisses my lips sweetly then whispers "thanks" in my ear. Hurting him is the last thing I want to do, so I'm setting a deadline for myself. If I don't feel any differently in another month or two—at the most—then it's going to be over once and for all. He can't put his life on hold for me; I would never expect that of anyone.

As he returns to his chair, I gulp down my red wine. The server comes over and refills my glass. Jarrod and I finish our salads quickly and begin discussing work-related issues involving our one joint project. Our entrées soon follow, and before we know it, the evening is over. I wasn't in the mood for dessert, so we leave after settling the bill.

We drive back to my house in comfortable silence, and I appreciate him letting me escape in my mind for some valuable introspection. When he walks me to my front door, he bends down for a kiss. It starts out as a soft brushing of our lips, but he quickly tries to deepen it by parting my lips.

With this kiss, he's trying to show me what he has to offer. He's trying to show me *we're good together*—it's a reminder kiss. It should be toe-curling, mind-bending, earth-shattering. But, it's not. I still kiss him back. Sadly, it feels clumsy. The taste of his desperation and effort of trying too hard is clinging to my tongue like a coating of sorts—it's not a good start.

A thought filters through my mind, *Wes would have a skilled tongue and kiss like a dream.*

Hopefully, I don't have a guilty expression. My eyes pop open to see Jarrod's reaction—to see if he can sense my hesitation, but his eyelids are closed since he's lost in the moment. He groans through the kiss, and I let him plunder my mouth. Still no *zing.* I'm not going to fake anything or lead him on. I said I'd try, and I am, but I can't create feelings of love by pulling them out of the air.

As he reluctantly pulls back, Jarrod gives the tip of my nose a peck and croons, "Goodnight, sweetheart. I'll talk to you later. Thanks for giving us more time."

Yes, *time,* that pesky four-letter word that eludes me. I'm much more fearful of time than the other four-letter word—love.

Giving him a tremulous smile in return, I bid him goodnight. Unlocking my door and walking into my house allows me to think for a minute. Having some space is necessary for me after tonight's events. I may have given him—us—another chance, yet it still weighs heavily on me like a weighted blanket.

Ash is whining away from the kitchen. I smile at hearing him, having a little buddy in my life to come home to. After removing my sandals, I place them on the shoe rack in my entryway closet. As I'm doing it, my dog struts over. I start grinding my teeth.

"Okay, you little escape artist, you're in big trouble," I huff but then can't stay mad at him because he's too damn cute.

He yelps, and I scoop him up in my arms and kiss his little head. A baby gate will be purchased tomorrow.

***

Olivia

With the evening not going according to plan, I need to unwind. Two glasses of wine is my limit, which I indulged in at the restaurant. So more alcohol and further imbibing is out of the question. And I'm not really in the mood for a bath either.

I'm in my panties and an old T-shirt from college, sitting on the edge of my queen-sized bed. My knees are drawn up to my chest as I hug my legs, a slave to my thoughts. I put Ash down for the night after taking him for a walk around the neighborhood. The heat wave upon us doesn't even dissipate once the sky darkens. The comfort of my air conditioning is a life source right now, but with my house being so old, it's still stuffy in my upstairs bedroom. Running my hand through my sweat-slicked hair reminds me I need to cool down.

My nerves are in need of calming, and the only thing I can think of to relieve the tension is to pleasure myself. Inviting Jarrod in for sex is a selfish thing, and I would never use him for that. If we soon become intimate again, and I'm feeling something for him in that regard, then so be it—I'm not a user or abuser and won't sleep with him if my heart's not in it.

My feet meet the throw rug on my hardwood floor, and I pad over to my bedside table, taking out my purple vibrator. As I go to lie down on my mattress, I strip off my shirt and underwear. I'm flat on my back and push the covers down to the bottom with my feet. There's no need for covers because, not only am I alone and in the privacy of my home, but I also can't stand anything touching my skin at the moment because of the humidity. I'm going to be even hotter once I make myself orgasm, so it's a moot point.

As I blow out a long breath, I hold the vibrator in my right palm. With my left hand, I begin pinching my nipples to kickstart my journey into ecstasy. Teasing my breasts is sending sparks right to my core, and it tightens in the most delicious way. I lick my lips and close my eyes to lose myself as I enhance the sensations being stirred in my body.

After a few minutes, I switch on the vibrator and lower it to my sex. I rub it around the entrance to my pussy and coat it with my feminine juices. Then, I leisurely move it toward my clit, causing me to immediately cry out. It's so pleasurable, I'm already seeing stars.

After switching the vibrator to my left hand, I place two fingers of my right hand inside my channel. I moan and bend my legs at the knees so I can reach deeper within myself. My tissues are ultra-sensitive, and I'm so keyed up—I can't wait to come. *Yes, this is what I need.* I let my mind flit to some images of Jarrod. Maybe thinking about him will help me solidify something between us.

My mind brings forth memories of Jarrod, naked on top of me in his favorite position—missionary, always missionary. As I've said, he's got a great body, and he's easy on the eyes. Toned in all the right places, firm buttocks, and average-sized cock, with the personality to boot—the total package. I try to picture him on top of me moving back and forth, sucking my neck, kissing my breasts; *I just wish he'd bite them.* He's not rough or adventurous by any means.

The orgasm I thought was upon me is now nowhere to be found. *What happened?* Maybe I'm concentrating so hard on trying to get off that I'm not letting it happen naturally. So, I try to let go and focus on breathing and clearing my mind of everything—even of Jarrod.

However, my mind has a different agenda. Because suddenly, images of a very adult, virile Weston Thorpe are conjured directly from my psyche. I have no idea what he looks like today, but my imagination has exceptional taste. I'm envisioning those tumultuous eyes of his staring right into me like he can see into my past, present, and future. My pussy starts to spasm in gearing up for what is sure to be a phenomenal climax. His gray irises continue to bore into mine, and he's breathing heavily. His cologne enters my nostrils, and I hug his midsection to me.

Performing a mental observation of his features, I scan my gaze up and down his taut, gorgeous body, taking everything in. His naked torso has abs for days. His nipples are a tempting shade of brown because of his tan; I love the hair on his chest with incredible pecs. I continue to wander down to the smattering of dark hair below his bellybutton that leads to his groin. Then, it's imperative I take a deep breath before I reach his manhood—I need to collect myself because the sight will demolish me. When I gawk at the impressive length and girth of his captivating dick and testicles, my mouth fills with saliva, and I have to wipe away the drool.

"Mmm," I moan.

Right now, there's no room to feel guilty for thinking about him—I can worry about guilt later and berate myself. In this moment, though, my sole attention is on Wes. Since I opened the floodgate and let thoughts of him back into my life that have lain dormant for so long, well, I've awakened a beast inside me, and she wants to be fed. She craves Wes in the worst way.

My fingers plunge into my slit at a frenetic pace, and I turn up the speed on my purple battery-operated toy. I'm so close. The exquisite torture of hovering right on that cliff, waiting to free-fall into pleasure, is exhilarating. Wes's image is doing this to me. My body is his to control—my everything is his. I picture him whispering naughty things to me and licking the shell of my ear in the process.

"Wes…," I groan his name aloud.

In my fantasy he responds to me, "Yeah, baby, that's it. Let yourself go for me. Wet my dick with your cum. Nothing else in the world matters except you…"

I can't take any more. I'm not even sure what else he says because that's when I lose it. I arch off the bed and free-fall off that cliff. My body overheats as jolts of electricity zap me from the inside and outside. Both my heart and breathing are erratic.

I remove my hand and toy from my pussy and clit. My arms and legs flop to the sides as I'm totally spent.

Oh. My. God!

I'm unaware of how much time passes before I finally open my eyes and return to reality. *Mmm, that felt so good. So why do I feel so satisfied and sad at the same time?*

I know why. The experience may have fulfilled me in one way, but it also robbed me in another aspect—there's no Wes, except for in my head. So, I can't do that again. I can't pleasure myself with thoughts of him and be beholden to a desire that will never come to fruition—the poor she-beast will have to suffer right along with me.

There is no Wes out there for me!

Chapter 8: On Di*splay*

Olivia

"I'm so glad you came over. I really needed a girl's day," I tell my best friend.

It's the following Saturday afternoon. The heat wave finally broke, so I'm hoping to do something outdoorsy later like plant some new flowers in my garden. Or maybe visit the nearby dog park so my little buddy can roam freely in a massive grassy area.

She snorts, "Yeah, after the week you've had, I'd say so."

We're watching one of my top three favorite movies. *Steel Magnolias* gets me every time. I know all the scenes and practically every line, yet I still cry and laugh as if it's my first time watching it. Sammy's not into chick flicks, but she tolerates them for my sake. Ash is seated on her lap; I knew he'd grow on her. She's oblivious that she's stroking his soft fur from his head to his tail, and he's sleeping away. I'm grateful Tom let me borrow her for the day. Her husband is awesome, and I certainly don't mind hanging out with him, but a girl's day is heavenly.

"What's Tom up to?" I tuck an errant strand of hair behind my ear that escaped from my ponytail.

"Oh, he's golfing with some buddies. He'd probably enjoy this movie more than me; you should've asked him," she giggles.

I can't help but laugh too because she's probably right.

"I'm glad you're here, though. And, clearly, Ash is happy you're here." I eye her and motion down to the pup with my head.

She stops rubbing him, finally realizing what she's been doing. "Oh shit! I guess he wormed his little way into my heart after all."

"I knew he would," I tease her.

The baby gate has been purchased. I got it the day after I went to dinner with Jarrod, and Ash hasn't escaped since. Jarrod and I have seen each other at work twice this week when I've gone into the office, and I've talked to him on the phone a few times. We're taking things slowly at my behest; he accepts that. We may even go to lunch one day next week.

My dad came over Monday night and met Ash, and he's come over each day since to let him out during the day—even when I've been here. It's a riot watching the two of them together. I'm sure he'll pop over today at some point to check on his buddy. A part of me wonders if I should get him a pet of his own so he won't be lonely, but I think visiting my place gives him something to look forward to.

"So, are you and Jarrod doing better?"

The question doesn't surprise me because I expected to discuss my boyfriend with her this afternoon. I had called her late Sunday night to fill her in on what happened at dinner. Of course, I left out the part about my solo performance in the bedroom, but I feel like we need to discuss the reasons behind my ability to reach release. As I've previously mentioned, I haven't ever told her about Wes, so this will be a doozy.

"Yes and no. *Yes* in the sense that I'm trying and willing to give this a shot to see where it may lead. He made me think I shouldn't be too hasty in ending things. But also *no*. The *no* is why I need to talk to you."

"Uh oh. Spill it!"

Turning my body to face her on the couch, I settle in for this important conversation. Criss-crossing my legs, I make a nice little hole for Ash to lie in. Without calling him over, he automatically gets up from Sammy's lap and plunks down on my legs, yawns, and goes back to sleep. I give his head a few rubs, and I'm glad he can comfort me while I try to tell my friend about the man who's haunted me for years.

Already feeling vulnerable—not because she'll discount my feelings—an uneasy shiver runs up and down my spine. I'm nervous because I don't want to come off as ridiculous or pathetic for pining after him. Sammy naturally acts like a strong person—much stronger than me, and I'm jealous of that trait. I'll have to summon her strength.

Clearing my throat, I start to impart a secretive piece of my past. "When I was a junior in high school, a new student moved here halfway through the school year. His name was Weston Thorpe. I had a crush on him—like a *major* crush. Well, maybe 'infatuation' is a better term for it. Anyway, it only got stronger during our senior year."

Licking my lips and swallowing are necessary as my mouth goes dry. "I ended up asking him to the prom because he hadn't asked me, or anyone, for that matter. I thought I had a chance. But...he shot me down. Ugh, my chest was splayed open, my beating heart bludgeoned, and I've never gotten over it."

I'm looking to her for any sign of pity, but her face is blank.

She parts her lips to speak, but I jump in there again, "I know, cue the violins and throw up the curtain for this performance. I swear, I'm not being dramatic. I. Loved. Him."

My lip quivers as I take a much-needed pause. Those feelings of disappointment and anguish are hitting me all at once. She now wears a perplexed expression on her face—the kind that asks *where is she going with this?* Sammy nods for me to continue once again—I'm sure she can sense I'm not quite finished.

"Erm, I'm *still* in love with him—never got over him, actually. He broke my heart without even knowing it. Jesus, we didn't even date, but it went beyond a simple case of: girl meets boy, boy's not interested, and girl loses boy, even though she never had him to begin with. Like I said, it wasn't a simple case. It's like a bad dream that won't leave my mind, and I'm a prisoner to what happened. The memories just cling to me—sharper than cat's claws. I'm probably not making any sense and sound pathetic, don't I?"

Burying my face seems logical, but I'm a grown-ass woman. I'll face the music with whatever my friend has to say.

"Liv, I don't think you're pathetic at all. There are some people you just can't get over. Whether a person is a teenager or an adult shouldn't make a difference. By all accounts, I think it's evident you reached maturity before high school. What you went through with your mom, I imagine made you view life and love differently than the average person."

Sammy grabs the hand that's tucked in my lap and looks in my eyes. There's no pity there, more empathy than anything. No judgment or signs of her dismissing my feelings.

"Thank you," I all but whisper and choke back a sob.

"What're friends for, eh? Hurt is hurt. Love is love, and sometimes neither of those things go away. And not to sound dismal, but maybe it's something you'll *never* get over. It all makes sense now with Jarrod! Since this is your first serious relationship, I would venture the second you felt he was getting too close, you started thinking about this guy—Weston's his name, right?"

She has a point. Ash stretches on my lap, and I need to come clean about the next thing.

"Well, I call him Wes—but Weston will do. Not like it matters; I haven't seen him in sixteen years. Although, I feel awful—I climaxed the other night to an image of him in my head."

Now I do hide my face. I cover it with both hands like I'm a frightened little girl. It's embarrassing admitting this, but I blurted it out anyway. I'm in need of reassurance that *it's going to be okay.*

"Shut up! You did not!"

I shake my head indicating, *yes, I most certainly did.*

"You little hussy," she jokes and breaks off into a fit of laughter.

Removing the shield from my face that my hands created, Ash stands up in my lap licking my cheeks like a wild man, wondering what my problem is. I purse my lips and cock an eyebrow at her so she can see I'm partially annoyed with her giggling away at my expense.

She finally calms herself to tell me, "Don't hate yourself for it. It's perfectly natural and normal. As hot as Tom is, and as much as he satisfies me—repeatedly—I still masturbate to someone else's face sometimes. Hell, I even do it during sex. There may be a certain scene from a porno we watched, or some actor I'm lusting after who just does it for me. You're thirty-freaking-four years old. Do what you want!"

I love her attitude. She doesn't apologize for anything and can usually put my mind at ease about a subject. Since she's a married woman, I had no idea women did that. Clearly I'm naïve.

"I thought that was like a form of cheating or something?" I awkwardly admit.

"Hell no! I'm sure most sex therapists—not that I'd know because we don't need one—would tell you it's even considered healthy. My God, Tom pictures some hot-ass actresses sometimes, and I'm not jealous in the slightest because I'm the one he's banging, and I'm the one he comes home to. Whatever gets either of us off works for both of us. And it's not like I do it every time."

This makes sense. "Wow! Okay, well, I won't beat myself up about it then. See, this is why I needed time with my bestie."

Gingerly moving Ash out of the way, I throw my arms around Sammy, clinging to her like my life depends on it. She hugs me back fiercely. I don't know what I'd do without her. The movie still plays on, but I lost my interest in finishing it so I turn it off.

She clucks her tongue and looks at me with a mischievous grin, "Okay, so now you're gonna spill the rest. Tell me all about *him.*"

I sigh. "Well, we're going to need wine for this!"

***

Weston

The yard is mowed, both front and back. The hedges are clipped, and Grant and I are finishing up with the weed whacking. We took turns visiting with Mom, and Mal is supposed to be home shortly so we can take her to dinner. Of course, my best friend and I will have to run back to our apartments to shower and change because we're disgusting. At least the unbearable humidity has disappeared; otherwise, we'd be melted on the sidewalk by now.

Mom seems good today. I was worried after talking to my sister last weekend that she was in another downward spiral, but it's not as bad as usual—I'm wondering if she switched medications. The antidepressants do wonders, and in her case, I swear by them. There's so much bullshit medication-shaming out there these days, but I know first-hand some pills work. No one will ever catch me judging anyone for using them when warranted. However, I can't get too excited because it's only a matter of time before she's pulled back under again by the depression.

"Hey, slowpoke!" Grant whistles at me to get my attention. "The weeds aren't going to trim themselves."

"Yeah, yeah. I've done more in five minutes than you've done in an hour," I jab back.

"I did the whole back and sides; now I'm helping you with the front. So, who's really done more, asshole?"

When I'm all done, I wipe my brow with the back of my hand and walk over to the porch to drink some water. Grant joins me, and we sit on the steps viewing our handiwork and nodding our heads in approval.

He takes a swig of water from his bottle, and we fist bump each other. I tell him, "Thanks, man. I do appreciate your help."

He replies while grinning, "You owe me so much—the list is longer than our fire hoses, brother."

I laugh at that comment. It's true, though. I'll never be able to repay him for the favors—not that he makes me feel that I have to. He does things because he wants to and because we're family. Hell, he even calls my mom "Mom."

Grant's family history is an interesting one. His parents are non-existent in his life. They basically disowned him years ago. His mom and dad didn't see eye to eye with him on religion—they're very devout, and Grant's not. Even though I feel I had a hell of an upbringing, it was my teenage years that sucked ass, not my whole childhood. But Grant, he had it rough from the time he was born.

My sister pulls up in her little car. It's not lost on me that Grant watches every move she makes from the moment she steps out the driver's side, to the moment she's standing in front of us. His lips part while gawking at her, and I'm trying to refrain from growling at him in warning.

Mal has no idea how people subconsciously gravitate toward her. Since she was a teen, men have noticed her and even leered at her. Her features favor our mother. Before Dad went to prison, my mom was always well put-together. But after…you wouldn't know that she and Mal are cut from the same cloth appearance-wise.

The innocence in my sister's blue eyes is there for the world to see—making me fearful someone will take advantage. Being that she's a hairdresser, her current color and style is aptly named *unicorn hair*. The vibrant colors of the rainbow are weaved throughout the blonde locks of her shoulder-length haircut. She wears black-rimmed glasses on occasion to be stylish, and she's always a trendy dresser who finds the best bargains at thrift stores or discount clothing shops. My sister represents what life should be—free, beautiful, and fun.

"Hey, guys! The yard looks amazing. Jeez, you have to stop spoiling me like this or I might get used to it," Mal smiles, her eyes sparkling like sapphires glittering in the sun.

Her smile is always infectious. Everyone around her adores her—that's what makes her dangerous. She's too sweet, too innocent, and too naïve. Although, when she wants to be assertive, that side of her will come out as well.

She laughs and informs us, "I would give you a thank you kiss on the cheek if you weren't so sweaty." Then she wrinkles her nose to acknowledge our state of sweatiness.

Grant is a first-rate flirt, so I'm not surprised when he asks her, "Do we both get a kiss, doll?"

Shit!

A red hue creeps into her cheeks—she's full-out blushing. *Damn, don't be charmed by him, kiddo!* Grant grins like a fucking loon. I elbow him in the side and shoot him a death glare that says, *back the fuck off!* He clears his throat.

She bites her lower lip and looks back and forth between us, clearly aware there's something going on that she's not privy to. Then she nods. "Well, I better get inside and get Mom dinner before we go out. What time do ya think you'll be back for me?"

"Hmm, give us about an hour to get ready, kiddo," I say, looking down at my watch.

When I glance back up at her face, now she's beet-red—it's not from blushing; now it's from embarrassment. And I realize my mistake was calling her "kiddo" to her face. Grant has warned me, yet I did it anyway.

"Okay," is her melancholy reply.

She quickly passes right between us—we're still seated on the steps—to run and hide inside. After I hear the door slam, I let out a slow breath and mutter, "Shit!"

"Yup, you're in the doghouse now. I tried to tell you."

Sighing in frustration, I admit, "I know. Sometimes I just forget she's a grown woman. It's hard to view her like that. And you don't help in the matter by flirting with her."

"Eh, think nothing of it. It's harmless. You know I do it with every girl. My bad."

Grant stands up and turns to offer his hand to help pull me to my feet. It's time to get home and get cleaned up. I'm looking forward to spending time with Mal, and hopefully my best friend will behave.

Chapter 9: Fuego!

Weston

Grant and I let my sister pick the place for dinner. She decides on Mexican—and for that, Mal's the best. She's a no-fuss girl and will eat like she's hungry, not just sit there nibbling like a mouse. It's the perfect place for us to go since Mexican is my favorite.

I made it back to my mom's before Grant showed up, so I was able to apologize to Mal for embarrassing her earlier. Also, I got to visit with Mom a little longer.

We arrive at The Green Chile Restaurant and slide into a booth, settling comfortably on the green pleather cushions. I'm seated next to Mal, and across from us is Grant—although, it didn't escape me that he sat directly opposite my sister rather than straight across from me. *Interesting.*

Focusing my attention elsewhere, I look at the menu. As always, there's too much to choose from, but this place makes a mean guacamole. I'm serious when it comes to my guac, so I'll slather it on everything that goes into my stomach tonight. All around the room I hear the sizzling of fajitas arriving to eager patrons, and I inhale the most mouthwatering spicy scents that can only be found at an eatery such as this.

Our server comes by to deliver drinks and complimentary chips and salsa. The three of us attack the basket like we've been castaways at sea with no food for weeks. We're downing margaritas—I drove all of us here, so three of these babies is my limit. Because I'm a protective brother, I'll also make sure my sister steers clear of shots because I want her level-headed. Subconsciously, I know it's mainly due to a certain someone seated across from her that I want her of sound mind.

My lime margarita tastes like the freshest frozen drink I've ever had. I glance at their glasses and notice I take mine with salt while Mal and Grant opted for sugar on the rim. Thankfully, my best friend and I can imbibe tonight because we don't have to pull a shift until tomorrow evening.

The vibe in this place is great, and there's no cheesy music that grates on my nerves like some establishments tend to blast through the speakers. Carnitas, tamales, chimichangas, and empanadas are what we order—Grant and I can put away a lot of food, but we're going to share family-style. This was the best idea to go out with my little sis and catch up.

"So, how's the hair biz going?" I ask Mal while stuffing a chip in my mouth.

She's mid-chew when she puts her hand up to her mouth and smiles. I caught her off guard, and she's as serious about her salsa as I am about guac.

"It's going well. I like the current salon I'm at. They're fair with pricing, so it'll do for now. I'd actually love to open my own shop one day."

I almost drop my next chip to look at her. Having no clue that this was even on her radar, I'm speechless.

Grant jumps in, "Wow, Mal, that's an awesome idea! You should totally do it."

There's that damn blush again in her cheeks, and this time it travels down her neck. I've never seen her blush around a guy so much. Now I'm thinking, *this dinner would've been an even better idea if I'd uninvited my buddy.*

Clearing my throat to get both of their attention, since they're staring into one another's eyes like they're damn lovers, I say, "Yeah, Mal, that's great. I had no clue that was something you'd want to do."

She shrugs in nonchalance. "It'll probably never happen, but it's an idea. I know I need capital—which I don't have—and I doubt I'll qualify for a small business loan. Just gives me something to work toward one day, ya know? Something I can pin to my dream board."

Her mouth turns down, and she nibbles on her bottom lip almost as if she's trying to squash a sad thought. She's probably thinking that as long as she's saddled with Mom, her life will never move forward. *God, I'm so fucking sorry, kiddo.* I vow right then and there I'm going to try harder to change the situation she's in.

"You'll make it happen. A smart, beautiful, and resilient woman like you will get it done. Trust me, doll," Grant professes and then immediately looks down into his margarita.

He doesn't see Mal's reaction. I notice, of course. Mal responds to him like I used to with Liv. The sun rose, set, and repeated when I was around that girl. She was the forbidden indulgence that would have tasted so sweet, but I was not lucky enough to take a bite from. Even with the serpent in the garden telling me to take what was mine, I had to leave her—the juicy metaphoric apple—hanging on the branch. *A regret?* Hell yeah! But I can be proud I didn't complicate her life; I wouldn't have been good for her. Sometimes my self-loathing rears its ugly head at the most inopportune time.

I have to wonder if it would be *that* bad if Grant did date my sister. And then the thought disappears faster than it came because I'll reiterate: it'd be too weird! Worse yet, if it ended in disaster or he hurt my sister in any way, our friendship would be over—it would crush me either way, losing my sister or the guy I consider a brother.

Mal doesn't say anything more about a potential entrepreneurship. And somehow the conversation shifts to me.

"Any new girlfriends you want to tell me about, Wes? Like a certain blonde named Della?" My sister—looking all smug—asks me, then bites into an empanada that was just dropped off to our table.

How the hell?

"Umm, first of all, you know I don't do the girlfriend thing, and Della was like two weeks ago. Second, how the hell do you know about her?"

My little sister sits there grinning like she's all innocent.

"Come on, girls talk. This chick—*Della*—came into the salon, and Nicole styled her. The entire time she was getting frosted, I had to hear all about how 'hot' this firefighter guy was. She described your tattoos in great detail, and some things I had to cover my ears over. I was only a chair away. It wasn't difficult to figure out who she was talking about."

Damnit, sometimes this town is too small!

I didn't even think Della was from around here. The bar is far enough away that the woman could've been from anywhere. And it's embarrassing my sister had to hear shit about me no sister should have to hear—this is the first, but quite possibly not the last time. I guess I'll have to be more careful.

"Plus, you went to high school with her. I just think she was a few grades below you," Mal informs me.

"Fuck!" I murmur under my breath as best as I can.

That woman probably knew more about me than I realized. I'm sure she knew my family history and targeted me. Most people around town have forgotten about my dad—he's old news to them. But, his name comes up on occasion, and I have to relive my past in stark clarity.

To take the heat off me, I throw Grant under the bus about that night too. "And what about Grant? His name come up? I'm sure, what's-her-face—Kylie?—would have some stories to tell too."

Finally registering what a dick move that was, I see Grant stiffen at the mention of the chick he had been with. My sister drops the fork she'd been eating rice and beans with. It clatters onto the plate loudly, serving as a reminder I screwed up again.

There's the old adage *where there's smoke, there's fire*. Well, in my case, where there's smoke there's *me*. Because I always seem to be at the root of causing pain—I'm the catalyst that allows the smoke to billow.

Grant stands up. "If you'll excuse me, I need to get some air."

He won't even look my way. His eyes are only on Mal's face, which is now marred with a defeated expression—a look I've seen on her many times over the years, but usually because of something to do with my family, not me in particular. Being thick in the head sometimes does happen to me, but tonight I know what's going on. I suspect her sudden change of mood is due to hearing about Grant with some other woman.

Before Grant turns on his heel and walks away, he places his hands on the tabletop and leans in to tell me menacingly, "Her name was Kelly, by the way. I don't forget names—I care too much to forget things like that."

Staring after his retreating form, I don't miss his anger; it's noticeable in the way he's carrying himself even if he didn't showcase it in his tone. We've known each other too damn long for me not to be in tune with certain things. We'll no doubt have words later.

Rubbing the slight stubble on my jawline, I turn to face my sister. *Shit, was that a tear she swiped at with her fingers?* She doesn't resume eating and instead starts downing her margarita. I eye her suspiciously.

"I lost my appetite, okay?" she explains without me having to ask.

Putting my arm around her, I squeeze her to my side—a thing I've done a million times as her big brother. "I'm sorry." Then I cringe asking her this next question, "You don't like Grant, do you?"

"N-n-no. Why would you ask me that?"

"It's just a feeling I have. It's in the way you look at him and talk to him. But if I'm wrong, I'm wrong."

A part of me doesn't believe her, but she doesn't lie to me. She never has, so I'll give her the benefit of the doubt.

"Well, I don't. Besides, even if I did, it's not like I'd do anything about it. He's your best friend, and I wouldn't jeopardize that." She licks her lips and finally faces me to look me in the eye. Then, her next words hit me square in the heart because of her vulnerability: "And I'm sure he doesn't like me like...*that*. I'm the baby sister to you guys. He's known me since I was a dorky kid, so it doesn't matter."

Feeling useless in this situation, I try to give her reassurance. Still silent, I realize I need to say something—anything—to make her feel better. But as I go to speak, Grant returns and plunks down in the booth again. "Ready for dessert? I hear the sopapillas are good here, at least that's what they said at the bar."

Mal slides away from me a little, and for her sake, I'm going to close the subject on this. It's better to leave some things alone. My prayer for her is to not develop feelings for him. Having first-hand knowledge of what a bleeding heart does to a person, I wouldn't wish it on my worst enemy. Hopefully, Mal never knows what it's like to love someone she can't have.

"Yeah, man, sounds good," I reply to him.

I try my best to shake it off, yet I have a feeling things will be awkward between the three of us from now on.

***

Olivia

It's Sunday evening, and I just left the mall, now heading toward home— back to my little pup whom I'm sure is anxiously awaiting my arrival.

Shopping is one of my least favorite things, but I promised Sammy after our girl's day yesterday we'd do a double date sometime this week. I know Jarrod will be up for it without even having to ask. And because I'm trying to give *us* a chance, I'm making the effort.

Since I thought a new dress was in order, I decided to venture where I'd have plenty of stores to choose from. Not only did I find a dress, but I also purchased new shoes and a bangle bracelet with a single pearl seated in the middle that joins the two sides of metal—a perfect complement to my earrings.

Tonight is a win in my book with my finds; even my bestie would be proud. Sammy would've gone with me had I asked her, however, I opted not to. My two-hour shopping trip would've turned into a four-hour ordeal because of her fashionista tendencies.

Glancing at the digital clock on my car panel, I see it's 7:42 P.M. I'm driving along one of my favorite highways in the Pines—well, it's my favorite during the day. It's a stretch of drive lined with lush forests on both sides. The greenery always puts a smile on my face, and when it's not too hot during the day, I roll down my windows to take in the woodsy scents. Fall is the best time of year, and I can't wait for it because the colors always beckon me to jump in a big pile of leaves like I did as a kid.

It's pitch black out now that summer's ending. And though not as many motorists travel at night, it's best to always stay vigilant. I scan the road constantly, flitting back and forth looking for any sign of movement. I'm trying to see if my high beams illuminate any eyes from animals on the side of the road. Deer are notorious for grazing along this stretch of Route 71.

My radio speakers are at a respectable level, and the group Heart— a band from the 80s I adore—are singing and jamming away about dreams.

My singing skills are lacking and should never be forced upon any human ears, but it helps relax me, marginally. If I have something to focus on, I won't think about what's lurking in the night.

I grip the wheel nervously, despite the fact that I'm almost home. It's a fairly decent night temperature-wise; the humidity is at least bearable. So, I imagine nocturnal creatures will be moving about in comfort, and that's what has my hands sweating and my nerves ratcheted up.

Suddenly, my beams catch a flicker of light on the side of the road—there's barely any time to react.

Oh no!

The last thing I remember is veering to the right to avoid the deer running across the road like lightning. The buck with huge antlers is racing so fast, and he's so big that if I hit him head-on, I'll be creamed.

It all happens so fast when I swerve.

I instantly lose control.

I'm spinning and…*crash!*

Then, darkness takes me.

Chapter 10: Wrecked

Weston

Shift started a little bit ago, it's now 7:50 P.M. Grant and I agreed to do a twelve-hour stint since two of our crew members were pulled out to work a forest fire in another county. My best friend and I haven't discussed the disaster that was dinner last night—or my sister, for that matter—but, eventually we'll have *that* conversation. It's an unspoken understanding, one in which it seems we need to forget it ever happened…for now.

The two of us are on the engine tonight with one other member along with our captain, Keith, while the other two on the rotation are tasked with manning the ambulance. We're just shooting the shit and running a hose drill with our training equipment. We're always training if we're not out on a call or cleaning.

After ten minutes, that sound I love so much, a buzz that seeps into my bones with both dread and a thrill because of never knowing what the call entails, comes across the radio. The crackling sound begins, and then there's a set of tones that indicate Central Dispatch is about to deliver an important message.

"Task Force 21. Highway 71 at cross-street Five Mile Road. Rescue Assignment," dispatch announces with a few more crackles before it goes silent.

"Woo hoo, boys. We got a rescue. Jobtown! Gear up and move out," our resident Jersey shore boy Dex hollers.

Grant and I are already in action suiting up. We're like a well-oiled machine, he and I. When he moves, I move—it's just the result of working together, side by side, for so long. There's a code we live by to have each other's backs. Quickly pulling on our turnout gear consisting of boots, pants, gloves, and coats—we're already wearing our navy cargo pants and *Pineville Task Force 21* T-shirts—we grab our helmets to put on when we get on scene. No need for air packs since it's an MVA (motor vehicle accident).

I'm the first to hop on the truck with Grant right behind me. We jump in our seats and strap in. Dex is driving, and our captain takes the passenger seat up front. The other two guys, Rick and Joe, are in the ambulance to offer ancillary support.

Being the first to sign on and respond ahead of the ambulance, Keith takes command to radio in our response, "Engine Eleven responding."

"Copy Engine Eleven."

We roll out. The Q (engine siren) roars in warning to the public to move out of our way. The lights are flashing—it's hypnotic. This is where my adrenaline starts pumping, and I'm not even concerned about how humid it is. I typically don't focus on those things because there's a life hanging in the balance. Each move we make, each decision executed could mean the difference between life and death. Obviously, we take our jobs seriously, and it's the moment of truth when faced with a person desperate to live. We do everything in our means and power to save them.

What makes calls more complicated is when we know the person. Our town is a decent enough size that I don't know *everyone*. But in smaller towns, hell, chances are the squad members are friends with the victim, related to them, or an acquaintance of theirs.

Five more minutes and we'll reach our destination. Station One is only ten minutes from the location of the MVA; we have two stations within the township. Central Dispatch comes back on the line with more information. As details become available, they share the data so we know what we're walking into.

"Engine Eleven, single vehicle MVA into tree. Caller states possible entrapment, and driver is unconscious."

"Engine Eleven copies."

My blood is pounding in my ears. My heart is thumping. My veins are screaming to jump into action. I have to tell my muscles to *calm the fuck down!*

We finally arrive on scene, and state troopers are diverting traffic to the other lane and setting up a perimeter for us to work in because our apparatus needs space. Looking to the vehicle, I wince for the driver who did a number on their car. The smashed two-door sedan crashed into a tree, and fresh tire tread-marks, where they probably swerved, are visible on the roadway. My nose registers the smell of burning oil permeating the air and overtaking any other smells. Neither the pine trees, the humid night, nor our body odor in our uniforms can compete with the oil.

My Halligan tool will not do the job to pry open the door or gain us entry at another point. We need something more heavy-duty after assessing the state of the vehicle. The EMTs are setting up their gear and pulling out the stretcher. My captain is taking control of the scene and calling for the spreaders, so I lift the compartment door by the bumper and grab a set. They're operated by hydraulics, for which Dex will flip the switch on the engine to make them functional.

In the background, I faintly hear Keith confirming to dispatch it's *a single person involved, female, unconscious.* We don't know the extent of her injuries, so it's vital we work efficiently and carefully. One wrong move could turn into a nightmare when extraction is involved: for every action, there is a reaction.

When our chief shows up, he'll take command; for now, Keith is in charge. Grant grabs the cribbings to secure her vehicle. No one can afford for the car to move when we're cutting since this is precision work. Moving into position, I'm ready to go with the spreaders—we're doing a classic door pop extraction. The driver's door—thankfully—is only bent; it's our best chance of getting her out. The passenger side door is practically wrapped around the tree, so that's a no-go.

Joe and Rick are trying to rouse the patient. No one knows her information yet, and since we can't get to her glove box or locate a purse, she remains unidentified.

"Ma'am, Ma'am, can you hear me? Ma'am?" Rick asks her over and over again with no reply or movement on her end.

I haven't even really looked at her because my mission is to get her out, not focus on her injuries—I'm not an EMT tonight, I'm solely fire rescue. Joe covers the unknown woman with a blanket in case glass or other pieces of the car go flying in the process.

Captain Keith is calling out directions and giving orders, and I take a deep breath while looking for a perch point in the wrecked metal to jam my tool into. It's always crowded in these confined spaces we have to work in. The EMTs complicate things without meaning to, but they have to stay with the patient at all times to ensure her well-being.

They're holding her head to steady it, and that's when I finally look up at her face. There's blood everywhere. So much blood. I don't panic on her behalf, though, because I can see there's a laceration at the scalp. Head wounds typically bleed profusely. It's nothing I haven't seen before. She'll get stitched up and be fine; I just hope the rest of her body is okay. She looks about my age, if I had to guess. The light-brown hair and blood practically smothering her ensures I can't identify her—she could be someone I know, but I doubt it.

State police are conversing with Keith and parts of their conversation filter to my ears. "….she apparently tried to avoid a deer. I'm sure this isn't your first rodeo on this highway, so as you know, the speed limit's sixty through here. When she swerved, she must've spun and lost control, crashing into that tree. I don't think alcohol's involved. Just a classic case of one of God's creatures running in the Pines."

I try to ignore the conversations and concentrate on my mission. With the spreaders being hydraulic-powered, they're not noisy. All I hear now is the metal of the car crunching and trying to separate under my hands—it's like smashing a soda can. I have to work the tool in there until it bites by gripping the metal. Remaining calm is of utmost importance—calmness equals power in these delicate situations. Finally, the door gives way and comes completely off. I toss it to the side, and everyone converges on the hole I just made.

Not that I want a pity party, but my arms ache like a motherfucker. Holding up the tool for long periods of time kills my muscles, even though I'm pretty buff. I was going to ask Grant to take a turn, but I got the door off before that happened. I stretch my arm for a second, then jump back into the fray after placing the spreaders out of the way.

Joe takes c-spine on the woman's head, effectively stabilizing her neck. This is where we especially need to work together as a team. It's a trauma call, so all hands on deck. We firefighters did our part, so it's time to assist the EMTs with the lift. The stretcher is right behind me, and we move the backboard into position to make it a smooth transition from each piece of equipment.

Carefully turning the patient's body, we maneuver her so her feet are aimed toward the center console. We continue to pivot her out of the seat then slide her upper half onto the backboard. Rick c-collars her. Then, the final move is to pull her completely out onto the board, slide her onto the stretcher, and strap her down. She still hasn't regained consciousness, but they'll work on her in the ambulance.

Our chief arrived and said the paramedics are down the road, so they'll take over for Rick and Joe. The main goal is to align her spine, and we accomplished that. While they're further embolizing her head and strapping her down, her shirt rides up.

Holy fucking Christ!

There's a strawberry-shaped birthmark on the patient's right hip. I can't help but think I'm very familiar with that mark, familiar because I've dreamed about it.

I say aloud without meaning to, "I know her!"

God, don't let it be Olivia.

And before I know it, I'm thrust into a memory—a memory I have replayed thousands of times in my head as if it was yesterday and not sixteen years ago.

***

Weston

Surely by now Olivia realizes I'm a stalker.

Staring at her whenever she's near is a dead giveaway. It's probably creepy as fuck, but I can't help myself. She's my obsession—a secret I keep all to myself because I don't want to share even the very idea of her with anyone. That's how much she consumes me. She's the reason I don't skip school and want to make something of myself. I'm going to become a firefighter because of her. I want to feel I'm "something" in this life, even though she's not mine.

Prom is in a month. I want to ask her to go so badly, but I'm sure all the guys are lined up around the block to take her. My old man would never let me go anyway, so there's no sense in trying. No money to get prom tickets and no money for a tux—yet I'd wear jeans if it meant I could go. And if I could ask one girl, of course it would be her. Fuck, I'd run away with her tomorrow—that's how serious I am. But if I disobey Dad, he'll take it out on Mal and Mom, and then they'll finally get the unpleasant treatment I've been given all this time. I can't let that happen; they're too innocent for that.

It's unseasonably warm today. I had to wear long sleeves again to cover up the bruises; people probably think I'm on drugs, but I don't care because that'll keep most gawkers at bay. The last thing I need is for one of my teachers or another faculty member to notice the horrific bruises. Hell, I have no friends, and I like it that way. No friends means no questions asked, and therefore, no prying into my business. This way I don't have to divulge details because inevitably that person would tell someone I'm an abuse victim, and my life would be over.

My desire is to get close to Olivia, but not too close. I want her to notice me, but at the same time, I don't want her to really "see" me. Because then she'll see all the parts of me I'm ashamed of. I'm weak. I'm a loser. I can't be a man, so what good am I to her? She needs a good guy who's strong and can protect her from the monsters and horrors of this world.

I'm not worthy of her.

Fuck, I love her, though. Is that even possible at seventeen?

I don't know. It's not something I want to talk to my mom about. If I had a normal dad, I'd confide in him and ask him the wonders of the world, but the only fatherly advice he gives me is "to not be a pussy and don't ever cry when you're taking your licks!" Yeah, that's what I get. I guess that's what I deserve.

We're sitting at lunch on a normal Tuesday afternoon at school. She's about six tables away, conversing with her friends.

Olivia…I say her name in my mind and sigh longingly at her, my fingers itching to reach out to caress her skin and play with her soft hair, if only she were seated closer.

And then, Olivia locks eyes with me as if I've said her name out loud. She couldn't have heard me; I didn't voice it. Smiling away, she gives a slight wave toward me. I grip the edge of the table until all the blood drains out and my knuckles turn white. Every teenage fantasy flashes through my mind of the things I want to do to her.

I turn around to see that no one is behind me and that she actually meant to wave to me of all people. I'm stunned there's no one else in sight.

I'm considered the weirdo in this place, right? The outcast? Shouldn't she be waving at a jock? I can't even play sports because once again, the old man wouldn't allow it. I have two thoughts on that. On one hand, I should play because I'll have an excuse for the bruises and marks that line my body. But on the other hand, I think Dad's afraid that if I play, I'll get bigger than him. That would pose a threat to his existence and the hold he has over me.

As I turn back around to look at her, she laughs and clamps down on her lips with her teeth to stifle her giggling at witnessing my confusion.

She does something next that I never expected. Pushing her chair back, she walks over to me and stands before my seated form. She's all curvy and all perfect with luscious skin, caramel-colored hair, and violet eyes that shimmer like jewels of the Nile.

Oh shit, I can die right now a happy guy.

"Hey, Wes," she says sweetly, those heavenly lips of hers shiny and perfectly plump.

Internally, I groan at her beauty, gulping aloud because it's hard to believe this girl is giving me the time of day. She's too precious. Too much of a treasure to be consorting with the likes of me.

"H-h-hi, Liv."

Damn, she's every boy's dream in the flesh. Her eyes smolder, and I want to get lost in any part of her.

"I noticed you're sitting over here all by yourself…" she trails off and looks around at the table.

There's no food in sight in front of me. I don't eat. My dad doesn't give me money—even though my mom thinks he does—and I'm not taking handouts from the school. It's okay; I get by the best I can.

She looks confused by my lack of lunch but shrugs and continues, "Mind if I join you?"

Fuck me! I want nothing more than to hang out with her. Keeping her at arm's length is a must, though. It's for her own good. She'll get hurt because I'll end up breaking her somehow. I'm tainted. Destroying her will kill me, and I love her too much to subject her to my life.

My hesitation is evident. I'm sure she can see in my face—see in my eyes—the raging inferno that is my emotions. It's a bitch to want something you can't have. And I'll never have her; it's just the way it is.

"Uh, I'm sorry, Liv. I was just about to run to my math class because I forgot my book."

Her face falls at my rejection. Damn, I'm no good! I end up hurting her no matter what—trying to protect her from myself still leads to hurting her. And I'm still stunned that she even wants to be around me.

As she runs her hand through her silky, wavy tresses, her T-shirt lifts from her torso. On her right hip I see a pink mark—I guess it's a birthmark—shaped like a strawberry. For some reason, I find it sexy and want to lick every inch of her, starting with that spot.

I avert my eyes and scramble to find a way to smooth over what I said, to take some sting out of my words. I rush to add, "Maybe another time, baby."

FUCK!

Cringing, I realize I just fucked up by calling her "baby." I can't help it. It slipped out as if my heart and mind wanted it to be out there.

Her face transforms, and she beams at me like I'm the fucking moon, stars, and sky above her. I breathe deeply through my nose, willing myself to stay seated and not sweep her up into my arms. Hope just entered her eyes, and I fucked up by teasing her with something I can't give.

"I gotta go, Liv. I'll see you around."

I scurry out of there faster than I've ever tried to run from my dad. Fucking up big time is what I'm known for. It's what I do best.

"Stay away from her!" I tell myself. She's off limits.

***

Weston

I'm brought back to the present. In my vision I only see a strawberry—it's burned into my brain for eternity. I'm frozen in place, not registering anything else around me until Grant shakes me roughly. "Wake the fuck up, man; what's gotten into you?" he yells.

Coming back to myself, I realize the paramedics have entered the ambulance and started cutting off her clothes—it's obligatory in a trauma to assess injuries. They're taking vitals. *Fuck!* I don't want anyone to see her like this. She's so small and vulnerable. Her little five and a half foot frame seems even smaller lying on the gurney.

Joe shuts the back doors so I can't see Liv on the stretcher any longer. I'm panting. My heart is beating wildly like it will fly out of my chest.

"I know her, Grant."

"Know who?"

"The patient. She's my...she's the...." *Love of my life.*

Swallowing back the words, I squeeze my eyes shut, overcome by memories of the girl my soul never let go of.

"Shit, I'm sorry, man. Who is she?"

Chapter 11: Painful Reminders

Weston

The ambulance starts to pull away with lights and sirens going. Across the radio, Rick tells Central they're en route to Lakeview County Hospital—the nearest trauma center.

Our job is far from over here. I can't just take off, even though everything in me is rebelling against following damn protocol. The voice inside my head is screaming to go after her and make sure she's okay. The bitch of it is, I can't even ask my fellow squad members anything related to her when they return from the hospital because it's a HIPAA violation. I'd never compromise my integrity or somebody else's.

Besides, it's not my place to go after her—I'm nothing to Liv. I just hope she has an emergency contact they'll reach out to on her behalf. The state troopers were able to search the vehicle and find her purse and phone, so it was tossed into the ambulance before they took off. The hospital should be able to contact someone utilizing her belongings. Passing around documentation and reports, troopers do confirm it is, in fact, thirty-four-year-old Olivia Kay Watson.

The confirmation wasn't necessary, but the pain of truly knowing it's *her* stabs me in the gut all over again. Bracing myself by leaning forward and clutching my knees, I take in mouthfuls of air to get a hold of myself. All I can do at this point is finish my shift and pray the next ten-plus hours go by fast.

I left my friend hanging, and he's standing here patiently waiting. I'm sure my expression says it all as to how shaken I am.

"Okay, so her name's Olivia from what the report just said. How do you know her?"

How do I even begin to explain who she is and how I was fortunate enough to know her back then?

My lips move and blurt it out. It feels good finally giving recognition to it. "She's a girl I knew in high school. I was in love with her; she just didn't know it. I can't explain how I know I was in love with her since I had to stay away from her, but it's true nonetheless. My dad would've fucked up both our lives if I got close to her."

Grant's eyes widen at my admission. Then, his brows knit together in anger, and I know it's because he's hurt on my behalf that I had to give something—someone—up because of my lowlife father. Why I never told him about Olivia, I'll never know because he would've understood.

"What can I do?" he asks me and places a comforting hand on my shoulder. I barely feel the touch through all my gear, but that gesture means the world to me coming from my brother.

Straightening back up, I stare at him, sorrow filling my eyes. "Just keep me from losing my shit until we get off shift. Keep me from doing something stupid I'll regret later. And I know it's not your thing, but say a prayer for Liv, please."

***

Weston

It's the next morning. I'm done my shift. My time in the trenches is over, and the unbearable torture has ended.

Not wanting to waste any more time by stopping home, I shower and change at the station. Rushing off to the hospital to see Olivia is all that's driving me forward now. Nothing is more important than her. Fuck, she probably won't even recognize me or remember me, but I still have to see her with my own eyes.

After I make it to the hospital, the attendant at the information desk tells me I can find her on the third floor in the recovery ward. Luckily, there's no problem with me visiting as her *friend*.

Hesitantly, I enter her room. She's lying on the bed, eyes closed—probably just asleep. Her body and mind need recovery after what she's been through. The intensity of a car accident alone takes it out of a person. I doubt she's still unconscious or has serious injuries because she's only hooked up to an IV and a heart and blood pressure monitor. No ventilator—she's not in a coma and not in the ICU wing. So, I'm assuming she's only being kept for observation.

Most likely they ran the battery of tests, including a CT scan and MRI. Liv's not still wearing a c-collar, which is the best sign yet, meaning there's no damage to her spine. Her head is bandaged, but there's no telling if she got stitches. I can't imagine she didn't, though, with the gash she sustained.

Dried blood coats her honey-brown hair, and she still has streaks on her forehead and cheeks from where they tried to clean her up. Little abrasions dot her face, probably from the air bag deploying or from debris that flew during impact. But nothing can hide her appeal. Liv is still gorgeous. With her hair out of her face, I can see how time hasn't changed anything, and yet it's changed everything.

She's certainly a grown-up woman—a stunning woman. More pronounced, luscious curves grace her small frame. She has a round face with those pink-tinted cheeks and lips I still drool over. I wish I could see her eyes. Those amethyst beauties could always bring me to my knees.

The front of her hospital gown slid down from her left shoulder, and a very dark, garish purple bruise is present. I suspect it's from the seatbelt tightening since it's a perfect diagonal mark that disappears under the rest of the gown. Hopefully, they've got her on some pain killers because no matter what, she'll be sore from the accident.

All I can think about is scooping her up and holding her to my chest to know she's real—to know she's safe. It's almost as if she's a figment of my imagination. Maybe I'm dreaming this whole thing because I can't imagine I'm this lucky to have been reunited with her after all this time. I look at her left hand, and her ring finger sits empty. Dare I hope this means she's not with anyone? And then I squash that thought because it doesn't matter.

I'm standing on her left side closest to the door. A part of me realizes I have no business being here, and I'm essentially trespassing. I should leave.

The nurse walks in, startling me with her presence, though I should've expected a nurse coming in since they frequently check on patients as they make their rounds.

"Hello," the friendly woman says while unwinding a stethoscope from around her neck.

"Uh, hi. How's our patient doing?" I ask.

She smiles warmly. "Ah, you must be the boyfriend. Her dad said you'd be coming by."

Fuck my life! A boyfriend?

I feel sick, an absurd thing to feel considering this is what I expected, but I still hoped she was unattached.

And what the fuck were you going to do about it if she was unattached? my psyche questions.

The nurse is unaware of the sucker-punch she delivered and goes about checking over Liv, who has yet to awaken. Roughly shoving my hands in my pockets, I try to conceal my jealousy. "Um, no. I'm not her boyfriend. I'm just a…friend."

"Oh, okay," the nurse replies. Then, she walks around the bed and writes something down on her chart.

"She's doing good. Letting her rest is best, though, and she should wake up on her own. Her dad should be back soon; I think he ran out somewhere. So, I'll let you be until it's time to check her again," she tells me and offers a reassuring smile.

"Thanks," I mutter.

I keep staring at Liv, scared shitless that she hasn't woken up, but also scared that when she does, she'll hate seeing me, or I'll freak her out.

Walking across to the other side of her bed, I pull the hospital curtain so it's draped across one side, separating her bed from the other, even though the other bed is empty. The nurse closed the door when she exited so we have a little more privacy.

Shit, Liv starts stirring, and because I'm a pussy, I duck behind the curtain so as not to reveal myself. Old thoughts and feelings of how I'm a creepy stalker weave their way through my brain. But I couldn't help myself back then, and I can't help myself now. The fire inside me has been stoked. The embers were jabbed with a poker, and new logs have caught ablaze. I left her alone once; I can't see myself doing it again. What rises from the ashes now is a ravenous creature, burning and dying to consume everything in its path.

***

Olivia

My eyelids are heavy. I feel drugged, but I'm doing everything I can to force my lids open.

This is the third time—I think—I've woken up since I was told I was in the hospital. Since I was told I was in a…a…car accident. Still hard to believe it happened. I've driven down that highway so many times since my teens, and I'm always so careful because my dad has drilled it into my head enough times about the dangers.

Something made me wake up. I have the feeling I'm not alone, but as I squint through the low lighting, I don't see anyone. There's no sound of movement or anyone breathing. *Strange.* It's probably the medication making me feel weird or hallucinate or something. There's no telling what doctors put in my IV because I wasn't awake when they did it.

My dad was here when I woke up the second time, I believe, but he's gone now. *Where'd he go?* I try to sit up. Not knowing how to work this dang bed, I plan to push myself up on my own. Planting my hands firmly at my sides, I struggle to lift my own weight. I'm so weak. My muscles are like jelly. Collapsing back down, I decide the prospect of sitting up isn't that important. I'll wait until a nurse comes in. Breathing heavily because I exerted a lot of energy in trying that little stunt, I lay here helpless and grit my teeth in frustration.

Not having any memory of last night sucks. I wish I would've been alert to thank everyone who rescued me—surely it was a big hoopla. When I finally became conscious, I learned from Dad the state troopers said no one else was involved—thank God for that; I would've been devastated if my accident caused anyone else harm. We were also told I was trapped in my car, and I had to be extricated. I groan aloud realizing my car is totaled.

Ash!

Now I remember, Dad ran home to check on Ash—okay, I can settle down a little more with the assurance he's being taken care of at least. My poor dad is worried sick about me and doesn't need more stress.

Everything still feels jumbled and scrambled in my head. Parts are fuzzy, but I'm confident I'm making sense of things. I know the buck that ran across the road was huge, and I know I swerved. Those details are concrete.

And I remember the final thought that assaulted my mind with crystal-clear sharpness—sharpness making the picture in my head seem like it was in high-definition. Despite what survivors say, for me it wasn't my life flashing before my eyes. Instead, it was just an image.

A singular image. A beautiful, painful, surreal image. I saw my dad with my arm around my mom, laughing and so very much in love. And I saw Wes with his arm around me, holding my face tenderly with his other hand. The calm in his stormy eyes told me everything I needed to know.

That image hurts more than the pain I sustained from my injuries.

I'm fine, though. No permanent damage done to my body—my heart is another thing. All tests came back normal. There's a dull ache in my head, and I reach for the spot above my forehead where I hit my steering wheel, if I had to guess. That second time I woke up, I was told I received thirteen stitches to close the wound—again, nothing serious. What is serious is the hole in my heart left in the wake of the accident. Because when I woke up, it was just a harsh reminder that my mother is dead, and I'll never have Wes.

What a tease that image was. What a cruel thing for life to show me.

"Wes...," I whisper to the cold, clinical room.

And then I hear someone suck in a sharp breath. Chills run up and down my spine.

I'm not alone.

The hair on the back of my neck stands on end. Goose pimples race along my arms—not in a good way. A lump is stuck in my very dry, parched throat. "Who-o-o's there?"

Chapter 12: I've Died and Gone to Heaven

Weston

Fuck!

Never did I expect her to hear me. She said my name. How the hell would she know I'm here? Is her current boyfriend named Wes? My mind is going wild.

The sound of her voice is like coming home—as if I can finally feel whole again. It's a more mature tone and huskier now that she's older. I'm a sick bastard since my dick twitches in my cargo shorts. Breathing through my nose as quietly as humanly possible, I try to calm myself. Not having heard that beautiful sound in sixteen years, it's like getting an injection of erection medicine straight to my cock.

"Please…," falls from her lips, "if someone is there, please say so," her voice cracks, and I hear the fear in her words—that was never my intention.

Still from the other side of the curtain—because I'm afraid to move just yet—I reply, "It's okay, Olivia. It's me, Wes."

***

Olivia

I died in the car accident.

It's the only logical explanation for the mind trip I'm experiencing. In heaven, I'd be reunited with Wes. In heaven, I'd see my mom again. Looking all around my room anxious to see her gorgeous face, I realize my mom's not here. I'm so confused. Gently rubbing at my temples, I'm hoping I'll figure out what the hell is going on—something's not right.

I heard Wes; I know I did. Only it wasn't Wes's voice like I remember. This was a deeper version of it. Almost like how it would sound today—the manly version. Maybe I didn't die. Maybe I'm hallucinating like I previously suspected.

"Am I crazy?" I say rhetorically.

And then there's that voice again. "No, you're not."

Using every shred of strength I have, I manage to sit up by gripping the bed rails I didn't think to utilize earlier. I turn my head to the left, and the hospital curtain slides back. Before me stands Weston Thorpe.

An angel, an apparition?

"Weston?" I croak. Now goose pimples are cropping up on my arms for an entirely different reason.

How is it possible he's here?

"Olivia...," he breathes, practically sighing—there's also an undercurrent of reverence in his tone.

Surely my heart rate spikes—I wait for the monitors to start beeping. My respirations have increased at the sheer shock and surprise of the situation. I'm basically panting. So many emotions are overtaking my body. I close my eyes because this isn't real. *Wake up, wake up!* I open them, and he's still here.

"How?" I say in a choked sob.

He seems to understand what I'm asking—*I don't even know what I'm asking.*

"I'm the one who rescued you," he rasps out.

A strangled sound escapes my mouth, I'm stunned as I hold my hand up to my lips. "You're a firefighter." It's not a question. When I last saw him, that's what he was pursuing.

"Yes. I became a career firefighter and EMT. I was one of the lieutenants on duty last night when the call came in. God, Liv, I'm so sorry this happened to you." He steps closer toward me and reaches out a hand.

He must think better of it because he pulls it back and sticks that hand in his pocket. His teeth gnash together, and I see the click in his jaw. It's the same face I saw so many times when we were teens—him restraining himself for some reason.

There in his eyes is the chaos, the smoke that swirls and glides through the gray, making them more vibrant and tempestuous. My favorite eyes—the only eyes I have *eyes* for. My heart folds up like a piece of paper into a neat little square, protecting itself because I won't survive him again.

"Thank you for saving me."

"Anytime, Liv, anytime."

Not sure what to think of that comment, I bite my lip because, as ridiculous as it may seem, I'm embarrassed he's seeing me like this. Feeling increasingly ashamed when I think about what I must look like—though I haven't looked in a mirror—I reach for the sheet to cover myself, pulling it up to my chin.

This is a crappy situation seeing him, of all people, in my current state. Because there he stands looking like the most stunning model, carved from stone. He still possesses a determined oval-shaped face with dark brows and the same dark brown hair, just a tad shorter than I remember. That makes sense since he's a first responder.

The most noticeable difference is his size. He's huge! Muscular, so freaking muscular. It's one of those things I need to look away from—I'm obviously overwhelmed—but I *can't* look away from. I'm gawking, my mouth hanging wide open. His black T-shirt is tight across his chest and arms. He has a tattoo on each bicep, although I can't make out the full design. *Holy crap, he has tattoos?*

God, when I masturbated to a vision of him, I got it all wrong. My mind was not prepared for the actual adult equivalent of this man.

Groaning, I apologize, "Sorry. I know I must look a fright."

He shakes his head. "God, no, Liv. You are and have always been…," he trails off and runs a hand over the back of his head like he's floundering for a word.

"…Timeless," is what he settles on.

Of all the things to say to me, that word detonates in my chest like I was internally hard-wired to go off. I always thought of *time* as my enemy. It's the most ironic thing he could have said to me.

There are so many questions bubbling in my throat wanting to be spit out. Thoughts are throwing grappling hooks at me, hoping they'll catch, and I'll finally produce something sensible. I grimace in pain, tugging the skin at my wound because of the expression I'm making. Putting my hand to the bandage, I check for blood. When my fingers come back dry, I'm still not satisfied.

He must notice my distress. "Can I get you anything?"

"Am I bleeding?"

He comes closer to me, close enough so his thighs are pressed up against the side of the bed, and his torso is against the rails. So close I inhale, and I'm introduced to the manly scent of his new cologne—not the one he used to wear all those years ago. His face hovers over mine, and I hold my breath.

"I don't think so. There's no blood seeping through. I don't wanna peel away the bandage because then it could potentially bleed. I think you're fine."

He gazes down at me with hooded eyes. The drugs being administered intravenously have nothing on the euphoric agent zinging through my veins with his intoxicating ruggedness. Butterflies flutter happily in my belly. Breathing on my end still ceases to exist. My core tightens because of his nearness. My nerves curlicue up like a ribbon, the weight of the situation registering in my mind how twisted this is.

Placing my palm flat on his chest, it's like touching steel. As I finally exhale, the contact between our skin scorches me like I'm being burned alive. I meant to push him back in order to get some clarity, but I find myself gripping the front of his shirt in my hand and pulling him closer. Closer, closer still.

"Wes, we need to…" I don't get to finish my sentence because the door opens.

Immediately, I let go of Wes's T-shirt, and he steps back. The moment between us vanishes without a trace and in walks my dad with Jarrod in tow. My eyes widen at seeing my boyfriend. He rushes to my side.

"Sweetheart, you scared me half to death," Jarrod says, reaching for my hand while delivering a kiss to my forehead.

The moment I just experienced with Wes felt so different than the moment I'm having with Jarrod. Not wanting to sound bitter, I ask him, "How'd you know I was here?"

"Your dad called me, and I came right over. I would've been here sooner had I known. I called Sammy for you; I think she'll be by later."

My best friend will give me an earful once she hears where I was before the accident, and how I should have been with her. I'll call her later if she doesn't come by first because I'm sure she's worried sick, just like I'd be if the situation were reversed.

Looking from Jarrod to Wes, then from Wes to Jarrod, I'm suddenly more tired now than I've ever been in my life. My mouth is agape, having no clue what to say to either of these men. Dad stands there with a bouquet of fresh flowers looking almost as confused as I am.

Out of my peripheral vision, I see Wes and Jarrod sizing each other up. Jarrod is by no means the jealous type, but it seems like he feels threatened—I can almost taste the testosterone in the air like a heavy fog that rolled in.

"You're the boyfriend?" Wes questions and crosses his bulging arms across his broad chest in a stance that no doubt conveys *don't fuck with me*.

Jarrod, ever polite, stretches his hand across the top of my bed in greeting and replies, "Yes. Jarrod Donovan. And you are?"

Wes makes no attempt to move, no attempt to shake Jarrod's hand. Not understanding the hostility emanating from Wes, I look at his face. He must sense it because he stares down at me into my pleading eyes, finally coming out of his trance.

He shakes Jarrod's hand practically in front of my face. "I'm

Weston Thorpe. Liv and I went to high school together."

It doesn't escape me that each man squeezes the other's hand tightly like they're trying to crush one another. Rolling my eyes, I look to my father.

"I assume those are for me?" My face splits in two as I smile at my dad, loving the sight of him and the flowers he brought, a comforting gesture.

Jarrod and Wes break apart and stand on opposite sides, both now crossing their arms in identical poses.

"Of course, hon. How're you feeling?" Dad comes over and kisses the top of my head after setting the flowers on my side table.

"Sore, but nothing I can't handle right now. The medication is helping, but I don't want to rely on it too much because I'm sure when I go home, I'll just be prescribed ibuprofen." As I adjust myself on the bed, my follow-up question I should've asked sooner is, "How's Ash? My poor little puppy."

My words come out in a rush. With all that's going on in the room, I almost forgot to inquire about my little guy.

Dad nods. "Doing fine. I fed him, let him out, and played with him. I'll run by later again, of course."

I'm so relieved, I sigh then sag back on the bed because it's good to know my fur baby is taken care of. I tell my father, "Thanks."

"I can let him out later," Jarrod pipes up and offers.

My dad looks to my face for a clue as to what to say. Thankfully, he figures out that I don't necessarily want Jarrod's assistance at this juncture.

"Uh, thanks, Jarrod. I'll let you know if I need help. Besides, it's giving this old man something to do." My dad grins.

"You're not an old man, Dad."

He chuckles, and I smirk at him. Then, Dad finally focuses on the other man to my left, the man who has me so flustered. "So, you say you went to high school with my daughter? What brings you here today?"

Before Wes can respond, I answer, "Dad, this is the man who rescued me. He's a firefighter."

My father's eyes fill with tears as he walks over to Wes. "I must shake your hand. I owe you a debt of gratitude, Weston."

Wes looks uncomfortable by the praise but shakes my dad's hand in return. "Please, Mr. Watson, call me Wes. You owe me nothing, sir. It's my duty and my honor to help people. I was *one* of many rescuers—there was a whole team of us. When I learned it was Liv, I had to come see her."

"And call me Robby. Well, I thank you from the bottom of my heart. Liv is all I have left in the world, so she's everything to me," my father explains.

Tears coat my lashes. My dad is an amazing man.

75

"Yes, she's definitely everything to us," Jarrod parrots off what my dad said.

Wes's sharp breath at Jarrod's words have me reeling. And I'm startled by Jarrod making such a declaration in front of my father—whom he's only met a handful of times. Here I am thinking we're taking things slow, yet that comment has sped things up without my consent.

"I gotta go," Wes grits out.

No!

Always running when he was seventeen, and running still. It's déjà vu.

"You're leaving?" It's a stupid question, but I ask it anyway.

"Sweetheart, you need your rest. It was very kind of your friend to stop by, but now that we're here, surely he's needed back at the station." Jarrod comes closer to my side and rubs my arm like he's marking his territory.

Wes's eyes are glued to that spot Jarrod's rubbing. He clenches his fists—some things never change when it comes to Wes's clipped responses, mood shifts, and departures.

"Yeah, Liv. I'll be by tomorrow if you're still here."

Having no clue if I'll still be here, my dad seems to have the answer. "Yeah, they're keeping her until at least tomorrow afternoon for observation. You're more than welcome to come by any time. Thank you again, Wes."

Jarrod grumbles something, but I can't make out what he said.

"My pleasure," Wes murmurs, and he's out the door before I can say *goodbye* or look at him.

Biting my lip and almost drawing blood, I'm sick to my stomach over the prospect I may never see him again. Sleep is the only thing that will give me a break from the pain slicing through my body.

Hurt runs deep, and hurt has a name.

Chapter 13: Bits and Pieces

Weston

Visiting Liv yesterday just about killed me.

I had to get the fuck out of there. As soon as her smarmy boyfriend showed up, it changed something in me; my skin crawled, and I got a bad vibe. I don't like him. Staying longer would have made me come apart at the seams. As it was, I almost snarled at him with a guttural outcry at the injustice of it all—as if I were some feral animal.

When I left the hospital, I went to the gym to work out. Burning energy and exorcizing some demons by way of kickboxing alleviated the pressure building up. Grant met me, and I was grateful for the company. Even though we didn't talk about anything significant, he was there by my side as we did our normal workout routines after a few kickboxing rounds. And he was able to talk me out of going back to see Liv until today.

At one point during yesterday's visit with Liv, I thought she wanted me to kiss her. Conjuring the fortitude of a thousand warriors so I wouldn't slide my mouth over hers was an exhausting feat. Taking her lips would have been wrong. Taking anything from her would have been wrong.

Yet, there were moments when both of us seemed to send subliminal messages to the other like one calling to their mate. My reaction to her has intensified, not waned. I'm starved for her. My hunger was teased like having chocolate cake waved in my face, only to have it pulled back and be denied the bite I crave.

Time, I need more time with her.

My cock lengthens thinking about seeing her again. I'll lose my shit if that dickwad is there again. Another encounter with him will be too soon and could spell disaster. However, I have a pit stop to make before going to the hospital; which may give me a chance to calm down.

There are so many things I should have said to Liv. This morning, I can only hope things will be different. Maybe we can start over. Maybe even pick up where we left off when I last saw her: a day forever engrained in the history book that is my life.

**

Weston

Overhearing some guys talking about Liv in the courtyard a few minutes ago has me seeing blood-red. They said she's going to Florida for college and how they "missed their chance to score with her"—that part made me so angry I wanted to punch one of those jock fuckers in their filthy mouth. I hate guys like that.

Her leaving is better this way. She's getting out of here, and it's a clean break. I'll promise myself not to go after her, not to look her up—just let her be. I'll quietly slink away into the shadows, and time will heal the hole she'll leave.

It's graduation day. While other students are planning parties and futures, college aspirations and careers, I'm planning how I can endure my world without Liv. When my dad hits me, I focus on the good. Liv is the good. After a beating, the thought of seeing her the next day at school propels me to take whatever comes my way. It's been like that since the first day I saw her. She's what gets me through.

There's no good now, only the ugly. My training to be a firefighter will have to be my new method of coping; knowing my mom and sister are safe is my other.

No Liv.

Immense pain jackhammers my insides, chiseling away at vital pieces needed for survival. How will I say goodbye to her?

The ceremony just ended. My diploma doesn't bring me satisfaction like it does for those around me. They're moving on, and I'm staying behind. My mom, sister, and dad are somewhere in the crowd, probably trying to find me here on the ground level of the stadium. My father will pretend to care and put on a show for my family's benefit. God, I hate him so much. He's evil. He's winning, and that's the worst thing because of Liv going, and somehow I blame him for it.

"Can I talk to you for a sec, Wes?" Liv questions from behind me.

Shaken to the core with anger about thinking of my dad sitting smugly in the stands earlier, I clench my fists but summon a sense of calm to wash over me. I turn to the girl whom I'll carry a torch for in this life and in the next one.

When I'm face to face with her, those amethyst eyes disarm me. "Yeah, Liv."

The knife twists deeper in my soul. I'll have to catalog every feature because memories will be all I'll have. Sweat breaks out on my skin as she stands there twiddling with the tassel to the cap she pulled off from her head. Her wavy hair blows in the breeze, sending shockwaves through me.

My robe is itchy. Thankfully, there's no need for long sleeves today since I'm wearing the cap and gown; it successfully covers the fresh marks from yesterday's abuse. No one should have noticed anything.

Finally, she speaks, and I wait with bated breath. "I just wanted you to know I'm going to school in Florida. I leave in a month so I can settle in down there sooner rather than later." She bites her lip as if telling me this news is somehow hurting her— it's her decision, though.

"That's great, Liv. I wish you lots of luck," I bite out.

Fuck, I sound like a jerk—I hear the animosity in my inflection. My tone is acrimonious, but I can't help but feel abandoned. Partly because I need to give her the final proverbial shove and push her away for her own good, and partly because I'm mad she's leaving. I'm mad because she doesn't feel for me the way I feel for her. She could never learn to love me.

Her chin lifts in determination, despite her quivering lip. "Well, I just wanted to say goodbye. So, bye." Turning on her heel, she stalks off, and that's the last thing she says before she walks out of my life.

I whisper several minutes after she leaves, disappearing into the crowd of caps and gowns, "Goodbye...Olivia."

***

Weston

It was a long time ago. No need to dwell on the past again, even though it's something I do often. Once that shit's in a person's head, it festers and engulfs the mind like a disease. What's done is done, and I can't change what happened then. I can only move forward. *Sound advice, so believe it,* I tell myself.

Visiting my mother wasn't on the agenda today, but I feel it's necessary—the necessary pit stop I have to make. Mal must be at the salon because when I pull up to the house, her car is gone. I have a key to their place, that way I can check on Mom when I need to. Knocking on her bedroom door and peeking in, I can see she's resting in her sitting chair, staring out the window which faces the street. She likes to watch the cars drive by.

"Mom," I say, hoping to get her attention.

There's no flicker of movement, no stirring of the eyes indicating recognition or responsiveness. She's in her medication-induced coma-like state. Mal and I hate seeing her like this. I wish I could do better for her. Maybe one day I can.

A part of me thinks she blames herself for what happened, and she's locked herself away, too overcome by losing so much in such a short span of time. Eventually, I hope she finds her way back to herself.

Bending down, I kiss the top of her head. I sit on the edge of her bed and watch out the window with her. Even if she won't talk, I will. Once in a while you'll get a noise out of her, but when she's fully under the weight of the medication, it can last for quite some time. Mal has to help her bathe, dress, and tend to her basic needs. Putting her in a nursing home is not the route we want to take…yet. We keep hoping she'll snap out of it, and there won't be a need to put her in a home.

"I kept a lot of things inside over the years, and I shouldn't have. I should've told you about Dad. At the time, I thought I was protecting you and Mal. I was wrong." My breathing is shaky as I swallow the golf ball in my throat. "I never told you about Olivia either. But I'd like to tell you about her now."

My mom blinks. It's a reaction—it's something.

"She's the love of my life. I've loved her since the moment I saw her in my junior year. I let a lot of things get in the way of pursuing her, but she's back, and I'm going to try to capture her heart like she has mine."

A tear slides down my mom's cheek. She remains silent. If I weren't looking directly at her, I wouldn't even have known she was listening.

Sliding forward so I'm closer to her sitting chair, I pat her folded hands in her lap. "It'll be okay, Mom. Mal and I are fine. We're going to take care of you…always."

We sit in silence for the next thirty minutes. Before I leave, I help settle her into bed. Kissing her forehead, her eyes flutter closed, and I look upon her wrinkled face lined with years of depression and marred with so much hurt. She's still a beautiful woman underneath it all.

As quietly as I can, I make my way out of the house and get in my vehicle. As I'm driving, I think about all the unspoken things between me and my mom. Between me and my sister. Between me and Liv. It has to change. *I* have to change.

Arriving at the hospital, I make my hasty exit from my truck, so anxious to see her. My skin is energized like I have some kind of fuel powering my body, crackling as pinpricks of awareness sustain me and cause the organ in my chest to beat frantically. I knock on her door, and her soft, melodic voice tells me to enter. My eyes dart around the room, looking for any sign that we're not alone.

"He's not here," Liv says while sitting up in bed.

I know she's referring to her boyfriend, and as we lock eyes, I'm relieved there won't be a round two. *But when's he coming back?*

She answers my unspoken question, "I told him I'd call him when I got discharged today. My dad's supposed to be springing me from this place in a few hours."

She smiles, and I about fall at her feet. So gorgeous. She looks like she showered, and the dressings on her head look they were changed. Her hair is doing its natural wave. No more dried blood-streaks line her face. Her tiny cuts are healing nicely.

"You look good today, Liv," I compliment her with a throaty tone.

"I feel good today. Tests confirm I'm fine," she swallows then continues, "Y-y-you look good too."

Concealing my shaking hands, I thrust them into my pockets. Today, I'm wearing one of my firehouse T-shirts with the emblem for our station. She stops looking at my eyes and fixates on my shirt. "Task Force 21? I guess that's your fire company?"

"Yeah. We have two fire stations we work out of. Two firetrucks and two ambulances that each have a number. And everything makes up the entire Task Force unit when we're called into service."

"Wow, I can see the passion in your eyes when you talk about work and hear it in your voice. I'm glad you found your calling, Wes. You seemed to…struggle…a lot in high school."

Breathing in deeply, I'm reminded of how and why I was that way back then. Her face showcases the lingering effects of how we parted. It's amazing how a person can be so enamored—so in love with someone— and never actually have *been* with them.

"Yeah, things were a lot different for me when I was a kid," I say nonchalantly, knowing full well it offers her no explanation and is vague in nature.

Licking her lips, she asks, "You ever think things could've been different—between us—if I hadn't gone off to college so far away?"

I gulp, not fully prepared for this conversation despite what I told myself this morning. "No, Liv. I don't."

As if I gave her whiplash—like she most likely sustained from the car accident—she rears back against the bed.

I'm sorry. I did it because I love you. If only you knew…

***

Olivia

That stings. His response hurts. Always ambiguity and vagueness to his explanations—I'm always left with more questions than when I started.

What the hell am I supposed to do with that response?

My brows automatically furrow. Weaning myself from the medication this morning might not have been the best idea. Once again, I'm confused by this man because I don't understand why the hell he's here. He seems reluctant to delve into our past, so what's the point of me being associated with him now or in the future?

The alpha male routine yesterday had me all hot and bothered, I admit. I couldn't help myself, before he spoke just now, I wanted to fall all over him as my mind flooded with memories of our time in high school. So many close encounters that never led to anything—missed chances, missed opportunities. One such encounter in particular still niggles at me in the deepest recesses of my mind.

***

Olivia

It's junior year. The new boy in school, Weston, is a godsend. Losing my mom has made my life dark, bleak, empty. I put on a smile for Dad and act brave each day, but it's a show. When I see Weston, everything changes. I light up, coming alive again like warmth and solace have touched me with a healing hand.

The beautiful boy with the somber expression —whom I admire from afar— captures my attention. He's so quiet, broody, pensive. A loner. I'm drawn to him and can't explain why. Since the first time I saw him, I've had sleepless nights.

We're in gym class and have free time to intermingle as long as we're doing something "athletic," according to our teacher. I pretend to dribble a basketball, acting like I know what I'm doing on the court, just so I can watch him sitting in the bleachers. He has a volleyball in his hands, rolling it between his palms—he's pretending like me.

Vacillating between going over to wrap my arms around him because he looks so sad and staying put because I don't want to be creepy is my latest dilemma. Both of us need comfort and protection. Both of us are joined by some unknown common thread—a bond. I sense it without even having officially met him.

The decision is made for me because my feet start walking in his direction of their own volition. As I make my way up six steps onto the bleachers, my foot catches on the rail, and I go flying into his lap. He drops the volleyball from his hands and catches me so quickly, like he was waiting for me—waiting to welcome me with open arms.

His face, just inches from mine, causes me to blush, and I'm holding on to his frame while he cradles me gently. Feeling his puff of breath on my lips sends tingles to places I've only dreamt about receiving pleasure. My breath catches, and our eyes are locked as if seeing right to the very depths of our souls.

All too quickly, he sets me upright, and I immediately lament the loss of contact.

"Y-y-you're Weston," I stammer.

"And you're Olivia," he says confidently.

I'm thrilled he knows my name.

His eyes are glazed over with something I can only describe as the way a man should look at a woman. My sixteen-year-old self is tingly everywhere now, and I'm sure I'm wearing a look that reflects this.

Our balls had bounced off somewhere when I fell into him. We'll have to do something athletic so we don't get in trouble. I'm about to ask him what activity he thinks would constitute such a designation—testing out my flirtation skills—but our gym teacher blows the whistle signaling free time has ended.

I'm torn. Not wanting to leave him—and it appears he's having similar thoughts because neither of us has made the effort to move—we linger in our own little bubble where no one can reach us.

"C'mon, Thorpe! Let's go, Watson! Break it up," our teacher screams at us.

Bubble burst! Poof! Reality has set in. Both he and I turn and everyone in the gym is looking right at us since we're the only ones not lined up on our respective sides that separate the boys from the girls. We're both trying not to laugh at the spectacle we've made.

"I don't wanna see you get in trouble, Liv, so I'll talk to you later. Nice to meet you," he tells me and holds my gaze. I'm loving the fact he called me "Liv."

"Nice meeting you too, Wes."

We walk off to join our respective lines. When I reach my spot, my heart about explodes in my chest as I think I've just fallen head over heels in love with the most beautiful boy I've ever met.

***

Olivia

"Liv…Liv…Olivia!" Wes says firmly.

Startled as I'm brought back to the present, I look around my hospital room. Now I'm angry after recounting the times we've been so close yet so far—stolen moments that never came to fruition.

"Why are you here?" I ask with a sardonic tone. The lingering frustration from my flashback still clings to me like a shield.

His nostrils flare. He owes me an explanation, and I'm going to make him give me one. I'll wait him out as long as it takes.

Finally, he replies, "Because I needed to see you."

"That's not an answer, Wes. Try again."

The storm is brewing in his eyes. I'll keep pushing him. I'm looking for a fight, the fight we should've had senior year. It's been a long time coming. He stayed, and I left. I would've stayed for him, though, if he'd given me a reason to.

"Because now that you're back in my life again, I can't see myself staying away," he replies huskily.

The butterflies in my stomach have returned with the force of an army. Breathing deeply through my nose is taking effort so as not to give away how affected I am. My chin trembles. The onset of tears is upon me, but I'll keep them at bay.

"Am I *back* in your life? Define what that means exactly. Because if you recall, I tried so many times for us to get close, and you always pushed me away. I always felt I was on a tilt-a-whirl with you and couldn't get off the ride—never knowing where I stood. Hell, I convinced myself for years you must've hated me." *It was easier to cope with that explanation.*

He vehemently shakes his head *no,* and his face transforms into a sorrowful expression.

"Fuck no, Liv. Hated you? God, never. You couldn't be more wrong about anything in this world. Liv, I could never, ever, hate you—or anything about you. You're what got me through school."

Astonished is the word to describe my current state as I press my lips together. I cross my arms over my chest, hugging myself. Am I missing something?

"How do you mean?" I question.

He audibly closes his mouth, and that broody look I always fell for is back with a vengeance. "Do we have to get into this right now?"

"Get into what? You're not making any sense." I practically whine.

"Can we not revisit the past right now? I know you must have questions. That maddening, sexy, fucking beautiful brain of yours always has. But can we just start over and get to know one another as we are *now*?" His eyes meet mine, and the storm has calmed.

Momentarily thrown since he called me sexy, I shake my head to clear it and focus on our conversation. I don't even know this man, and I realize that's the whole point to his plea—he wants me to get to know him…*as the man he is now.* I must be crazy for considering this. Sixteen freaking years have gone by. We're right back to where we started, which is nowhere.

"And how do you propose we do that?" I eye him like he has two heads.

"Let me take you on a date when you're feeling better."

What I'm about to say is the truth, yet a small part of me feels like I'm using Jarrod to my advantage. "But I have a boyfriend," I remind him—as if he's forgotten.

"A boyfriend you sent packing. A boyfriend who isn't here right now. There's a reason I'm here and not him. I know you feel it too," he coos, his alluring voice dripping with that sexy tone—it does things to me.

"For the record, I didn't send him packing. Me saying I'd *call him later* isn't giving him a kiss-off. Sure, we've had our problems here and there, but I'm trying to work through things with him like I promised I would." *Why am I telling him all this?*

Crossing my arms again as a protective method is necessary because I blurted all that out, volunteering it so easily. I'm always so vulnerable around him as if he wields some kind of magic power over me. My mother's earrings are at home tucked away in my jewelry box;

otherwise, I'd be rubbing them to soothe my frazzled nerves.

"We don't even have to go out on an actual date. We can keep things casual. I'll make you something to eat at your place or my place—wherever you're more comfortable. I've become accustomed to cooking at the firehouse, and I'm always looking to test out new recipes on willing taste-testers. Let me do something nice for you while you're recovering."

He smiles my way like he knows he's already winning at wearing me down. This isn't some game for me, though. So as not to perpetuate the growing void between us, I'll give him what he wants because I want answers—and if this is the way I'll get them, then so be it.

"Okay, dinner at my place then. I'll be out of work for the next two weeks, but I'll be working from home, so any night is good. My best friend Sammy—you probably heard her name mentioned yesterday—came by to see me after you left, and she arranged everything on my behalf with our employer. So, what night are you off-duty?"

"Starting tomorrow, I'm on for forty-eight hours and then off for forty-eight hours. How about Saturday I come over?"

"That'll work. Saturday it is. Let's say five o'clock?"

"I'll be there," he confirms. Then he grins, "So…you know there's just a few important details we're forgetting."

"Yeah, like what?"

"Oh, like where you live and what your cell number is." He chuckles.

Eyeing him dubiously, I ask, "You're not going to harass me and send me some kind of pervy messages if I give you my number, are you?"

He laughs at my question. "No, Liv. I'll keep it completely platonic. Scout's honor!" He uses his fingers to make an X on his chest for crossing his heart.

I giggle at that action. "Somehow I doubt you were a scout." Biting my lip, I'm not sure if I'm relieved or disappointed he's promised his messages will be *platonic* in nature.

He gestures toward my phone sitting on the table next to the bed. "Let me program my number in your cell. Then you can text me your address."

I unlock the screen for him. Handing him my phone, our fingers brush, and I suck in my breath. The slight touch is enough to warm my skin. It's enough to send my libido into overdrive and make my heart go *thump-thump*.

As he's plugging in the information and biting his cheek trying to stifle a smirk, I have an inkling I'll have to check my phone and see what he was up to.

While he's still typing and looking at the screen he queries, "You know what else I don't know?"

A ton of stuff about one another. "No, what?"

"What you do for a living."

"Oh, yeah. I guess I never mentioned it. I'm an environmental engineer. And Sammy, Jarrod, and I all work for the same engineering firm."

His jaw clicks at the mention of Jarrod. "That's amazing. I knew you'd go on to do something either helping the environment or people."

"Well you're one to talk, Mr. Hero. I just design things. You actually *save* people."

"I'm no hero, Liv."

"To me, you are."

He clears his throat and walks over to grab my hand that's resting at my side. I dare not move or breathe for fear of spoiling the moment somehow. With him lifting my hand to his mouth, I watch every millisecond unfolding and burn it into my brain.

"I'll let you rest. See you Saturday, baby," he murmurs against my skin.

Baby...

I'm not sure if he realizes he said it or not. Not thinking too much into it, I shrug it off. He gently places my hand back to its former position. And now, my normally guarded heart is anxious to see what Saturday brings.

Chapter 14: Big Engine

Olivia

Saturday

After Wes left the hospital from Tuesday's visit, he texted me not more than fifteen minutes later. Shocked by his hastiness, but also flattered, I found myself grinning like a loon when my phone chimed. Instead of him plugging in his name under my contacts, his number came up as "Big Engine 911." *That crazy man!*

Tears were streaming down my face, and I practically choked with laughter at the designation he gave himself. Never did I expect him to program *that* into my phone, but as funny and playful as it was, I immediately changed it to *Wes*. I didn't need a tease like that blaring at me from the screen whenever we communicated.

Our text conversation was brief; however, it packed a punch that was difficult to ignore and not overanalyze.

Wes: Feel free to contact me anytime if you need anything.

Me: Thanks!

Wes: So no comment on the name? You're just going to leave me hanging?

Me: None whatsoever. I think the name says it all.

Wes: I suppose it does.

Me: Are you flirting with me?

Wes: I am. You know you like it.

Me: No comment.

Wes: Your lack of comment says it all.

Me: You're so bad.
Wes: You have no idea.
Me: I'm not encouraging you!
Wes: That's probably a good thing.
Me: Why's that?
Wes: Because of what you do to me.
Me: Do I want to know what that entails?
Wes: Probably not. Some things are best left unsaid.
Me: There are a lot of things not said between us. I seem to be left with more questions than answers when I'm with you. You're a very cryptic person. It's driven me crazy since high school.
Wes: That's not my intention. But I'm glad I've driven you crazy all these years.
Me: That's not what I meant!
Wes: Oh? So what did you mean?
Me: Never mind. Some things are best left unsaid.
Wes: I thought so. Now who's being cryptic?
Me: Well, it takes one to know one.
Wes: I'm going to have a lot of fun with you on Saturday.
Me: No comment.
Wes: I rest my case.

Since then, texts with Wes have remained flirty in nature, but nothing bordering on scandalous; I wouldn't do that to Jarrod. I'm not dangling my boyfriend on a hook—at least that's not how I view it. Jarrod and I have talked on the phone, and he came by to see me when he was done work on the night of my discharge. Tuesday night was awkward to say the least.

My inkling is it's best to keep Jarrod at arm's length. He's trying too hard to compete with Wes. However, there's no competition. Wes and I aren't *a thing*. A platonic relationship is all we have. I'll see Wes tonight as planned, and now more than ever, my once-upon-a-time seventeen-year-old self needs closure—whether that involves a beginning or an ending.

There are no expectations on my side as to what can or could happen between Wes and me. Feelings are being stirred; memories are emerging, and my mind is running wild, but it doesn't equate to a potential romantic relationship. I would have to get out of my current one first, and I'm a noble person. Wes used to be the great equalizer in my life—it's why I'm still holding on to the past.

The Wes I knew then might not be the Wes of today, but it's hard to convince my soul of that when I feel fingers reaching out from inside me to grab him in a death grip like we belong together. All I know is whatever happens tonight could be monumental.

***

Weston

It seems I've waited an eternity for Saturday to arrive. Now that it's upon me, I'm an anxious, jittery, unbalanced fucker.

Deciding it's best I try to alleviate the burn and ache in my cock, I make the decision to jack off before I see her tonight. Maybe it'll help settle me. Words like *possessive, claim,* and *envious* are racing through my brain. She has me off-center. How one woman can upend my world so effectively boggles my mind. As much as she's always been a part of me, I learned to live with her absence. Now that she's back in my life, I don't know how to function without her around.

I lie back on my bed in my apartment, close my eyes and let the world melt away. Ignoring the sounds of the outdoors and my incessantly dripping faucet, I concentrate on images of Olivia. Her beautiful skin, hair, and those fuck-me-eyes are all I see. The hue of her eyes is so vibrant I could fall into the purple pools and never resurface. The allure of her lips summoning me from across the room in my mind's eye has my balls tightening. Liv's luscious curves are revealed to me as her womanly figure is stripped of any layers, and she's lying here bare.

Imagining her juicy cunt has me groaning aloud. Reaching to the waistband of my pants and boxers, I tug the material down past my groin. I fist my cock in my right hand and angrily tug at it, sliding my palm up and down my engorged shaft. Nothing will feel right unless it's her touching me. Nothing will satisfy me until I have her fully. This will have to do for now until I have the real thing.

Envisioning her gorgeous tits in my face is an easy task. There was no way to hide her figure from me at the hospital, even in the ill-fitting gown. I was even gifted with the sight of her body during the rescue. Now that she's safe and the dust has settled, I don't feel like such a pervert for reminiscing about her curves. Liv's perfect pink nipples would be sucked until she comes. My fingers would be soaked with her honey while I lick them clean and eat at her for hours.

My hand is working my cock up and down furiously, harder and faster, getting closer and closer to release. All this pent-up frustration and push and pull between her and me is driving me mad. Fucking her is not going to resolve the issue. For the first time ever, I want nothing more than to make love to a woman. I want to make love to her and only her. No other woman can stabilize my existence.

Groaning again at the idea of driving my dick into her hole over and over as her body welcomes me home, I pump two more times and that does it. "Fuuuuccccckkkk!" I yell as my cum shoots off all over the bed, my stomach, and on my hand.

"Olivia," is what I rasp out to an empty room as I'm coming down from my high.

She makes me out of control. This woman makes me lose my shit. She shatters me and puts me back together. I've always loved her and will always love her. This time around, it will be different. I handled it all wrong back then when I was younger. I'm a man now, so no excuses. This time around, I'll make her mine!

***

Olivia

My doorbell rings. Ash starts barking and races to the entryway. My heart is thundering in my chest, and the cacophony of barks mixed with the pounding in my ears is overwhelming. With sweaty palms and all, I take a deep breath and amble to the door.

"It's okay, Ash," I assure him and pat his head as he runs around at my feet excitedly.

Tugging on my pearl earring while closing my eyes and saying a little prayer for the strength to survive tonight in Wes's presence, I finally open the door. Before me is a male model. No other guy has anything on Wes. He wears sexiness and ruggedness like a banker wears a suit. These attributes fit him like a glove, and that makes him more dangerous and appealing. Biting my lip in appreciation, I work my hungry gaze from his head to his shoes.

The fitted gray ribbed shirt matches his stormy eyes. Dark-colored jeans accentuate his lower half in the most incredible way, which has everything south of my bellybutton on high alert. His massive thighs and delectable ass are flawlessly squeezed by the denim. Hints of his tattoos are peeking out from the short sleeves, and I wish I could see the full artwork. Finding myself drooling, I lick my lips and proceed with caution as I inhale his scent—it's dizzying. My eyelids feel heavy, and I'm sure my irises are hazy with lust as the drugging agent that is him takes effect.

He chuckles at my reaction, and it snaps me out of the fog. In each hand he's holding grocery bags stuffed to the brim with items. He sets them down then moves in to hug me, cradling me in his strong arms while he kisses my cheek. The stubble grazes my skin and sends prickles of desire to my center.

"Hi beautiful," he murmurs.

Managing to squeak out a "Hi," I quickly pull back. Returning to my senses, I realize I so easily give myself away each time I see him.

"How're you feeling? As always, you look stunning."

90

Clearing my throat and ignoring his comment because I don't trust myself not to say something stupid, I give a simple reply. "Feeling good. A little stiff, but getting around fine."

He smiles at me, and Ash barks again at my feet to announce himself. Wes looks down at my pup, and instead of petting him, he scoops him up with his meaty hands. "And who might you be?" he questions with a grin.

"Oh, this is my dog Ash. I just got him from the shelter. My dad was taking care of him for me while I was in the hospital."

"I remember your dad mentioning something about that. You still volunteer at the shelter?"

He looks at me with the warmest expression like he'll melt into a puddle. *It's because of you; you inspired me,* is what I want to say.

"Yes. Not as often as I'd like, but I can't give it up. It's a part of my life I enjoy so much. I've wanted to get a pet for a while, and I couldn't resist this little guy."

"Well, how could you with a name like Ash? It's an interesting coincidence given my profession, wouldn't you say?"

Wes catches my eye and gives me a lethal wink coupled with a predatory smirk. Gulping at the sudden heat in his eyes, I focus on my dog. "He was found by a burn pit, so his rescuer gave him the name, and it stuck. So…dinner?" I give him the not-so-subtle hint as I motion with my head to the bags on the ground.

He puts Ash down, grabs the handles to the groceries, and steps inside. We make our way to the kitchen, and he starts pulling everything out of the bags to line up on my counter. Based on the ingredients, it'll be a Mexican dish.

"What're you making?" I sidle up next to him and play with my necklace, running the heart pendant back and forth along the chain—a distraction technique I'm employing to avoid the electric current running between us.

"Enchiladas, of course. There's no other meal that'll do. Instead of trying a new recipe, I decided to make you my signature dish. Although, I never asked you if you like Mexican, so I hope that's okay?"

After I nod enthusiastically, he shakes his head in approval and asks me where a cutting board and knife are, which I happily retrieve for him.

He starts slicing green chilies as I grab a baking dish, which he coats with cooking spray. As he's assembling the tortillas in the glassware and cooks the ground beef on the stove, I shift my weight from one foot to the other so I don't tire out my legs. They're still sore from the accident.

Wes casually interjects, "I know the experts say there are five food groups, but they forget about the sixth one, which is enchiladas—that's in a category all by itself." He looks to his right where I'm standing with a lopsided grin.

"That's how I feel about chocolate. So maybe there are seven groups?"

We both start laughing. He finishes prepping the meal and puts it in the oven. After setting the timer, I realize we have twenty minutes to hang out.

He pours us both a soda, and we head into my living room to relax on the couch. Wes takes one end of the sofa, leaving plenty of room for me to join him, but I opt for the opposite end to put some distance between us. I'll end up in his lap if I sit next him. The dog's timing is impeccable because the lap is where he goes—not in mine, but in Wes's.

Taking the plunge first, I jump in, determined to get the answers to those questions burning a hole in my brain much like money in the wallet of a shopaholic. "How's your family doing? If I recall correctly, you have a younger sister."

Admittedly, I don't know much, or remember much, about his family. There were a handful of times he talked about having to watch his little sister, and it was one of the many—albeit justified—excuses as to why he could never hang out with me.

"You have an exceptional memory. Yes, I have a younger sister; Malory is her name. She's doing well. She's a hairdresser now and no longer the little girl in pigtails who used to follow me around wanting to play dress up and have tea parties."

The affection shimmering in his eyes at the mention of her is plain as day. It brings a smile to my face knowing he has someone he feels like that about.

"And your parents?"

Immediately, his face transforms into a scowl at my asking, and I'm worried I overstepped. *How could I have known this was a sore subject, though?*

"Mom could be better. She's had some rough years, lost in her own world these days. Depression has taken her from Mal and me. Medication somewhat helps. She has her good days and bad days."

He's vague on the details, and I can understand. Not wanting to pry but at the same time wanting to be closer to him, I'm walking a tightrope that's challenging to balance upon.

"I'm sorry about your mom." I bite my lip, feeling terrible he's uncomfortable. But this is how you get to know a person, and it's the adult thing to do—to converse. Hesitantly, I ask next, "And your dad?"

He inhales a sharp breath through his nose, and the hands that were sweetly caressing my puppy are now balled into unyielding fists. His arms are clenched tightly, the muscles bulging and corded in various places. That jaw is squeezed together and locked down like a jail cell—I'm afraid he'll break all his teeth.

"You mean you don't know?" he grits out.

Where's this vehemence coming from, even though I don't believe it's directed at me?

"Know what?"

"Nothing."

"Should I know something?" I ask nonchalantly.

His nostrils flare, and for some reason, he's completely bothered by this subject. Everyone has their family issues.

I rush to tell him, "Sorry, you don't have to answer that."

Wes hasn't looked my way; his eyes are still off somewhere, trapped in a state of anger. I scoot forward on the couch and put a hand to his thigh. "Wes. Wes. Wes!"

His head finally snaps my way, and I move my hand to cup his cheek. I run soothing circles with the pad of my thumb across his cheekbone. *God, it feels so good to touch him.*

"Are you okay?" I'm so worried.

"Yeah, sorry. I don't like to talk about…my father. Maybe one day, but not right now."

"It's no problem, really. Talk about—or don't talk about— whatever you want." I try to sound upbeat and cheery as I remove my hand from his face, already missing the contact and connection, but I don't return to the other end of the couch.

"Well, Mal and Grant are who I consider my family. Grant's my best friend, but he's more like a brother than anything. He was also there the night of your accident—he's the other lieutenant on our squad."

"Oh, wow. I'd love to meet him sometime and thank him as well."

"He'd like that; I'm sure of it."

We're silent for a moment. Ash snuggles back into Wes's lap and begins to drift off while we both stroke his ears.

"Your dad seems like a great guy. Protective and quite perceptive of your feelings. I like him."

Smiling at that remark, I tell him, "Thanks. He is. My dad's the best."

Seeing that fist balled once more, I know something dark and twisted went down between Wes and his dad. Sensing it's painful to hear the "my dad's the best" comment, a twinge of sorrow lances through me. His father has hurt him somehow—I assume he didn't have what I have with my dad. The urge to comfort him again is strong, but I resist.

He takes a deep, calming breath, then shifts gears to me. "What about your family? Is your mom around?"

Now I'm the one who's distressed. Immediately, I begin rubbing my earring. Wes grabs my free hand and holds it. Fighting to swallow back tears, my voice cracks when I go to speak.

"I know we never got around to talking about these things in school. It seems we were always in some little bubble when we were together, oblivious to the world around us. I wish I would've talked to you about her back then. She died right before you moved here, actually. I always thought her leaving and you arriving were connected somehow."

That sounds ridiculous even to my own ears. He probably thinks I'm an idiot.

"Liv, I've always felt we were meant to be in each other's lives somehow too. We met at a time when I needed something good and wonderful in my life more than ever. My darkest days were after we moved here. There was only one beacon of hope. One star that lit up the sky…it was you."

My heart is hammering. When I asked him in the hospital if he *hated* me, it's because I didn't ever want to hope or believe he returned my feelings. I didn't want to get hurt, but I managed to get hurt anyway. He said things wouldn't have been different if I didn't go off to college—I don't know if I believe that now. Little bits and pieces are starting to take shape, and before long, I'll have everything I need to decipher this underlying message that has spanned over sixteen years.

"So, when you said at the hospital I *got you through school*, you were referring to these *dark times?*"

He responds with an unequivocal, "Yes."

Wes stares into my eyes. My apprehension, past pain, fears, and insecurities fade into the background. It's just him and me in this moment. Automatically, our bodies shift toward one another, and he moves in slowly for a kiss. Closing my eyes and parting my lips, the drugging effect is upon me again. Never did I mean for this to happen, but I can't stop this freight train from rolling down the tracks.

He's a hair's breadth away as his scent washes over me and completes me in a way I'll never experience with anyone else. Wes holds my face tenderly, reverently, like kids hold a soap bubble not wanting it to disappear because the wonder and magic will vanish. Before his lips meet mine, the timer to the oven goes off.

Chapter 15: Mouth to Mouth

Olivia

Poof, the moment evaporates before us.

Opening my eyes, I lick my lips, and we stare at each other. We both recognize the moment is gone, yet neither of us makes a move to pull away. Finally, he lets go of my face and stands to turn off the timer.

He opens the oven door, and I hear him moving around in the kitchen; I assume he's finishing whatever needs to be done for our dinner. My insides are a tangled mess. This thing between us is bigger than I could have imagined.

I'm going to end things with Jarrod, that much is clear—this conscious decision is what's best for all involved. Whether anything blossoms with Wes doesn't matter, and it has no bearing on the Jarrod-decision. What this thing between Wes and me has proven is I'll never have this passion, this heat, this longing, with Jarrod, or anyone else. It's not fair to me or the man who doesn't hold my heart—there is, and only ever was, one man who does hold it. I won't deny any of us the chance for happiness and fulfillment.

It's impossible to sprinkle water on this relationship with Jarrod and have it magically grow. I can't invent a spark or ask to get bitten by the lovebug for the sake of sparing his feelings. Our relationship was stunted at the beginning, and there's nowhere to go from here. It will be a difficult conversation, but a necessary means to an end—my mind's made up.

Rooted to my spot and captive to my thoughts, I'm startled when Wes puts a hand to my shoulder. Clutching my heart at the scare, I laugh softly when he chuckles at my jumpiness.

"Dinner's ready."

"Can't wait," I tell him.

He holds his hand out to me, helping to pull me to my feet. I hadn't even realized Ash jumped down from the couch and was waiting in the kitchen for us. Smiling at my little guy, I dutifully follow the sex magnet making me hungry for food and for other things.

The table in my eat-in kitchen is beautifully set. Clearly, he found my good china dishes I inherited from my mom. They were in one of my cupboards, and I'm delighted they're being used for this occasion. The delicate pastel butterfly pattern gracing the plates practically flutters at me with joy, splitting my face into a serene smile.

He follows my gaze to the china. "I hope you don't mind me using them. Although, I probably should've asked."

"Not at all. They're the loveliest thing I own, besides my mom's pearl earrings."

Reaching for my left ear lobe and holding it out to him, I showcase the jewelry. He regards the pearl then sweeps his hand out in front of him for me to sit down. My mom's presence is always with me—she's forever sending me little hints from above, much like how people believe in *pennies from heaven.*

We settle in our respective seats and heap the orgasmic-smelling enchiladas onto our plates. Digging in gratefully and with more gusto than I've mustered since the accident, I moan as all the flavors hit my tongue and explode like Pop Rocks candy.

"Mmm, my God, this should be illegal," I manage to say around a mouthful, while also groaning in appreciation.

"My cooking, or that sound you're making?" He raises a brow in my direction as his eyes darken. In turn, I almost choke on my food, not realizing I walked right into that one. Ignoring the comment, I keep chowing down.

After a few minutes, I want to elaborate on things about my mom. Sharing something like this with him is important to me—things I've never even shared with Jarrod.

"You're a good cook, I have to tell ya. My mom made one signature dish and that was pineapple chicken. Every once in a while, I make it for Dad. It's not as good as Mom's, of course. She made everything amazing, even when they were epic failures." I chew another bite and take a brief pause while he looks at me with understanding and patience.

"I think I mentioned to you that I cook for the firehouse quite often."

Nodding at his remark, I feel compelled to open up my world to him. "My mom would've liked you, and you would've liked her. She was the type of woman who used words like *fantabulous.* She was intermingling the

English language long before it became a popular thing to do. If only she were around today because she'd love the *awesome sauce*-type expressions people have come up with."

We both chuckle, and I continue to think about her stunning face and warm heart. He asks me what she died from, and I tell him about the dreaded "C" word that robbed her from our lives. "Ya know what I miss most about her?"

"What?" he encourages me with genuine curiosity.

"The notes in my school lunches. She'd always tell me what a fantastic kid I was. When we lost her, my dad was temporarily taken away from me too. Having no siblings to mourn with or anyone to lean on made me bitter and angry. Then…you moved here," I whisper the last part and look down at my half-eaten dinner, overwhelmed with heartache.

Moving at lightning speed, he's on his knees in front of my chair. Without asking and without any kind of warning, he swoops in and kisses me hard. He sensed I needed him. His lips are greedy. His tongue is brutal, but with that brutality comes the sweetest pleasure. I can taste his need. I can feel his desire radiating from him. Clutching to him desperately, my body recognizes I need to be close to him, not out of lust but from craving intimacy.

He's growling into my mouth, and I'm moaning uncontrollably. This has been building for sixteen years. This yearning that has lain dormant has risen with no sign of being tamed. His hands work their way up my back and under my shirt as he holds me to his frame. My breasts are pressed firmly against the hard planes of his chest. In response, everything inside me tightens and coils intensely.

The kiss goes on and on and on. My fingers are in his scalp, holding him in place. My body aches, but not from my injuries due to the accident. My stitches don't even protest the movements in my face as we devour one another.

He gives me life. He gives me breath. He gives me everything. And I hope I do the same for him.

***

Weston

She's my everything plus infinity.

Her mouth is divine. The flavors on her tongue send me straight into ecstasy, trapping me for eternity. Now that I've tasted this side of heaven, I'll never be able to leave. Growling into the recesses of her lush kisses, I revel with the knowledge her tits are smashed against my chest, sending electrifying sparks straight to my dick. My hands ravenously rub the bare flesh at her back—I want more. I crave more. This one taste is pleasure and pain at the same time. It's heaven and hell all at once.

My lungs are in desperate need of air, but I can't stop myself from claiming and consuming her. It's taking everything in me to be gentle. Her injuries are still present, and I'm holding back my passion as much as I can to protect her. I'll never stop protecting her. I've failed her these last sixteen years, but I won't fail her again.

Finally pulling back from her, which we're both reluctant to do, the aftermath of our need is written on our faces and expressed through our eyes. My feelings mirror hers—it's plain to see.

"Wow," is what she says breathlessly.

"This is all new territory for me, Liv."

"I'm breaking up with Jarrod," she blurts out.

A part of me wants to argue over this abrupt decision because I didn't mean to drive a wedge between them, and then the selfish part of me is fucking overjoyed beyond comprehension. She holds her fingers up to my lips to halt me before I can speak, but she's unaware I don't even have the words. I kiss the pads of her digits, and she smiles at my actions.

"Before you say anything, I want you to know Jarrod and I have run our course. It hasn't been working for a while. *You* are not the reason I'm breaking up with him. However, I'm not a cheater, and whether this thing between us," she gestures at the space separating our bodies for emphasis, "goes anywhere or not, I'm still ending things with him. I'll tell him tomorrow."

Nodding because I don't know what else to say or do, I lace my fingers with hers. This will have to be where things stand for now. We'll take it one day at a time. I'd never think she could be a cheater, but I have so much respect for her regarding her loyalty. My love and appreciation for her as a person has grown exponentially. She's the real deal—the tried and true perfect woman for me and the love of my existence.

Liv purses her lips and smiles slightly. "There's one important thing I must know before anything else happens."

Holding my breath because I'm still not ready to reveal the things I've kept hidden, I pray she doesn't venture down that road again about my father.

"So, what're your tattoos of? And can I see them?" Her eyes shimmer with excitement.

Thank fuck that's all it is!

Beyond grateful for a reprieve, I give her lips a chaste kiss. This request I can totally deliver. The gentlemanly thing to do would be to pull up my sleeves, but I'm no gentleman tonight. Whipping off my shirt, she gasps as my bare chest—with a set of rock-hard abs and pecs—come into view. Her intake of breath to calm herself pokes at my inner beast—

taunting him to come out and play with fire.

Goddamn, she makes me feel like a man.

Swiveling to show her my right bicep, she traces the outline of the firefighter with her delicate fingers. I shiver. I fucking shiver in response, and goose pimples line my arms. Then, I swivel again, letting her repeat the process with the other tat. She licks her pretty pink lips while touching my flesh. It's unnerving, and I want nothing more than to plunder her mouth again, then bury my head in between her legs to plunder her nether opening.

"This is beautiful artwork on you. They reflect you perfectly. And you still say you're not a hero?" Her eyelashes flutter.

"Tattoos don't make a person. They may tell a story, but it doesn't always mean it's true. Or they cover up things you don't want to show the world."

Her brows furrow at my words. She doesn't ask what I mean, and I assume she understands it's another hint at a checkered part of my youth I'm not ready to disclose.

"Well, they're beautiful nonetheless, and so are you," she murmurs then lets her fingers fall back to her sides.

"Thank you, Liv. But *you're* the beautiful one."

She bites her lip, and I stand up to put my shirt back on. After smoothing the fabric back in place, I sit down in my seat, and we resume eating.

We gobble down the remnants of our meal until we can't take another bite. I clear the table and insist she rest. Tonight must be a lot on her, and her weariness is starting to show. She watches me load the dishwasher and pet Ash in between my cleaning duties. Liv's dreamy glances have my dick taunting me for some relief. Rubbing one out earlier didn't do anything but fuel the inferno that is my libido.

Watching a movie will hopefully distract me from making any more moves on her this evening. We finally venture into her living room and settle in to view an action flick. She snuggles into my side, and I welcome it. Putting my arm around her, I hug her to me, feeling invincible when she's near—the world can't touch me or her.

After ninety minutes of a quality action-packed plot, the credits roll. She fell asleep about halfway in, and I stroked her hair the entire time while Ash laid across my lap. Nothing has ever felt more right or real, and it's as if I've been given a gift—the gift of glimpsing the future and seeing how things can be in my life. I just pray to God I don't fuck this up. There's nowhere in the world I'd rather be than right here, right now with her. But she needs a restful night of sleep, and I have to leave soon before I end up inviting myself over for a pajama party.

My hands scoop up one sleepy Ash, and I place him to the side of the couch on the floor—the poor dog doesn't even rouse from slumber. I find his owner isn't much different. Carefully extricating myself from her snuggles, I pop up from the cushion and scoop her up in my arms. Carrying her upstairs to her room is not a difficulty. I locate her bedroom easily and use the front of my foot to kick open the door.

Laying her down with ease, she rolls over to her stomach and lets out a contented sigh. Since she isn't wearing shoes, I don't have to remove them. I finagle her body to get under the covers and make sure she's comfortable. I don't like leaving her like this, so I decide to fashion a note.

Downstairs, I find a pen and paper and scribble down some words. Ash must have woken up at some point because he's dancing around by my feet. I take him out to her backyard and let him piss and run around for a minute. Earlier, I noticed his dog bed by the refrigerator and the gate to the entrance of the kitchen was propped up on the wall. It occurs to me this must be where he sleeps. He gets lavished with rubs from me before I lock him in there for the night.

After making my way up the stairs again, I head to her bedroom once more. I place the note on her bedside table and take one final moment to admire her beauty. I bend down to kiss her on the cheek and linger longer than necessary—inhaling the sweet fragrance of her hair as I go. Reluctantly, I turn out her light and swing her door around so it's slightly ajar.

After exiting her house and making sure I turned the hardware to self-lock behind me, I am overcome with the weight of this evening. It's a night I will never forget. Her scent hangs in the air. The feel of her skin is forever imbedded in my brain and branded on my flesh. And the flavor of her mouth has left its calling card upon me.

She may think I rescued her that night, but really, it was the other way around.

Chapter 16: Fired Up

Olivia

Waking up, I stretch my arms high above me and mewl at the sensation of my limbs getting relief. Surely there's a goofy grin on my face because I feel happy, content, and whole. Finally, last night comes back to me, and I rocket up from lying down into a sitting position.

Wes was here last night; we had dinner, and then I must have fallen asleep. I don't remember walking up to my room, so he must have carried me. Clutching at my chest is necessary to keep my heart from flying right out of my ribcage—my heart knows it's been set free by last night's revelations. Sniffing the air, I would put my hand on stack of Holy Bibles and swear I can still smell his mouthwatering scent permeating my bedroom.

It's after ten in the morning when I check my bedside clock, and I notice a folded note to its left. It's Wes's handwriting, which I'd recognize anywhere no matter how much time has passed. It's because I used to stare at his name on the top of his assignments whenever we'd sit near each other in classes.

Smiling to myself, I lift the white notebook paper with *Liv* scrawled on the front and read the contents.

> *Olivia,*
>
> *I wanted nothing more than to stay and watch over you last night, but it wouldn't have been right. Don't worry, I put Ash away.*
>
> *Thank you for a memorable evening. Being near you again has turned me inside out, in*

> *a good way. I have many years of dates to make*
> *up for, so when can I see you again?*
> > *Hope you slept well. I know I'll be*
> *dreaming of you all night and day.*
> *Kisses,*
> *Wes*

Words escape me at the moment—even in my own mind. This whirlwind romantic cyclone we've been swept up in is unexpected and perfect all at once. It's also poetic in the sense that it's so representative of *us*. We couldn't get it right as teens, but I sure hope we get it right as adults.

Ash starts barking from downstairs, and I realize I have to get my lazy bones up. Wes is such a thoughtful, caring man—he always has been. His protective instincts, pride of civic duty, and his strength irrevocably draw me to him. The preponderance of evidence mounting in favor of Wes and me working out is staggering. As I analyze and normally catalog my life into neat little columns—much like a monthly planner—I find myself not wanting to categorize anything this time.

Live in the here and now!

Embracing a future of possibilities is on the horizon. Mom taught me to look for the signs, and more and more are coming into focus instead of remaining blurred in the background. Ash barks again, reminding me I have many things to do before I see or talk to Wes again, starting with breaking up with Jarrod—tonight.

***

Olivia

"We've been over this, Jarrod. My mind's made up."

"I don't understand why you're throwing away a chance at a future for some fireman who seems like a brute."

We've been at this already for ten minutes over the phone. It's not the bravest way to break up with someone, but I knew if he came over, he'd never leave. It's no surprise Jarrod is putting up a fight—again—and trying to do everything in his power to convince me to remain with him. The difference is this time it is *the last time*.

"Jarrod, please try to understand. It's. Over. That's it! I wish to remain friends and colleagues, so I hope that's possible," I sigh deeply in obvious frustration.

"Olivia, he's not good enough for you. You'll see, and you'll be sorry—it could be too late by then for me to take you back."

The nerve! This side of Jarrod is so off. Maybe I *have* taken advantage of his good nature for so long, not realizing that under the carefully controlled exterior, he's just a hurt little boy. More than ever, I'm doing what's best for all involved.

"Let me be clear and reiterate what I said earlier. This decision isn't based on Wes. I'm not going to lie or pretend I don't have feelings for him, but I'm ending this with you because it's never going to work. Don't bring him into this. It's between you and me. Please, just finally accept it." *I didn't need a month or two to come to this conclusion—I'd set the deadline and it turns out it wasn't necessary.*

My voice has a whiny sound to it, and I'm not a whiner. It seems Jarrod is bringing out this side of me. Hopefully, he's pacified, and if not, then I did my best. Hanging up is the only other option because I've entertained this conversation long enough.

"You slept with him, didn't you?"

Sucking in a sharp breath at the venom and accusation in his voice, I reply with an emphatic "No."

He's a desperate man grasping at straws. I don't provide him further explanation or reasons why he's wrong—he doesn't deserve my time, and it's none of his business. I didn't cheat. A stolen kiss was wrong, but I'm not sorry for it, and it doesn't constitute cheating for me. Most people have their own definition of cheating, and mine extends to sexual acts, which doesn't include kissing.

"Goodbye, Jarrod. I pray you come to your senses and will see things differently in a few days."

Not waiting for his reply, I hit the button on my cell to end the call and hang up. I want to throw the damn, defenseless thing against a wall. At least it's finally done and over with; the breakup is a thing of the past and not hanging over my head. Standing up from my couch, I walk into the kitchen to get a drink of water and try to relax. Jarrod's words have disturbed me and gotten me all riled up.

After letting my dog outside, I wander back into the living room and curl up with a blanket on my comfy cushions. I call my dad to check in—he always makes me feel better. It's too late to invite him over for dinner now, but I need to hear his voice.

He answers on the second ring. "I was just thinking of you. I haven't seen you in a few days, so I need to check on my girl and my boy."

I love how he includes my pup in everything. "Hey, Dad! Yeah, Ash and I miss you. We both are due for a visit."

"Well, how about tomorrow night?"

"That'd be great! I was actually thinking about inviting Wes. How do you feel about that?"

There's a long pause, and I lick my lips while I absently play with the frayed ends on the afghan covering the lower half of my body.

"I'm fine with it, but the question is, how does Jarrod feel about it?"

This is my dad's subtle way of getting information, even though I'll gladly volunteer some things to him. "I just ended it with him."

"Ah."

"It hasn't been working for a while."

"At the hospital, I could tell there was...tension between you two. I figured Wes had something to do with it."

Breathing out through my nose, I chew on my lip in contemplation. "There's something *there* with Wes. There always has been, and even if nothing comes from it, ending things with Jarrod was inevitable."

Despite sounding wishy-washy, I'm trying to keep my budding romance with Wes to myself for a little while longer—well, I guess until tomorrow night, that is.

"Honey, it's your life. And this old man doesn't need to stick his nose in it. I just want you happy, and I know your mom would want that too."

A tear slips down my cheek, but I also chuckle as I once again try to convince him he's not old. He laughs at me for telling him so, but I know I'll never sway him on this concept. My dad and I make plans for dinner, and after a few more minutes of chatting, I end the call.

I just hope Wes is free to attend. He's the next on my list to converse with. I'll text because it's harmless, and I have no clue if he's busy at the moment.

Me: Thank you for the note and for putting me to bed. And for locking Ash up. Lol. A lot of thank yous.

Wes: Hey! I wondered when I'd hear from you. I didn't want to press my luck by stalking you. Believe me, I was tempted to just drop by. You're welcome, by the way.

My insides feel like there's a school of fish swimming around over the idea of him coming by. *Stalking* doesn't sound off-putting considering that's what I felt I did to him back in the day.

Me: Are you free for dinner tomorrow night? My dad is coming over, and I thought it would be fun to do a family thing.

I hit myself in the forehead over the word *family*—it's too premature for that. I wince when I make contact with my stitches. Thankfully, they come out tomorrow when I go to the doctor for my checkup.

Wes: I'd love to. However, I promised Grant and Mal the other day we'd do dinner.

Me: Bring them along, of course!

Wes: That would be great. Grant and I both work Tuesday. It's funny because I was going to ask you if you wanted to come with

us out to dinner.

    Me: Well, how about we make this one big get-together, and I'll also have Sammy and her husband Tom come over?

    And here I thought Wes would run for the hills over the prospect of a big family thing. With everyone coming together, I would think it would be slightly awkward for them to bear witness to Wes and I beginning our journey together. I shouldn't stress so much.

    The dot moves across the screen as he's typing. I'm back to playing with the blanket and using my foot to rub Ash's furry spine. My pup's already fallen asleep by my feet.

    Wes: And what about Jarrod? Is he coming too?

    Well, I didn't want to tell Wes like this, but I'm an idiot for texting him instead of calling or inviting him over for a face-to-face discussion.

    Me: I told him earlier it's over.

    Wes: Are you okay?

    Me: Better than okay.

    Wes: That's good to hear.

    Me: What are you up to right now?

    Wes: I came to the station to work out. A certain somebody has me needing to blow off some steam.

    My legs are restless as I squirm and squeeze my thighs together—it doesn't do anything but make me squirmier. The thought of having this man *turned inside out over me*—his words, not mine—is a heady notion. He holds all the cards; he just doesn't see it. In my mind, I've already shown my hand and laid my two pair upon the table.

    Me: You couldn't be referring to me, could you?

    Going the coy route is my next hand, and I'll ante up—there's no need to call my bluff.

    Wes: Liv, there's no other woman who could ever make me work out for three hours straight and at the end still feel like I'll combust if I don't exert some more energy.

    Throwing the blanket off is essential to my survival because now I'm overheated by the thoughts snaking through every brain cell. An image of him exerting all this energy on me has me swallowing the excess saliva that has pooled under my tongue.

    The dilemma over taking things slow and now moving too fast has me stopping to think about the right course of action. However, I shouldn't worry what people think. It's how *I* feel about myself that counts. Venturing down this path with him is new because I wouldn't have behaved like this as a teen. As an adult, I can do whatever I damn well please. Being an unattached woman, I can flirt all I want without guilt or shame.

    Me: I know the feeling.

    Wes: Do you now?

Me: Yes. I need to exert some excess energy too. Just not at the gym.

Wes: And how are you going to do that in your injured state?

Me: I'm not that injured. It's been a week.

Wes: So what do you have in mind?

Slowly blowing out a breath, I decide I got myself into this, so there's no turning back. I hate being lame, yet I can't help myself with my next line.

Me: What are you wearing?

Lame, totally lame!

Wes: Gym clothes.

Me: More specific.

Wes: What are you doing? Are you flirting with me? Olivia, I'm shocked by this behavior. And quite frankly…it's about fucking time.

Me: You never answered my question fully.

Wes: You're a demanding little thing.

Me: Wouldn't you like to know?

Wes: Absolutely!

Biting the tip of my thumbnail and staring at my phone, I cluck my tongue, carefully deciding my next line—minus the lameness.

Me: Well, I suppose tomorrow night you'll see for yourself.

Wes: Is that a threat lol?

Me: More like an invitation.

Wes: Bring it on!

Me: You're on.

Wes: Oh Liv, you don't know what you've started.

Me. Maybe I do. And maybe I should have started it years ago.

Wes: What am I going to do with you?

Me: I hope everything.

Wes: Baby, I'm going to go take a cold shower now and pray to God I can stay away from breaking down your door tonight.

Gah! There's that *baby* again!

Me: Okay, I'll behave. I won't tease you any more tonight.

Wes: Too late. I'll talk to you later. Get some rest—you're going to need it.

Me: You too.

Chapter 17: Grilled

Olivia

Monday

Sammy and Tom are coming for dinner this evening. She's even taking me to my doctor's appointment to get my stitches out, so we're on our way there now.

After I stopped texting Wes last night, I ended up working on one of my new building projects to take my mind off things—it barely helped. I spent the remainder of my night fantasizing about Wes and my battery-operated toy got quite the workout.

Sammy got the highlights from his and my text conversation. Her reaction is what I expected. "I still can't believe you officially broke up with Jarrod. It's about time! And now I can't wait to meet Wes and see how he measures up. How you've kept all this history with him from me over the years, I'll never understand."

She sticks her tongue out at me as maturely and demurely as only Sammy can deliver, and I reciprocate.

"Like I told you, no one knew about Wes," I whisper. "Please don't be upset with me, and besides, you know you can't stay mad at me for long. It's not that I didn't *want* to tell you; it's that I *couldn't* tell you. I buried my feelings deep in the ground for so long, they just couldn't be dug up— not even with the assistance of a heavy-duty backhoe."

She snorts. This was going to be difficult for my bestie to accept, yet I knew she would eventually concede. After all, if the situation were reversed, I would be disappointed she'd never told me; however, I'd get over it.

Wes invaded my thoughts for so long that when I moved away and went to college the only way to cope was to forget he existed. Moving back here was a fresh start for me in a lot of ways. The memories were always there, but I didn't have to acknowledge them until the accident.

"What if it doesn't work out with Mr. Wonderful?"

Biting my lip, there's a stabbing sensation that hits my heart and pierces the shield around it. I've resigned myself to the fact that it's a possibility we won't work out. There's no sense of permanence that hovers between us. The only permanence is how I'll forever feel about him.

Swallowing hard, I tell her, "Then it doesn't work out."

"Just like that?"

"Yes. I'll tell you one thing: I'll never settle again. The expression of *having to kiss some frogs before finding your prince* is not something I want to do. I found my prince at seventeen, and he's the only prince for me. Maybe it's just like it was for my mom and dad. There's only one great love of your life, and whether we work out or not doesn't matter. It doesn't change how I feel."

"Damn, girl, that's too heavy for this early in the morning. We're getting coffee ASAP so I can handle this conversation."

Chuckling at her way with words, we pull off into a coffee shop. My appointment isn't for another forty minutes, so we have time. Before we exit the car, I thank her for taking me today. I know my dad would have brought me, but I needed to let Sammy know about everything before tonight's dinner. Being my bestie, it's a given she needs to be up-to-date on my love life. She's fearless when it comes to telling someone how it is, and I don't know if it's a good or bad thing when it comes to introducing her to Wes.

My phone vibrates in my hand. It's an incoming text from the man himself. Sammy hears it and winks at me, knowing full well what has me smiling.

Wes: Let me know how you make out at the doctor, and before I come over tonight, can I ask a favor?

Me: Of course.

Wes: Can you come with me to meet my mom? I've told her all about you. It would mean a lot to me.

Moving my hand to my mouth to prevent the gasp that wants to escape, I'm bowled over by the fact he asked this of me. Thinking about him telling me how his mom isn't in the best frame of my mind, bless her heart, I am touched by this offer. Of course I'd like to meet her. I'd like to know the woman who gave birth to this glorious man. He has no idea what this means to me.

Me: I'd love to! Will I meet your sister too?

Wes: Not yet. She'll still be at work, but she's definitely coming to dinner. Let me know when you're done at the doctor, and I'll swing by and pick you up. I know it's a lot to ask in one day. I don't want to overwhelm you.

Me: There's nothing I'd love more. I'm not overwhelmed, I promise.

Wes: Okay, TTYL baby.

***

Weston

Liv and I arrive at my sister's place. Our clasped hands resting on the center console instill a sense of peace and purpose in me when I gaze down at where we're joined. Looking up into her sparkling amethyst eyes framed by the longest, thickest lashes, I end up losing my train of thought. She does this to me all the damn time—then and now.

Not being able to help myself, I lean toward her and kiss her lips sweetly. "Ready, baby?"

This is a big step for us. It feels right, though. I need her to know a piece of me even if I can't share the whole story. Somehow with her meeting my mom, it solidifies this developing relationship.

If I'm right, this meeting will mean as much to Liv as it does to me. With her mother having left this world, I'd like to think she'd appreciate sharing this with me. Her hand is slightly sweaty. If she's nervous to meet my mom, I get it. I experienced the same apprehension when I met her father. Most likely, I'll always have a twinge of dread around fatherly figures. However, her dad seems like a great man, and I look forward to spending more time with him.

"Yes," she replies softly.

We walk into the house, and a pumpkin pie smell hits my nostrils. My sister must've been burning candles before going to work. She loves her fall scents even before the season starts. I'm excited for Mal to meet Liv tonight—I know they'll hit it off.

"Their home is lovely," Liv comments.

"Yeah, it's a nice place. Mal does a good job keeping up with everything." Then, I gesture toward the closed door, "My mom's in here."

I rap on the door once with my knuckles, and after looking in, I find Mom in her sitting chair. We're on another round of her being incommunicado. Sighing, I pull Liv along to stand beside the chair then kneel down in front of the woman who birthed me.

"Mom…" I give her a slight shake, hoping it will jar her.

No response.

"Mom, this is Olivia Watson. She's the woman I told you about." From my kneeling position, I whisper in my mom's ear so Liv can't hear, "She's the one I told you I love."

My mom closes her eyes, and I'm filled with happiness knowing it's progress. Maybe Liv can help me pull her from the darkness. Knowing what it's like to be down in that hole since I've visited it too many times myself, Mom probably feels like no one can pull her out. She loves us kids, but she's been so broken—we haven't been enough to fix her. If she sees we're happy and that what happened to us years ago won't stand in the way of a prosperous future, she may eventually come out the other side of this.

"Hi, Mrs. Thorpe. It's so nice to finally meet you. Wes was kind enough to bring me today. I'm honored to be here. I'm lucky to have crossed paths with him again. Not sure if he told you, but we went to high school together."

Liv rubs at her earring—something she does subconsciously—and proceeds to sit on the corner of the bed. "You have an amazing son," she conveys while smiling warmly in my mom's direction, then Liv locks eyes with me.

While I mouth to Liv "thank you," my mother turns to look up at me. Swallowing hard, my eyes are instantly filled with moisture. This is the first time in a week there seems to be life in her.

"Weston…," my mom croaks.

On the rare occasion she does come out of her fog, I cherish it. It reminds me of some of my Alzheimer's patients, but, of course, that's not what's wrong with her. I personally think her brain goes into protective mode so she doesn't have to deal or cope with what happened. We gave up a long time ago on therapists—it never helped.

"Hi, Mom!"

She opens her frail arms, and I'm enfolded into her welcoming hug. Hearing Liv sniffle from behind us makes me realize this is a special moment for all.

As I pull back from my mom, her eyes move to the right, and she asks, "And who's this beautiful woman?"

"This is my Olivia."

"Your Olivia?" My mom smiles with confusion.

"Yes," I confirm.

"Hi, Mrs. Thorpe."

They shake hands, and my heart thumps in my chest at the impact the three women in my life have on me—*I just wish Mal was home to see this.*

"Nice to meet you, dear. My, you have a pretty name," my mom says sincerely and follows it up with a yawn. "Excuse me, I think I'm really tired."

It takes a lot out of her to do anything. That's why it's imperative

Mal and I ensure she gets the proper nutrition since she doesn't get much movement or physical activity.

"No problem, Mom. We'll let you rest. I'm glad you got to meet Liv."

"Me too, my sweet boy. Goodness, you get more handsome every day. You look so much like your father." As she's saying this, her eyes glaze over. *Father* triggered her mental retreat.

As quickly as she came out of it, she goes right back in. Time is up. My mother is gone again. Looking at Liv, I whisper, "I'm sorry."

There's no need to apologize, Liv automatically understands.

Repositioning my mom so she's comfortable, I rub her hair and say a little prayer for her. I'm grateful for these moments we are gifted. Liv even wraps a blanket around the front of my mother, which only makes me love her more.

Liv and I walk hand in hand out to my truck, and before getting in, I dip her back and kiss her with everything I have.

Olivia Watson… My dream girl. My life. My everything plus infinity.

***

Weston

Two hours later, I'm right back at my sister's house, sitting in her living room. I promised Mal I would bring her to the dinner, and I always try to keep my promises. When I told Mal about our mother's progress today, she was crushed she wasn't here to witness it. Hopefully by bringing Liv around more, it will help. It might spark something in her.

Mal is so excited to meet Liv. She's practically bouncing out of her skin over the idea of having a *sister*. She seems to be putting the cart before the horse when it comes to my relationship, though. Rolling my eyes at her is all I can do because she's already got me walking down the fucking aisle. But I'll never make it anywhere with Liv if we don't get over to her house for dinner. My sister's fashion show is the hold up.

"Are you sure this looks good?" she questions from the doorway to her bedroom and does a spin to show off her umpteenth outfit.

"Yes, Baby Girl, it looks fantastic. But it doesn't matter what you wear. Not only do you always look beautiful, but Liv doesn't care what you're wearing."

Her hand flies through the air as if to say *nonsense*. "I just want to make a good impression for your sake, that's all. So, you're sure?"

I'm about to reassure her again when in walks Grant from the kitchen with a bag of chips in his hand, snacking away. Around a mouthful of crunching, he says, "It's perfect."

The blush in Mal's cheeks has me grinding my teeth. I suspect the outfit choice for tonight is more for Grant than it is for Liv. Mal disappears into her room, and I glare at Grant. He laughs his ass off, and I swipe his bag of chips, which is met with a huge protest on his end.

"You don't need to eat this shit."

"Fuck you! I work out way harder, so it's not like it matters. Go change your tampon."

Grumbling at his comment, I stand up and go check on my mom to make sure she's all set for dinner in her room. There's no way to convince her to come since she's in a catatonic state anyway. It's best to let her rest, and maybe she'll snap out of it when Mal is dropped off later. I'm second-guessing taking two cars. Earlier, I asked Grant to bring her home, and I'm a fucking idiot for just now realizing I'm practically delivering my baby sister right into his welcoming lap.

My original line of thinking involved the convenience of having my car there without having to take Mal home, just in case Liv makes good on her text messages from last night. I'm not going to go into this evening with any expectations because *saying* and *doing* something are two entirely different things.

Shaking my head as I enter my mom's room, I pray tonight isn't a shitshow with everyone being there. But no matter what, I'll get to see Liv—that's what matters.

***

Weston

It's a mild evening. The humidity is down from the oppressive wave that plagued us only a few weeks prior.

We're all sitting out back on Liv's small deck, watching Ash trying to catch fireflies in his mouth—unsuccessfully, of course. Dinner was delicious. Liv's dad manned the grill, and she had enough food to feed a small army. We each brought an accompanying dish or dessert to contribute. Any worries about our respective sides of the family meshing well were quickly quelled when the conversation played out like we've all known each other for years.

Every now and then, Liv tugs at her pearl earrings, and I revel in being part of her inner circle, privy to what that sign means. She's wearing makeup tonight, not that she needs it. Her wound is barely noticeable and now that the stitches are gone and her hair is swept to the side, no one would know that just a little over a week ago, she had a wreck—*and at the same time, wrecking my world in the best possible fucking way!*

Her skin is glowing. As the citronella candle flames dance in the wind, they cast light on her face, tempting me all the more. We're sitting next to one another. Underneath the patio table, I have my hand resting on her leg, lazily drawing a circular pattern on her inner thigh with my thumb. She squirms, giving away how affected she is, and I'm eating that shit up. *Oh, she's going to be fun to torture and tease later when we're alone.*

Liv's dressed in a black sleeveless summer dress with small flowers in varying shades of pinks and blues. Her sparkly sandals show off her gorgeous legs, and the ankle bracelet is driving me crazy—it's like the red cape to a bull. I want to kiss every inch of her, starting with her graceful legs and delicate ankles.

"No one wants seconds on my brownies?" Mal asks our group and pouts.

"I think I speak for us all when I say we're stuffed. But feel free to send some home with us," Tom tells her with a grin the size of Texas.

Sammy elbows her husband in the gut, and I hear her whisper about how she doesn't need or want the calories he's inviting upon them. She's a feisty one, and I like her. I have a feeling she's going to warn me off about Liv, though, or give me the typical best friend speech about chopping off my nuts if I break Liv's heart. I have no intention of doing such a thing, so if that discussion comes my way with Sammy, I'll set her straight.

It's after nine o'clock. We've eaten, socialized, and those who chose to imbibe have drunk their chosen poisons. The evening is coming to a close since it appears most have to work tomorrow. I don't have to be at the station until eight in the morning, but I'm used to running on little sleep, so I'm not worried in the slightest.

Liv's dad stands from the table and runs his hands down the front of his shirt, then he takes his glasses off and rubs at his eyes. It looks like he'll be making an exit soon.

"Leaving already, Robby?" I ask him.

"Yeah, it's time for this old man to get home. I'm up way past my bedtime as it is. You kids all enjoy the rest of your evening and thanks for having me over."

Liv rises to her feet to hug him goodbye and administers a kiss to his cheek. Seeing this father-daughter moment, I turn to Mal and see my sister is wearing a stoic expression. Then Mal meets my eyes as I'm conveying how sorry I am that she doesn't have this—she's been cheated of something I can't make up for. Out of the corner of my eye, I see Grant look at her the same way I am.

A chorus of thank yous rings out to her dad for grilling tonight. It was definitely some good eating, but I'm glad I've had time for my stomach to settle because my dessert is coming soon—it involves nibbling on one Olivia Watson.

Robby shakes all of the guys' hands and hugs all the girls. He gives plenty of rubs to Ash's head and then makes his departure.

"Well, I think we're going to head out too since we have a bit of a drive ahead of us," Tom remarks, and he and Sammy proceed to get up from the table.

Mal and Grant linger out on the patio talking and watching the dog play, but I follow Liv inside the house to see her friends off. As we make our way out to the front, Liv excuses herself to grab some leftovers to send home with them—minus the brownies. And I gather this will be the warning speech as Sammy fixes her steely gaze on me.

"Do I need to tell you that if you screw this up, there will be nowhere in the world you can hide?"

Snorting at her attempt to intimidate me, I also find myself smiling. Her protectiveness is endearing. She's concerned about the most important woman in the world, which is something I can appreciate.

"Sammy." Tom gives his wife a look to say, *what the hell?*

"Don't *Sammy* me. Liv deserves nothing but the best, and I won't let her get hurt."

She stops throwing daggers at her husband with her eyes and spins back around to concentrate on me. It's like I need to check my back for grill marks matching the chicken we ate earlier—Sammy is trying to barbeque me.

"I can assure you, I've lov-...liked Liv for a *very* long time. I have no intention of hurting her," I convey sincerely.

Fuck! I almost slipped with the "L" word. My family more or less knows, but it's something I want to tell Liv first before I share it with her best friend. Sammy assesses my features for a few more seconds then nods in satisfaction.

Liv walks in with a bag for them and stops in her tracks when she appears to sense the tension in the air. "Am I interrupting anything?" she asks cautiously.

"Not at all. We were just saying goodnight to your rescuer over here."

Hearing Liv whisper the word "behave" into Sammy's ear as she hugs her goodbye has me stifling the hearty laugh that wants to escape from my mouth. Eventually, the couple pulls away in their car, and I put my arm around Liv. We walk back through the house to rejoin the other two on the deck.

When we step back outside, I see Mal brushing a piece of Grant's hair that had fallen across his forehead out of the way. She doesn't even notice our approach. If Grant does, he sure as hell doesn't act like it. Clearing my throat, my sister pulls her hand back into her lap faster than a gun shot. My fists tighten at my sides, and Grant sits there with a smirk—

the bastard!

"Do you need me to drive you home, Mal?" I question in a firm tone.

"Uh, no thanks. Erm, Grant still doesn't mind taking me home, right?"

Her eyes rove over to his face. There's so much hope and admiration in her expression. I must be deluding myself into thinking I can possibly keep these two away from each other forever. *Who am I to judge when I can't stay away from Liv?* A part of me wants to accept something could happen between them, but at the risk of sounding like a broken record, I'm fearful my family dynamic will forever change if it doesn't work out between them.

"I've got this. You and Liv just enjoy the rest of your evening." Grant waggles his brows at me. "You ready to go, doll?"

My sister nods effusively, beaming at him like he's hung the fucking moon for her. Opting to clench my jaw instead of growling seems like the wisest choice. Grant and I will be having a damn come-to-Jesus moment. Clutching on to Mal as she hugs me goodbye, I can't help but close my eyes and see ribbons still in her hair along with childhood innocence. Then, Mal hugs Liv and gushes over tonight's gathering.

After walking over to Grant, I clap him on the back and grip his shoulder, squeezing with all my might—he gets the message. Off they go, and even though I should concentrate on the goddess left by my side, I can't help but stare ahead of me long after my best friend and baby sister have left.

"You okay?"

Snapping out of it, I shake my head to clear the fogginess. "Yeah, sorry. It's just hard. They're my only family."

Liv nods in understanding. She then bites her lip and reaches for my hand. "I can't say I *get it* because I don't have a sibling, but it's no secret how protective you are. Mal's lucky to have you. Haven't you noticed the way those two look at each other, though? It's magical," she sighs dreamily.

Breathe in, breathe out. Breathe in, breathe out.

"I have." *Because it's the way I look at you.* "But Mal said she doesn't like him like that. I have no reason not to believe her."

She giggles at my logic. Any other time I'd laugh with her—this isn't one of those moments.

"Grant's great! It's easy to see why you all adore him. You said yourself he's like your brother. You don't think you'd be happy for the two of them if they got together? Heck, I can understand why your sister likes him."

That does it! Her glowing endorsement brings out my jealous beast—I have many beasts lurking inside.

She yelps in surprise when I grab her in my arms—locked and trapped.

"What's this now? There will be no talk of finding my best friend attractive. You're in big trouble now, baby. You've gone and poked the bear." This time I do growl in warning because she provoked and ignited this passion.

Her breathing is erratic. The swells of her tits are moving up and down with her heaving breaths. My eyes can't help but wander to that exact spot, riveted by the sight before me. She follows my gaze, and when we look into each other's eyes, I'm lost to the purple swirls like I'm gazing into a galaxy of celestial exquisiteness.

"Tell me you don't want this—this thing between us, Liv. Tell me to leave you alone. Because if we start this, it will never end. Once I have you, I'll need and want everything from you. I'll never be able to live without you again. What we already have is intense, but it only works if you're with me. Are you with me, baby?"

She swallows, and I see her lips tremble. My hands are sweating at the small of her back where I have them laced together. My heart is beating so fast, I'm afraid I'll have to use my medical training on myself to regulate it.

Everything comes down to this moment. It's all or nothing.

Chapter 18: Sheets

Olivia

"Yes, I'm with you." *Forever...*

"Is this all too fast, Liv? Am I pushing you into something? You don't feel like you're getting out of one relationship to jump right into another, do you?"

So many questions—at rapid fire—but questions warranting answers. I've had many of my own. Some still unanswered, but I believe we'll get there when he's ready.

Resting my forehead against his chest, it's a relief to have some clarity. I may not always relinquish control to others. In this instance, I can embrace a future where we're together, and by all accounts, it sounds like it's for the long haul. We may barely know each other as adults, yet I know the important things, the things that matter: what's in his heart, the type of person he is, and how he treats me.

"No. It's not too fast. I've had similar worries, but I can't turn off a switch and stop feeling the way I do. You're not pushing me; I'm going into this with open eyes and open arms. We're in this together."

Lifting my head from where it's nestled, I look at his handsome face. I'm still trapped by his hold, and there's nowhere else I'd rather be.

He kisses the tip of my nose and tells me, "I don't deserve you."

Laughing at his absurd comment, I'm poised to protest.

"Let me finish. I mean it: I don't deserve you. In my line of work—and from what I've seen over the years—there are no guarantees in life. We're not promised tomorrow. Hell, we're not even promised today. But I would always regret not taking this second chance to be with you, despite not being worthy."

He has it all wrong. Speech eludes me. His impassioned words are still a blur streaking through my mind. One second I inadvertently make him jealous, and the next second he's professing his love—minus using the actual four-letter word. My brain hasn't caught up with processing everything, but he got the answers he wanted, so his mouth is on mine.

Not even a sheet of paper could be put between us. We're as closely pressed together as it gets. Flames of desire are licking up my spine and curling around my skin, making me burn with white-hot need. I could power a small city with the electrifying currents running through my body. Moaning uncontrollably into his frenzied kisses, I swirl my tongue to mirror his movements. The result has him groaning out his own call of need.

As he's sucking and tasting, he murmurs, "You're fucking timeless, baby."

That little verbiage sends zaps of excitement right between my legs. I'm rubbing my body up and down the front of him to create friction—the craving is unbelievable. I want to cry because it's never been like this with anyone. Never have I felt so alive. Never have I been so desired by another human being, and the culmination of suppressing my feelings for over a decade has left me completely overwhelmed.

Moving my lips to his neck, I suck and lave the area. Continuing along his jawline, I lick right where his stubble has formed. I nuzzle my cheek against it so it scratches me, giving me a reminder he's real and this isn't a dream.

He pulls back momentarily and stares me down while cupping my cheeks in his strong hands. I turn my face into his hand and kiss his palm. That gray cosmic storm brewing in the depths of his eyes is the sexiest, most erotic thing. I can't imagine he's ever looked at another woman like that; those looks are reserved for me.

"Are you sure you're feeling up to this? Don't push yourself. Fuck, I want you so goddamn bad, I'm going insane, but I won't risk hurting you," he breathes out.

"Yes. I'm fine; my checkup today confirms it. God, I want this more than anything. I'm yours. I've *always* been yours, Wes. Take me!"

He throws me over his shoulder—an action I imagine is considered the *fireman carry,* and I squeal with delight. We leave the back porch, and he stalks through my house with me laughing at the situation. I slap his biteable jean-covered ass. For good measure, I grip the denim-clad buttock, and it's just as firm and muscular as expected.

"So, you're an ass girl?"

It's awkward for me to talk in this position as we're now making our way for the stairs, but I do my best while practically hanging upside down. "Only for *your* ass."

"That's my girl."

As we enter my bedroom, he lets me down to my feet—slowly—and we're both smiling. This is why he's irresistible. He can be anything and everything all at once: sexy, playful, broody, bossy, demanding, and sweet. Ash is sitting at our feet, and we both look down at him in apology.

"Sorry, boy, but what I'm about to do to your mother isn't for your eyes."

Ash cocks his head to the side in wonder. Cracking up over his comment, I watch as Wes shoos the poor pup outside the door and tells him to *stay*. My dog complies and sits. Then, he closes the door with an audible click, causing a shiver of anticipation to run through me.

"Where were we?" he asks me mischievously, smokiness still weaving through his irises.

The predatory gleam he's throwing my way has my panties completely soaked. Unsure whether it's a rhetorical question, I choose to remain silent. Needing to do something, I reach for my sandals to unstrap them, but he halts my progress by kneeling at my feet. Raw power emanates from his every pore.

Dear God, I won't survive this!

"Allow me," he explains in a husky voice from his position on the floor.

He has my foot cradled in his hands, regarding my shoes with admiration. Wes expertly unbuckles the first strap, then repeats the process on the other foot. It's taking everything in me to stay still and upright. After the second shoe is removed, he fingers the silver bracelet on my ankle, lovingly, reverently.

His Adam's apple is working in his throat when he swallows down what appears to be nervousness. As much as he exudes the classic alpha male qualities, there's a vulnerable side to him—it's equally appealing. This night is the same for the both of us.

Tonight, time is my *friend*.

The fitted black shirt stretched across his broad, chiseled chest needs to be removed. I'm dying to see his chest again. Running the material of my dress through my fingers stops me from ripping his top down the middle—otherwise, I'd muster the strength to destroy the shirt Hulk-style.

He places his hand on the back of my calf and dips his head to kiss my ankle, swirling his tongue across the bone. Throwing my head back, I brace myself by gripping his shoulders for support. If outsiders were looking in, they'd witness me deep in the throes of passion. My core painfully clenches and throbs, begging to be filled.

"Oh my God, Wes!" I moan out.

He keeps up the torture by licking, sucking, and swirling his way up my legs. As he reaches my thighs, he tosses the skirt of my dress over his head, and not being able to see him makes it more intense. He lavishes more attention upon me—this time below my bellybutton on his way to my pubic bone.

After I cry out again at the bliss he's delivering, he plants light, open-mouthed kisses all over my panty-covered pussy. And then he does something that has me falling forward and clutching his head. He bites my inner thigh with expert pressure.

"Ahh!"

Nothing has ever felt so euphoric. And as long as I'm with Wes, I'll always feel this way.

***

Weston

Fuck! I never dreamed it would be like this with a woman. Sex has always been enjoyable, but nothing to this degree—nothing this incredible, and I haven't even been inside her body yet.

My love and lust for her is not an incipient fire. Oh no, it's a damn five-alarm fire!

Inhaling the fragrance at her pussy opening almost sends me over the edge. I can taste and smell her through her panties. After I lift my head from under her dress, I look up at her stunning face. Her thick, dark lashes flutter closed as she licks her rose-stained lips.

Remaining kneeling, I slide my hands between her legs and hook my thumbs in her black satin panties, tugging them down to the floor. She steps out of them, and they get tucked into my back pocket just because I can.

Her pupils go wide with each thing I do, and I'm eating up her appreciation for my skills. The sensual looks she's throwing my way captivate me instantly. Loving that her lower half is bare under the dress, my cock is rock-hard and pulsing. Relief is imperative or I'll blow my load in my pants, making a damn mess of myself.

Whipping off my shirt, I toss it over my head and rise to my feet. I toe-off my shoes and socks, and Liv wraps her arms around my neck. She admires my tattoos and kisses each bicep—an action that means more than she'll ever know. When she looks back up, I take the opportunity to kiss her deeply, passionately.

Hungry for more, my hands move to her perfectly-sized breasts that fit in my large palms and feel like they were made for me. Squeezing gently, she arches her back and thrusts them further into my hands. Kneading her flesh with the material still a barrier between us will not suffice. She needs to be completely naked. We need to be skin on skin.

Inching my fingers slowly up her legs to gather the hem of her skirt, I leisurely pull the dress off like I'm unveiling the greatest treasure in the world—and to me she is. When her bare pussy comes into view, my breath hitches. Seeing that strawberry birthmark on her hip floods me with emotions. Without even a second thought, I lean down and kiss the mark. She gasps at the contact.

Working my gaze up to her bra-covered tits, my dick continues to thicken and lengthen—something I thought was impossible because it's never been this engorged. She reaches behind her back to unhook her bra, exhaling loudly. I understand her anxiousness and nervousness because it's the same for me. Once the cups fall away, I lower my head to her hard nipples, which are inviting me to devour them. Her long hair hangs straight today, partially covering her breasts. The nipples are playing a tempting game of hide and seek behind her hair as she shifts her weight from foot to foot. *Almost a goner at this point.*

Liv's naked body is glorious with a taut tummy, rounded ass, and luscious hips. She has curves I know how to maneuver, tease, and please. Sheer heaven. Too beautiful for words, and too innocent for someone like me. However, I'm a selfish prick, and I need her like I'll die if I don't have her. How I survived this long without her is a mystery.

After a few minutes of my hot mouth nibbling on her soft peaks, I work my finger down the front of her body and swirl it around, right at the entrance to her cunt. She's tight and clamps down on my digit as I move it in and out. So wet, so very wet. The gasps and moans she's letting out transport me into a world of pure ecstasy. Not only do I hear everything she's doing, but I also feel it in my marrow, transfixed by our two beings about to become one.

"You don't know how long I've wanted you," I croon in her ear.

"I do. For me, it was the first time I saw you. Right then and there, something inside me came alive. These serendipitous moments are leading to something bigger than you and me," she explains.

More proof I don't deserve her. She has me on a pedestal I cannot live up to. What she describes was the same for me—from the first time I laid eyes on her.

"Me too, baby." Choked up with emotion, I get back to something I can take control of. "Now take off my pants."

Her eyes go wide as a squeak escapes from her throat. My fingers—now two in her hole—are greeted by a rush of more liquid due to my command. She fumbles with the button fly and has to try a few times. When the zipper goes down, her fingers tremble. I remove my fingers and watch her tug my pants down to my feet, which is so goddamn hot.

"Now the boxers."

She nods and licks her lips, and in turn, my dick jumps. Liv runs the tips of her fingers around the waistband then slides them slightly in to pull them off me. My cock springs forward, and I can't help but angle my hips, jutting my hard rod forward. My balls ache; my dick is screaming for attention.

"Can I touch you?"

"Baby, you never have to fucking ask."

She lightly wraps her hand around my shaft, and I hiss through my teeth, closing my eyes at the sensations. I thrust forward in her hand. *God, I need more pressure.* As if she heard me, she grips me firmly, and precum coats the head of my cock. My balls already want to draw up to shoot my load all over the front of her. *Patience.*

Her pleasure comes first above all else. We move to the bed where I lay her down gingerly before I continue working on her to bring her to orgasm. In haste, I forgot to grab the condom out of my pants pocket, so I rectify that. Once it's retrieved, I set it on the nightstand.

The naughty minx gives me a saucy grin when I return to her. I kiss the look right off her face. Then my hands find home again and plunge back into her heat—three fingers this time, stretching and preparing her to take my cock as I go. She rides my hand and whimpers into my mouth. I suckle her nipples and continue south, scraping my teeth along the way. When I taste her clit while flattening my tongue, she comes up from the bed like an earthquake moved through. It's not a race, but the fact I got her off so easily gives me a fucking shot of male pride straight to my dick.

We'll combust the sheets at the rate we're going.

Finally, her elegant, lithe body settles back on the bed. She emits a contented sigh from her swollen lips—lips I've punished with my kisses. Her sultry voice hits my ears as she thanks me over and over again—I'm the one who's thankful.

There are plenty more abilities in my arsenal I have yet to unleash. The devilish smile upon my face says so. Her hair is fanned out across the pillow, creating a crown fit for a queen—my queen.

"This is it, baby, no turning back now."

"I know."

Quickly, I slide on the condom and place the head of my cock at her velvety folds. I enter, and her walls immediately close around me. We both grunt and groan as I pull out and work back in until she adjusts to the feeling and size of me. Sweat drips down my hairline. My hands go into her crown of hair, tugging at the strands to anchor her to me. *Forever.*

I've branded her body now, and she's branded me. I've claimed her. She's mine in every way possible. Bucking and thrusting with expert movements, I bring her to the brink again. Not wanting either of us to come yet, I decide to switch positions to heighten the experience.

"Get on top of me, Liv."

She complies and her swift action, plus the brush of her skin on mine, makes me flinch in pleasure. *Ahh, I'm so damn close, it's painfully good.* Once she climbs on top of me, a thought occurs. She's about to impale herself, but I grab her ass with both hands, and she yelps in surprise.

"Nah, not like this. Spin around in reverse cowgirl."

She bites her lip. It's fucking adorable and a turn on. "I've never done it that way."

"Well, baby, you're in for a fucking treat. You'll feel it more intensely, and I'll be so far inside you I'll never leave."

Her mouth falls open at my words, and I smack her ass so she knows to spin around. When the rounded globes are resting on my stomach and her opening hovers over my shaft, I tell her to *do it*.

She lowers herself, and I fist the fucking sheets. "Holy shit!"

Not being able to see her face makes me hammer my cock harder inside her as she matches my rhythm and takes her cues from me. This erotic dance we're doing with our sexes couldn't get any hotter, sweeter, or better than this.

"Liv, you ruined me for other women years ago. And now you've fucking pulverized me. You'll never have another man's cock, and I'll never have another woman's pussy. You hear me?"

She moans, and I take that as a *yes*. Soon I'll take her without a condom, but since we never even got into the whole protection-kids-medical discussion, a rubber is necessary. A few more thrusts, and that'll be it.

"I'm about to come. I want you to come with me."

"Yes, I'm there," she cries.

"Now, baby!"

An explosion occurs in my body, detonating from every cell. My cum spurts out like it will never end, my veins and body straining from the force of release. Her cunt creams and covers me so thoroughly, it's maddening. Once I completely empty myself, the pulsing subsides. Her pussy seems to stop spasming, and it's only a matter of time before she slumps over.

Her hands go to my thighs where she's bracing herself. I can sense her exhaustion. Wrapping my arms around her, I pull her back, and my cock slips out from her—the loss of her heat already affects me.

I tuck her into my side and kiss her forehead, cheeks, eyes, and lips. Her breathing evens, and I wonder if she fell asleep. I hate to leave her even for a second, but disposing of the condom is priority. Getting up from the bed, she mumbles something unintelligible.

After discarding the rubber and washing my hands, I enter her room and clean her off with a towel—she doesn't even stir. I toss on my boxers and open her bedroom door where I find Ash asleep on the floor all curled up in a ball. That little dog has made me an adoring fan. Once I pick him up, he wakes up and starts licking my face gratefully. After letting him outside and making sure he's taken care of for the night, I check the house to ensure all the doors are locked.

Entering the bedroom again, I lie down behind Liv and spoon her, burrowing my nose in her hair. The heat from her body is soothing, and my eyes are heavier than I thought. My boxers remain on because I don't trust myself not to slip my big boy in throughout the middle of the night— whether it's unintentional or *accidentally on purpose*.

Sleep starts to take me, and for the first time in my life, I have peace. And for the second time in my life, true love found me again and brought me back... *She* is my life.

Chapter 19: E*Mmm*T

Weston

My phone buzzes while simultaneously chiming out my alarm tone, which means it's seven in the morning. Snagging it quickly so as not to wake Liv, I turn off my alarm notification.

At least I didn't disturb her. She's still passed out from last night's activities. There's only an hour until I have to be at the station. Since I work close enough from her house, I have enough time for morning sex, a shower, and if I'm lucky, some breakfast.

Two condoms remain in my pants pocket, so I sneak out of bed and retrieve one. Rolling it down my full erection, I'm ready to bury myself to the hilt again in her sweet honeyed hole—last night wasn't enough. It will never be enough. I'm desperate for her. A wake up call from behind will do nicely.

Spooning her once more, I insert my knee in between her legs, nudging them apart to spread her to my liking. I line my cock up to her opening, teasing her pussy lips as I go. Her body reacts instantly even in sleep, and I start inching my way in. My whole lower torso is straining and tensing because it's already too good. *Motherfucking hell!* Rubbing her nipples and kissing her neck has her stirring awake.

"Morning, baby."

"Mmm," is her only response.

While my one hand pinches her nipple, the other skates down toward her clit and lightly rubs the bundle of nerves. She pushes back on my shaft and ends up fully seating herself on me. We both moan at the action. Deciding to apply more pressure to her clit, I also speed up the in-

and-out motion of my dick pounding into her. She continues to arch and thrash, and I hold her to me so she can't squirm away.

"Oh my God, Wes. It's soooo good."

"I know. I'm already so fucking close. That's what you do to me."

It won't be long now before we both rocket off. I'm looking forward to spending quality time going down on her, and I can't wait until she sucks me off—I need to get fully acquainted with every delectable part. Oral sex is one of my favorite things, and normally I would have made more of a meal of it last night, but I couldn't wait to be inside her and claim her. I'll be working for three days straight, but when I'm done my shift, my ass will be right back here in this bed, going to town on her. That's a promise!

Thinking about eating her out and how good her mouth will feel on me has me hovering right there on the edge. My dick will start flowing with cum any moment like a damn volcano bursting with lava. The tingling in my balls has me making sounds low in my throat even I don't recognize. Her body's tremors already signal her impending release.

"God, Olivia, your pussy is so fucking tight and wet. Come for me and cover my cock with all your tasty juices."

My words get to her, and she screams my name as she catapults into orgasm. Following right behind her, I dig my fingers into her flesh. The fact that she'll wear my marks makes me quake longer, but I hope I'm not hurting her. Maybe it's a good thing she has a break from me for three days because I'd wear her out—I can't help it.

We both shudder with aftershocks, and I kiss the back of her neck and shoulders over and over again. I want to see her face. I need to see her lilac eyes. Pulling out of her, I grunt because I already want back in. She lies on her back, giving me a perfect view of her tits. There's not enough time for me to hold her like she's the most precious being, and I lament the fact I have to get moving. After administering kisses to her nipples, I slide out of bed to go into the bathroom, toss the condom in the trash, and start the water.

When I poke my head back into her room, I ask her to join me in the shower. She jumps up from the bed, her breasts bouncing with each step. *God, this woman has no idea what she does to me.*

As fast as I can, I soap us off and enjoy rubbing her body down with the sweet-smelling shampoo and soap. After I pay close attention to massaging her scalp, she does the same for me, and her hands feel divine— it's that good. These intimate moments mean the world. She doesn't voice it, but I get the impression she's never done things like this with previous boyfriends or lovers—neither have I in an intimate sense; it was always just sex. And because I'm possessive, I have to know for sure.

"There's lots of firsts you're giving me, baby."

"Huh?"

"I've never stayed overnight with a woman. Conversely, no one's ever stayed over with me because I didn't want that kind of relationship with anyone."

"Oh? Me either." *Confirmation.*

Now I'm satisfied. And I don't miss the blush that has crept up her skin to the apples of her cheeks, suffusing them with a luscious pink.

"For the first time ever, you have no idea how badly I want to call out of work and play hooky with you. For once, I don't want to be a responsible adult. Growing up fast at a young age had its advantages and disadvantages. I missed out on opportunities to just be a reckless kid—makes me want to try it now."

Her eyes flash with something—pain maybe? Pain for me? She needn't do that on my account. I survived. I only brought it up because it's how much I want to be here with her. Liv's features tell me she wants to ask more questions, and I know I opened that door by my ambiguity and evasiveness. However, I don't elaborate further, and she doesn't ask, being the loyal partner she's already quickly becoming. Instead, she rewards me with a kiss and a charming reply.

"I'd love if you played hooky too, but I know you're needed elsewhere. Trust me, I'll miss you. I guess I'll have to be patient and see you when your shift is over. When are you done, by the way?"

"I'm on for seventy-two hours. I can come by when I get done on Friday morning if you'd like?"

"I'd love that! Since this is my last week of being home, we might as well take advantage of it as much as we can."

"I like the way you think. And maybe if you're feeling up to it, you might want to venture over to the station and visit me?" I make the suggestion.

"Really?"

She's so easy to please, and the hopefulness in her tone has me cupping her cheeks as I move her out from under the spray to kiss her passionately.

"Really," I tell her.

"Okay, then. I'd like that."

"And if your body didn't need a break right now, I'd take you against this shower wall."

Her mouth hangs open in a large *O*, and her eyes widen in shock. Talking dirty to her makes me hornier than I've ever been. My dick jumps at the idea of the wall.

"Wow, I've never tried that either," she says breathlessly.

"Oh, don't worry, we will…soon."

We finish our shower, and I help her step out of the tub, toweling both of us off quickly. Liv's clearly loving being taken care of, as evidenced by her smiles and innocent touches. I'm so glad to be doing it; this is how it should be.

We enter her bedroom, and I throw on my clothes from the previous night.

"Oh gosh, you didn't bring any clothes to change into, did you?" She looks guilty, thinking she did something wrong.

"Nah, but it's all good. I've got stuff at the station. I only needed a shower. Believe me, I want nothing more than to have your scent on me all day, but I'm not sharing you—any part of you—with anyone."

She looks so fucking gorgeous standing there with a towel wrapped around her curvaceous body and one wrapped around her head. I find myself contemplating the whole hooky thing again.

"I know that look, and you'll be late if you don't get moving," she threatens.

Chuckling at her remark, I pull her panties out of my back pocket. Putting them to my nose, I inhale her feminine fragrance before handing them over to her.

"Oh my God, I can't believe you just did that," she whispers.

"Since I had to wash you off, I need your smell in my head until I see you again. Otherwise, I can't be held accountable for my actions if I go crazy while on duty."

She walks over to me and throws her arms around my neck. The towel wrapped at her breasts comes undone, leaving her standing before me naked—testing my control and patience to its limits.

I don't ever want to let go.

Glancing at the clock on her nightstand, I see I only have twenty-five minutes until my shift starts.

"I can let Ash out real quick for you."

"You don't have to do that."

"I want to."

"Well, the least I can do is make you something to eat to-go. How about some coffee too?"

"That sounds perfect, baby. I'll take it black, and whatever you give me, I'll eat," I add emphasis to the word *eat* and waggle my brows at her.

She giggles and walks to her dresser to put some clothes on. I leave her room and head downstairs to let Ash outside.

Ten minutes later, I'm getting in my truck with a to-go coffee and a breakfast bagel sandwich she put together. After buckling my seatbelt, I stick my head out the window to give her a long kiss goodbye with lots of tongue.

"You can come by today, tomorrow, or Thursday—whichever you prefer. Hell, you can come by all three days if you want."

"You won't get sick of me?" she jokes.

"Never, Liv. It's an open invitation. I'll text you when I can."

"Okay," she replies while biting her bottom lip devilishly, tempting me all the more.

As I pull away, I look in my rearview mirror at her standing in her front lawn in a T-shirt and a pair of pink cotton shorts with her long hair still wet from the shower. It's the hottest fucking sight. This feeling is more than addictive—I don't even have a name or term for it.

This is how I want to start each morning from this day forward.

**

Olivia

After Wes drives off and I watch him completely disappear from view, I walk back into my house smiling like there's a watermelon rind wedged in my mouth—I've never smiled this much.

One night with him confirmed that he's *it* for me. I knew we'd fit together perfectly in every aspect. When he made love to me the first time, and again less than an hour ago, I knew I belonged to him. He owns every part of me, inside and out.

My regret is not telling him I love him. It's ridiculous, but I wanted him to say it first. There's no doubt in my mind he does, though. I can't help myself, I just want the words. The fairytale ending all little girls dream of once upon a time hits me over the head; it's why I need him to say it first. We'll get there; I have to believe that.

He is right about one thing: my body is sore. There are parts and places on me I didn't even know could be sore—I don't think my body hummed and smarted like this even after the accident. Thinking it's best not to smother him this early on, I decide to visit him tomorrow at the earliest. As much as I don't want time and space between us, I think it's necessary.

In no way do I misconstrue the situation. I'm not jumping into anything with this man. In fact, I never climbed out from the crater when I fell head over heels for him over a decade ago. So, I can't very well have gone back in. This is new territory for both of us. Hearing how these are a lot of firsts for him—as well as a lot of firsts for me—we'll need to navigate through this together.

After finishing my breakfast and grabbing my own steamy mug of coffee, I mosey over to my couch to review some plans. My phone chimes with a text. Thinking it's Wes, I grin before even picking it up.

When I look at the screen, my heart sinks. It's not from Wes; it's from Jarrod.

Jarrod: My how quickly you move on. Already he's spending

the night? Nice to see we meant so much to each other since I could never stay over.

Staring open-mouthed at my phone, I'm frozen. First of all, he's the last person I expected to hear from. Second, my stomach twists over the thought that he knows Wes spent the night—that's disturbing on so many levels. Is he spying on me? That's really the only logical explanation.

And third, this side of him is making me uneasy. What happened to the sweet, corny guy who used to blow me kisses and make me catch them in the air? Something doesn't seem right here. Love pushes you to do crazy things, and I understand that, but this duplicitous behavior isn't normal and leads me to realize I never really knew him.

The thoughts niggling at me the first time we broke up—as well as this final time—should have warned me. Maybe I just didn't want to see what was there. The mask and persona he cultivated so well made it difficult to see through the façade. Well, I see now, and I don't like it. However, I'm not willing to tell Wes because he shouldn't have to fight my battles for me. It's not that I'm too proud to have a man swoop in, it's that I'm afraid Wes will do something foolish in my defense.

There's no way around it, I have to work this out on my own.

Jarrod's text doesn't warrant a reply from me. I'm not going to encourage this behavior, so I exit my messenger app and put the phone back on the coffee table. Reeling from that message, I decide to call Sammy. She may or may not answer depending on what's going on at work. Surprisingly, she picks up after a few rings and doesn't even say hello.

"I was just going to call you to ask how last night went. I want all the juicy details, and don't you dare leave a thing out because I don't believe for a second that he didn't stay over."

Did she even draw breath?

I'm laughing at her enthusiasm, but this is what she's been waiting for. For me to have my own Tom. But I don't want a Tom; I want a Wes.

Offering as many details as I'm willing to divulge, I give her a rundown of our evening and our morning. She gushes over certain parts of our conversation, which I find amusing since this girl doesn't need to live vicariously through me. She and Tom can do a number on burning up their own sheets.

Now on to the not-so-fun thing I have to ask her.

"Is Jarrod at work today by chance?" Somehow I know I need to come clean about how rattled I am by all this—surely she senses it anyway.

"I haven't seen him today, but you know I can go a whole week without seeing him sometimes. He's probably out at one of the sites. Why do you ask; is something wrong?"

My hesitation speaks volumes. "Uh, no. Just curious."

"What aren't you telling me? Even when you were dating him, you never asked if he was in the office when you were out. Spill, or I'm driving down there now."

"He sent me a weird text. He knew Wes spent the night."

"That's creepy."

"Which is why I wanted to know if he was there. Either he randomly guessed Wes spent the night, or he *knows*."

"What did you say back to him?"

"I didn't reply and have no intention to. When I come back to work next week, I plan to alert HR of the situation to avoid any potential problems in the office. I won't subject myself to a hostile work environment. Actually, I'm hoping he'll finally take one of the job offers and move to Chicago. Although, San Diego would be even better."

"Are you scared he'll do something? Be honest, Liv." Not only can I hear her concern, but I feel it come across the line.

"No. I think this will all blow over. He's just hurt and jealous—two things I can't do anything about. Listen, I need you to promise me one thing, though."

"Depends on what it is." That's why I love this girl; she's a feisty one.

"Just don't tell Wes or my dad? I don't need either one stressing out about this."

She expels an audible breath. Knowing full well she's not happy about it, I'm still going to ask this of her.

"On one condition: if Jarrod does one more creepy thing, then you're going to tell me, Wes, and your dad. Or maybe even involve the police if it's something serious. That's the only way I'll agree to this."

"Deal."

She seems satisfied with that and tells me she has to get back to work. We say our goodbyes and end the call. Feeling marginally better because Sammy has that effect, I get back to my plans that are spread out on the coffee table.

About an hour later, a text comes in. Cringing inwardly, afraid it's Jarrod, I reluctantly flip my phone over. This time it's my man. *Thank God.*

Wes: Do you know how hard it is to concentrate on work right now since all I can think about is you?

Yes, I do actually.

Before I reply, I tug at my pearl earrings, thinking about how I could get used to this. I want life to be like this with Wes from this day forward.

Chapter 20: Snapshots

Olivia

Thursday

Today's the day to meld our worlds together even further. The dinner on Monday was part of it—part one, basically—and by visiting the fire station, that will be the other part—part two. Nervous doesn't begin to describe what's going on inside me.

Acceptance is important. I want his friends and family to accept me. Admittedly, my viewpoint on a person being a firefighter is skewed because of watching TV shows that apparently don't accurately portray things, so when I go to visit him at work, I realize it will be enlightening.

What I imagine movies or shows tend to authentically depict is the brotherhood that exists among the members, like the way movies have captured the outpouring of love, support, and sense of family in the aftermath of September 11th. With the seventeenth anniversary of that fateful day having just past, I am reminded that life is filled with moments, moments in time that I can capture in mental snapshots that make up a picture book to revisit. And when I leave this world one day and that picture book goes with me, I will still have left behind snapshots in someone else's story.

Having one last look in the mirror at my appearance, I square my shoulders and take a deep breath. Pairing my skinny jeans with a silky turquoise blouse is the right choice to bring out my eyes. Last, I slip on my flats and straighten my necklace chain that has a pearl pendant dangling from it. I'm ready.

"Here goes nothing," I say aloud as I'm walking down the stairs to leave my house. The drive over to the station makes my palms sweat, and clenching the steering wheel proves difficult with the added moisture. A lot is riding on today.

It feels good to finally drive myself. Luckily, my insurance carrier issued me a rental car, which was delivered to me late last week. This is my maiden voyage since the accident, and even though I'm happy to be independent again, it's still a little frightening getting behind the wheel. However, my fears about my visit to his work are overtaking all else.

Pulling up to the station, I take a second to admire the building. The number of times I've driven by this place and never given thought to the heroes it houses makes me wish I'd noticed. The number of times I've driven by it and never run into Wes is shocking—it's so strange we never reconnected until now. How or why we were meant to find each other at this specific point in time, I'm not quite sure, but find one another we did.

"There you are, baby," Wes says huskily as he peers into my car window that's rolled down.

Almost jumping out of my skin at the scare because I didn't even hear his approach, I put my hand over my heart—feeling its frantic rhythm beneath my fingers. Laughing nervously, I tell him, "You scared me half to death."

He leans in and kisses my lips, murmuring his sorries—all is forgiven. I stroke his cheek, needing to touch him in some way.

"God, I've missed you. Texts and phone calls haven't been enough. You get any work done?" he asks me.

"A little bit here and there. I have a lot to do when I start back next week. I'm thinking I need to devote a full week of actually going into the office instead of working a little from home like I normally do." I leave off the part about how I dread going into the office on the chance I might run into Jarrod.

"Well, as long as you don't push yourself. So, does Ash miss me too?"

Not being able to contain my jubilance at seeing him after two days, I nod and grab the collar of his uniform shirt to pull him into a heated kiss.

"Hey, hey, hey. There will be none of that," Grant laughs a few feet away from us and proceeds to approach my car. "How ya doing, beautiful? Is this one still treating you right?" He angles an accusatory thumb at the man I love.

"Always," I say, staring directly into Wes's eyes.

"Get a room," Grant chuckles and walks off.

At his retreating back, Wes yells, "We would if we could."

I smack Wes playfully on the chest for that comment, and he winks at me. He's such a bad boy—it's so addictive.

"What's *that* look for?" He cocks his head to the side.

"Oh nothing. I was just thinking of how hot you are and how I love you in that uniform."

It's a simple navy blue set of cargo pants and a polo shirt with the firehouse emblem silkscreened on the front. There's nothing spectacular about it; however, anything on him looks fantastic and makes me take notice of his incredible physique.

"Well, I hope you'll like it better on the floor tomorrow when we're both naked and rolling around in your bed. I can't wait to reacquaint myself with your sweet little body and spend hours worshipping you."

An uncontrollable shiver zips up my back, and I swallow hard at the images he's helping create in my mind. His naked body fulfilling my every desire. His naked form enveloping me. Him on top. Me on top. Me writhing like a wanton creature. I can picture it all in stark clarity.

"C'mon, baby. We better get inside and do the whole introductions thing, or I'll drive off with you to the nearest bed and end up losing my job in the process."

"Okay," I say, smiling brightly at him.

This day is important to both of us—I can see it in his eyes. After parking my car and walking hand in hand into the station, I'm given a tour of the facilities and introduced to the other three guys and two girls on shift. They're a family unit here; that much is clear.

There are more members I'll have to meet some other time, and Wes assures me I'll get to meet his chief when he comes back from a meeting with the township. After hanging out in the lounge area for twenty minutes, Wes informs me he made us all lunch before I arrived and it's in the warmer.

The other crew members consisting of Grant, Rick, Joe, Lucy, Dee Dee, and Ethan all file into the dining area—Wes had mentioned he has a soft spot for the probie. They sit after grabbing plates and serving themselves buffet-style. I grab my own plate and join Wes, who immediately brings me into the conversation. He's always making sure I'm feeling comfortable and welcome.

Sniffing appreciatively at the casserole dish, salad, and rolls he prepared, I thank him and give him my compliments. "So, how long have you two known each other?" I ask both Wes and Grant about their friendship.

"It's been since we were in EMT school together. That was like fifteen years ago," Grant offers.

"Wow! I can't believe you two have been friends that long." I'm happily surprised by this news since Wes was such a loner in school.

"Me either," Grant jokingly grumbles out, and everyone around the table laughs.

"Oh, we call them the old married couple," Rick interjects.

"Quit your bitchin', Rick. You're just jealous he and I make a better couple than you and your wife." Grant gives him the verbal dig, and Lucy is practically choking on her drink.

There must be an inside joke I'm not privy to, but I still smile as the rest crack up over the comment. Turning my smiling face to Wes, I look at him and say with an undercurrent of sarcasm, "I'm just surprised he's had a friend this long. I tried to be his friend in high school, but he kept to himself."

"Well that all changed. I guess it's because I was with him the day his da—," Grant starts to say but is interrupted by Wes.

"Grant, can you go check the oven? I think I forgot to turn it off."

What was Grant about to say?

I look from Grant to Wes, then from Wes to Grant, puzzled by the non-verbal exchange they have going on now. Feeling left out doesn't begin to cover what this moment is like. My insides are bending and twisting; there's something not right about the situation. It's as if Wes doesn't want me to know something, and I'm finding it difficult to grasp because I can't imagine he wants to start a relationship forged in secrets.

Is this the Dad thing again? Why does it seem like it keeps coming back to that?

For now, I'll let it go because I don't want an audience. But Wes and I need to talk in private. Grant goes to check on the oven—although, I'm sure the oven was never the issue. Wes excuses himself and stalks off toward the kitchen.

Everyone remaining at the table starts talking about inconsequential things, and I sit here stoic and silent, my mind swirling with worry. However, I don't have too long to dwell on it because an alarm sounds. Suddenly, everyone's radios, which are strapped to their belts, simultaneously go off.

It's hard to make out what the call is because I don't understand all the jargon, but every member springs into action and leaves their unfinished meals where they are. Wes appears at my side.

"I'm sorry, baby, but that was a call for the Task Force. So, the engine and ambulance have to roll. We've got a structural fire. I'll call or text you later, and I'll see you tomorrow when I'm done my shift. Thanks for coming by," he explains urgently.

"No problem. I understand. Duty calls," I convey as I give him my best smile.

He then kisses me on the lips and chastely kisses my forehead. Wes races off after his team, and I hear a bunch of shouting and vehicles running in the bay next to the dining area where I'm currently sitting. The sirens blare on the firetruck and ambulance, and before I know it, all the flurry of activity stops. It's eerily silent—clearly, they left.

Deciding it's best to busy myself, I cover the casserole under the warmer and clean up what I can from the table of trash and empty items. It's the least I can do for them, considering they're literally out there saving lives and trying to preserve property.

As I make my way out to the car, I think about how I'm grateful for the opportunity to come today. Since I'm already out and about, I decide I'm going to drop in on my dad. He always helps calm my nerves by just being in his presence. I need to shake this dread I have in my gut regarding Wes.

Losing him again isn't an option. My heart won't survive it this time.

***

Weston

Grant almost fucked it up for me yesterday. Thank God we got that call. It ended up being a small kitchen fire that was no big deal, which I'm happy about for the sake of the residents. What I'm not happy about is Liv potentially knowing about my past. It's not Grant's fault, though.

It may seem ridiculous and unrealistic to keep that part of my life from her, but it's what I have to do. I thought I was going to tell her before we started seeing each other; however, I chickened out. My reasons are my own. It's mainly because I don't want that shit in her head. She doesn't need to be tainted somehow by my hellish history. Leaving it behind is where it needs to stay; I'm not dredging it up all over again. It's probably wrong of me, but I don't see how her knowing would make a difference. I moved on when he went to prison, so end of story.

Did you really move on? My conscience isn't convinced.

Only fifteen more minutes until my shift ends. I wonder if she's awake yet. Yesterday, I only texted her and never got around to calling— chickening out again because I was afraid she was going to ask me why I acted so weird.

I've maintained all along I don't deserve her. Her beauty. Her innocence. Her patience. Her love. Hell, she even tidied up the fucking place before she left. I hit the damn jackpot with her, and I know it. She's the best thing that's ever happened to me, and fucking it up isn't an option. Losing her again isn't an option.

Me: You awake, baby?
Liv: Yeah. Morning!
Me: Morning! I'll be leaving here in fifteen minutes.

Liv: Sounds good. I'll see you then.
Me: See you then, baby.

***

Weston

Arriving at her house a little after eight, I'm greeted by the loveliest sight when she opens the door. She's in a long T-shirt and nothing else—unless she's wearing panties I can't see.

Not giving her the opportunity to start in on me about yesterday, I don't even say *hi*. I dive right into her lips, kissing her deeply and ravishing her completely. She moans into my mouth as I move my hands to her hips. Feeling there's no waistband means she's definitely sans panties—which has me growling like a madman.

Lifting her off her feet, she wraps her arms around my neck and throws her legs around my midsection. After carrying her to the couch, I set her down. We're not going to make it to her bedroom, and that's fine by me. The couch will do fine for what I have planned.

"I'm going to eat at your pussy, baby. I've dreamt of nothing else."

Her violet eyes enlarge as her mouth pops open. I tug down the blanket haphazardly lying on the back of the couch, maneuvering it under her bottom so it'll be easy cleanup when we're done.

"Well, I didn't know you had this in mind first thing." She grins.

"You can't expect me to have gone three days without having you, could you?" I pull off my T-shirt, leaving my jeans on, and kneel down in front of her as she's perched on the couch.

"Baby, I have to touch you. Kiss you. Feel you. Taste you at all times. And if I can't have you, then I have to dream of you and all the wicked things I'm going to do to you. I'm a hungry man, and the only way I'll be satisfied is by eating your pussy right now."

"Wes...," she says, trembling at my words.

"Baby, you didn't even wear panties, so you must've known this would happen," I chuckle as I remind her.

"Okay, well sorta. But I thought we'd talk first."

"No talking. There'll be plenty of time for that later. Just relax."

Placing a hand to her chest, I gently push her back so she's lying against the cushions. She has her thighs pressed together, and that simply won't do. With a hand at each knee, I move her legs apart, and her gorgeous wet cunt is revealed. She moans as I grunt.

Licking the tops of her thighs, I swirl my tongue in a circular pattern. Her hands immediately go to my head. Smiling at the reaction she's having, I kiss my way to her pubic bone. This will be quick and delicious because I have no control or patience around her.

There's nothing that would give me more pleasure than dragging this out and mercilessly torturing her, but I'm always at a disadvantage with her. She will forever hold the power, and I'm helpless against it.

Inserting a finger into her channel, her smooth, soaked tissues grip me fiercely. After a few plunges, I insert the next finger. After more kisses and a lick to her clit, I finally add a third.

Once she's putty in my hands, I remove my fingers and begin working on her with my tongue. Licking around her folds and teasing her opening has her scoring my naked back with her fingernails—it feels so fucking good!

"Ahh...Wes!"

Keeping up my licking, I also blow on her wet clit, which elicits a full-body shiver from her. Liv's eyes are closed, and the faces she's making are so damn sexy. My hard-on is stabbing the zipper to my jeans. I hope she'll reciprocate and taste me next.

"I'm about to come," she admits.

She doesn't realize I already know. The signs were already there, but it spurs me on to finish her off thoroughly so she'll remember how good it was the next time she's alone and needs a reminder of how earth-shattering it feels for me to eat her out.

Plunging two fingers back into her passage, I concentrate on her clit. The sucking sounds my fingers are making as they move in and out of her, creating a suction, are so fucking hot. With her pussy being so juicy, I've never been so mesmerized by a sound like this.

My tongue flicks, laves, and kisses that spot as I pull back the hood of the nub to exert more pressure. When I gently bite it, her release is like fireworks going off as she shudders and screams. The liquid heat that meets my hand is erotic and breathtaking. She's such a stunning woman and the perfect lover. Hell, she's the perfect woman.

Once she's done quaking, I cease my ministrations and stand up. She finally opens her eyes, and they're shimmering with gratitude, happiness, and love. *Oh, I damn well know it's love.*

"Are you real?" she asks dreamily.

That question has me laughing because I've been wondering the same about her.

"Yes, baby. Real and in the flesh."

"Mmm. I don't think I can move, but it's my turn to play with you."

My intake of breath is clear as day. My dick moves at the thought of her *playing* with me, and I swallow hard because she's a dream come true.

***

Olivia

Wes manages to shatter me in the best possible way, but he also puts me back together. An orgasm like I just experienced should be illegal. He can't possibly be real. How I got so lucky with a man like him, I don't know, but I don't dare question it further.

He looks at me with such adoration, patience, and love. It's written in his eyes. The gray that makes me swoon has little hearts whirling about in the storm of his irises.

It's my turn to make him feel good. If I can deliver even an ounce of what he just did to me, then it should knock him on his ass. He reaches for the buckle of his belt, and I watch as he removes it from the loops. Licking my lips, I'm enthralled by him unbuttoning his jeans—his long, thick fingers have me biting my lip while tingles are radiating in my core. When he slides his pants down and only his boxers remain, I'm basically panting.

After the boxers come off and his huge cock juts forward, ready and waiting, I'm salivating. I understand his need to taste me because it's the same for me. I don't just need to taste him, I *have* to taste him. Just like breathing is necessary, well, tasting him and feeling him in every part of me is necessary. Connecting with him like this is the ultimate act of love and devotion.

Expelling a breath, I sit up and move a shaky hand to his shaft. When I close my fist around it, he groans like it's sweetly painful—I know the feeling since I felt that exquisiteness only he could so expertly deliver to my pussy.

"God, you're so big. I can't wait to have you in my mouth," I whisper as I stare at his thickness—I'm also testing out my dirty talk skills.

His only response is a guttural moan, so I'm obviously doing something right. He's so different than previous boyfriends. This was never my thing, but now I want it to be my thing more than ever—to master his pleasure. I move my hand up and down his length. I've given head plenty of times, but this time is special because it's him. Never have I wanted to wrap my lips around another man's cock so badly before. Wes makes me a desperate woman.

After a few more pumps, I move the head of his dick to rest in my mouth and slowly work him down to the back of my throat. My eyes sting and burn trying to take him all in, but I welcome the sensations. Getting my gag reflex under control finally, I begin to bob my head, and he groans each time his cock moves further in. Tasting precum has me moaning.

Everything in me tightens, and a ripple of ecstasy simmers

throughout at the knowledge I'm giving him the ultimate high. I pay close attention to the vein on the underside of his shaft and lick all around it. Sucking on his balls next has him gripping my hair roughly—I purposely left it down so he'd be able to run his hands through it. His heavy sack tenses up, and I'm thinking he's already close. We so easily turn the other one inside out, upside down, and backwards.

Thinking we'd talk before delving into anything intimate was an oversight on my part. I shouldn't have expected anything different when we're so drawn to each other. With more purpose and determination, I suck harder and faster, and before long, he's emptying himself down my throat with a salty-sweet flavor unique to him. I don't break the contact and love the taste and feeling of knowing I brought him to this point.

"Fuck! Liv!" he yells.

He pulls my hair harder, but it barely registers because the euphoria of administering this level of passion makes everything feel so good. Now I can appreciate how Sammy talks about there being a fine line between pleasure and pain and how pain can morph into pleasure. Wes could do anything and everything to me, and only because it's him would it be pleasurable.

Once he's done spilling his seed, I let him fall out of my mouth, and he slumps down on the couch next to me, spent. He's face down, and I giggle. Apparently, I did my job well. I wipe my lips and grin. As he turns his face out from the cushions, he still has a sheen on his chin from eating me out—I'll be shocked if it's not also on my couch. What a pair we make.

Running my fingers down his back, I notice a bunch of faded white lines like cuts that long ago scarred. They're everywhere. I probably didn't notice them before due to lack of lighting. Even his biceps under the tattoos have faint traces of some scarring. I rub at the spots.

"Hey, what's with all the marks on your back?" I ask casually.

He lifts his head up and gets into a sitting position. "Oh, they're nothing. Occupational hazard."

He moves in and kisses my lips. I still taste a hint of myself on his tongue. It seems we're lip-locked for a long time. When we pull apart, I feel sticky and forget what we were talking about—he once again distracted me with his incredible abilities. All I know is I need a shower. Standing up, I stretch and look down at him in his exhausted state.

"C'mon, Tiger." I reach out my hand to him.

"Tiger?"

"Yup, Tiger. It seems fitting at the moment. Let's get in the shower. I believe you promised me wall sex in there."

"Yes, ma'am!" he says.

I've never seen a man move faster in my life.

Chapter 21: Shelter from the Storm

Olivia

The following week on Friday, I'm enjoying being back to work. It's been hectic trying to get up to speed on new projects we recently acquired because it's not always easy to be briefed by phone or email. Coming into the office this week was productive and has put me in a good mood.

The best part is I haven't run into Jarrod. Maybe he's had time to think about everything and realized I was right—we had no future together whatsoever. There's a rumor going around—watercooler talk—that he may even accept a job offer in Detroit. It's not San Diego, but it's still far enough away. Jarrod hasn't attempted to text me again since the first night Wes slept over, so a piece of me wants to hope he's moved on.

As for Wes, he's been distracting me with sex—it's working. There have been opportunities for me to bring up what happened at the station, yet I haven't. I could force a conversation, but it's not my style. If he decides it's something of importance, surely he will tell me. We've only been dating for a week and a half, but I would like to think he could trust me to talk to me about anything—now or in the near future.

The sex has been so amazing, I'm surprised I'm not in a coma from too many orgasms. We haven't been using condoms. I hadn't slept with Jarrod for many weeks prior to our official breakup, and with all the bloodwork Wes has to have done for his job, we agreed we are safe. Wes was relieved to find out I'm on the pill.

So many things are running through my head. When Sammy walks into my office as I'm staring off into space, I jump because I'm lost in thought.

"Hey. How'd your first week back go?"

"Pretty good. It feels great to get back to a routine."

"I bet. And how's your fireman?" She arches a brow at me.

I naturally smile at her question because any time he's brought up, my heart flutters and my belly summersaults. "He's good. He's going to the shelter with me tomorrow to volunteer. And my dad's coming over for dinner on Sunday night."

"Oh, how domestic of you two. You're becoming quite the little couple so quickly," she points out.

Biting my lip, I look at her and rub my earring, "Wes asked me if this was all too fast. I don't feel it is."

"Oh, sweetie, I meant nothing by it. I'm so happy for you. It's your relationship and what you make of it."

"Thanks. I feel like we've known each other a lifetime already. I'm not gonna lie, it's been a whirlwind. But if he and I both feel it's right, that's why I haven't questioned it. It's real, raw, intense, and all-consuming. And…I'm *finally* happy," I say with moisture filling my eyes.

Then we hear a loud BAM! in the hallway—as if someone punched the wall. *What in the world?*

Sammy and I rush out my office, but there's no one there. She looks right while I look left, and I could swear I see Jarrod's profile turning the corner down the hall. Sammy doesn't turn in time to see him. We both spin around and see a slight indent in the drywall.

"That's creepy and weird. It sounded like something hit the wall and look, here's proof," she says while pointing at the spot.

"Yeah, strange."

My nonchalance isn't convincing, but I'm not telling her I think I saw Jarrod because I promised her if something happened again, I'd come clean with Wes and my dad—I have no intention of worrying anyone over nothing.

Maybe my mind's playing tricks on me, and it wasn't Jarrod. Maybe the dent was already there. Maybe the bang came from something else. I don't want to reach out to Jarrod and accuse him because I could potentially open Pandora's box. I alerted HR earlier in the week of the situation, so at least they're aware if anything occurs. We don't have cameras, so unless he confesses, there's no way of knowing.

Best to leave well enough alone.

***

Weston

"This place is amazing. I wish I wouldn't have stopped working here.

They've done many upgrades to it since I last visited," I remark, marveling at the shelter we're standing in.

"I'm so glad you came. And I'm lucky you had another Saturday off. How do you get so lucky?"

"Well, I switched shifts with someone else for today. So Grant's working while I'm off, and I'll have to work Monday to make up for it. I guess he'll have to get along without me."

We both chuckle because I'm sure she's thinking my best friend and I are too attached as it is.

"I'm grateful you could be here. This place has become almost a second home. I don't get to volunteer as much as I'd like, though. However, when I do, it gives me purpose and satisfaction knowing I'm doing something."

I reach for her gloved hand since we're cleaning the dog runs and give it a squeeze. No matter what she's doing and no matter what she's wearing, she always looks gorgeous. She makes even old clothes and janitorial supplies look fucking hot. She's an anomaly among womankind.

"You working in the office at all this coming week?" I angle my head at her while I'm sweeping the one kennel.

"Yeah. I'll probably go in a few times. At some point, I'm hoping to return my rental car and go car shopping. Wanna come help me spend my insurance money?"

"Love to, baby."

Sauntering over to her, I lean my broom up against the wall and embrace her while kissing her mouth hard. I can't help myself around her. I'll try to be good because there are probably cameras in this place—*that could also be fun, though.*

Resuming my cleaning duties, I grin thinking about how we'll have plenty of time tonight for me to devour her. It sucks I have to work Monday, but I'll see her on Tuesday. I've been staying over at her place every chance I can. She came over to my apartment for the first time the other day, just long enough for me to grab clothes. It's the typical bachelor pad, and she seemed to like it, but home feels like wherever she is. *Her* place feels like home.

When I'm thinking long-term, I can't help but wonder if I'll move in with her or if she'll sell her house, and we'll get a place together—we won't be keeping my apartment, that's for sure. No matter what, I just want to be with her, so it makes no difference where we live. I never wanted a nice house because with staying at the station so much, I didn't see the point. Now, I want things I never let myself hope and wish for: a wife, a house, kids.

"What're you smiling about, Tiger?" she questions with a giggle.

"Oh, nothing. Just doing a little thinking."

"Uh oh. Should I be worried?"

"Nah, it's all good stuff." *Wink, wink.*

"Like more shower wall sex?"

Waggling my eyebrows, I smirk. She makes me forget my name when she brings up anything sex-related.

"Well, *now* that's what I'm thinking about."

"Later," she promises.

"Definitely."

***

Olivia

Sunday

Staring at my phone, I'm thinking if I look long enough and hard enough, the letters will rearrange themselves to read something different. No such luck.

Jarrod: You two belong together if you stay with him after what I found out about his past. I think you deserve better though, Olivia. Let me know if you want the truth.

Not wanting to entertain his text, though my interest is piqued, I clear my screen and set down my phone. I refrain from responding to him and playing into this game or whatever it is, reaffirming to myself I won't worry about what Jarrod's up to. I'm not telling Sammy about this text. I'm not telling my dad. And I'm definitely not telling Wes.

"Hon, do you need help in there?" my dad calls from the living room.

"No thanks, I'm coming," I tell him and finish preparing the drinks I offered to make for the three of us. Plastering on a smile for their benefit and grabbing the tray, I make my way out to the living room then hand drinks to Wes and my dad.

"What shall we toast to?" Wes asks.

"How about to honesty and love?" Dad suggests while holding up his glass.

A lump in my throat forms, and I can't swallow it. Holding my glass up anyway, the three of us drink to his toast.

I probably look guilty. I probably look like I have a bad taste in my mouth from the face I'm making—it's not from the wine because it's delicious, but I can barely enjoy it. Moving my eyes over to Wes, I see he's wearing a similar expression. *To honesty and love.* What's with his face?

Must not think too much into it; must not think too much into it, I'll keep repeating this thought the rest of the night like a credo.

Chapter 22: Distance and Time

Weston

October 6, 2018

For the last few weeks, I've felt a growing separation within me. Almost like I have internal tectonic plates that keep shifting and moving, creating a bottomless gorge running right through my life.

There's something sinister lurking; I sense it even in sleep. I feel it wrap its tentacles around me and squeeze me breathless even when I'm awake. Not fully understanding why I'm experiencing this is the worst part about it. Not knowing if there's an explanation is even more maddening.

I've been pulling more shifts at the station—working as much overtime as I can. I have to escape from this doom and gloom to survive. I'm in survival mode again like I was as a kid.

Liv feels it—she must. But she's letting me have my distance. She's letting me have my time. But I can't seem to get out of the funk I'm in.

When she texted me yesterday asking if we could get together this weekend, all I could think was I needed a buffer, so Grant and Mal are meeting Liv and me for dinner.

As Liv and I arrive at the restaurant with her looking sensational, the churning in my gut batters me like an unrelenting hailstorm. Assailed with shame over the way I've been behaving, I try and suck it up as we make our way to the table where Grant and Mal are already waiting.

We came back to The Green Chile Restaurant. It's hard to enjoy my favorite place when I'm being hit from all sides and there's no shelter in place—the hailstorm will surely win.

Grant claps me on the back, and my sister gives Liv and me each a hug. When Grant kisses Liv on the cheek in greeting, I snarl. If either notices, they don't comment on my conduct. However, I do catch Mal's eyes riveted to everything Grant's doing.

We all settle in our seats, and after ordering drinks, chips, salsa, and guacamole, we venture into conversation. I'm doing my best to stay out of most of it, but of course, I'm dragged into it here and there.

"How's work going, Liv?" Grant inquires with a sly grin—the one he reserves for women he's pursuing.

What the fuck?

"Good, thanks. I'm back to working at home a few days a week since I'm caught up with my projects. Sammy wants to know when we can all get together again because she had a blast with you guys."

"Anytime you want. My schedule seems to be more flexible lately than his." Grant doesn't even look my way when he tells her this.

The smug bastard. This maneuver seems intentional. He's trying to piss me off and send me a message at the same time. As my best friend, he knows what my problem is, and he's going to run with it.

Mal shifts in her seat. Grant's flirting with Liv is affecting my sister. As much as I don't want anything to happen between the pair, and she's assured me there isn't anything, I also don't like seeing Baby Girl hurt. She so easily loves and trusts people. She so easily gives her heart away.

Maybe Mal really does like him. And then I squash that thought.

"Don't you have a rock to crawl back under?" I grit out to my best friend.

Liv looks from me to him, trying to decipher what Grant and I are silently communicating. He knows he's on dangerous ground. I warned him off the day Liv came to the station, and I made him promise me he wouldn't talk to Liv about me. It's not his business or place.

"Uh, why don't we ladies go freshen up and give you two guys a moment to miss us?" Liv offers.

Mal nods her head in agreement, and the two women walk off to the facilities. Glaring at Grant, I'm waiting him out.

"This evening is going smoothly, I must say," he states sarcastically.

"No shit!"

"Why don't you just fucking talk to her and get your head out of your ass? The timing couldn't be worse. I've seen you in moods over the years, man, but this degree is something I've never seen."

Crossing my arms and leaning back against the booth cushion, I don't engage in the battle he's trying to draw me into.

He sighs and approaches it differently, "You can't keep this shit inside you. Sooner or later, Liv is going to want to know what's going on. And you better damn well have answers for her. She deserves everything.

You said yourself she's *the one*. If that's the case, then treat her as such. Tell her why you are the way you are. Tell her what happened to you in high school."

"What the fuck do you know about it anyway? You've never been in love."

He gives me a challenging look as if to say, *You don't know what you're talking about.* I'm not going there with him.

"Just get your shit together is all I'm saying, Wes. Or…you could lose her."

Not being able to fathom that concept, I choose to ignore his advice. Instead, I turn the tables on him.

"You get your shit together, and don't lead my sister on or flirt with my girlfriend!"

"I don't have any intention of doing either of those things."

"Good. Then we're clear."

We continue to scowl at one another until the ladies return. I move out of the booth so Liv can scoot back in. When we are back in our seats, she kisses my cheek and looks at Mal sympathetically.

Maybe this evening's foursome was a bad idea after all.

***

Olivia

October 16, 2018

Time. That pesky thing I previously said was my enemy, and then became my friend, is rearing its head again—back to being my enemy. Still elusive. Still a traitor.

It's been a cyclone of activity for the last week and a half. Wes has been working extra shifts and keeping a crazy schedule. All over the news there's been coverage on the forest fires in the Pines, and because of that, he's on loan to the State. He has additional certifications in the Forest Fire Service, so he's lending a hand.

The nights have been lonely without him. My mind has played tricks on me thinking the separation is intentional. I'm being weak, insecure, and pathetic. The sad part is, either Wes senses this distancing between us and isn't saying anything, or he doesn't notice anything, and I'm just being ridiculous. I'm a coward for not bringing it up regardless if it's intentional or not.

What kind of relationship does that make?

Not feeling in the mood to go into the office today, I opt to work from home. It's been radio silent from Jarrod since his last text, and my engineering firm announced last Friday that Jarrod did officially accept the job offer in Detroit. He moves next week, and his going away party is tomorrow. I will not be going into the office then either to see him off.

One positive thing happened, at least. My rental car is returned, and I'm the proud owner of a new mid-size SUV. It was a little more than I wanted to spend, but at the time, I kept leaning toward a *family* car—I hope it won't be a regret to add to my list.

Ash jumps up on the couch, sensing I need comfort. Rubbing his head infuses me with serenity—he's like my built-in stress ball as of late. He's now a permanent fixture of this house that I never knew I needed but always wanted. I just adore my pup.

My mom's pearls temporarily settled me the last two days, but even they haven't helped completely center me. The source of my discontent leads back to the lack of communication with Wes. We need to fix it.

My dad came over the other night for dinner, and it was just the two of us. There was no doubt he knew something was eating at me. As I reflect on our conversation, I need to hold tight to what I learned and what I must do with this newfound knowledge.

"Honey, what's going on? You don't quite seem yourself," my dad questions with the years of deep-set lines in his forehead pinching together.

"Just a lot on my mind lately, that's all." I attempt to smile and continue pushing the food around on my plate.

"If your mom were here, she'd have some words of wisdom. This old man can't quite get all philosophical and stuff like she could, but I'll do my best." He takes a deep breath. "Did I ever tell you your mom and I separated when you were little?"

My intake of breath at the news confirms to him he never told me—neither did my mom, for that matter. I can't fathom this ever occurring. They were so in love. He's still so in love with her. It doesn't make any sense.

"What?" I ask with incredulity in my tone.

"You were about two at the time. I said some stupid things and left for about a week. I went to stay with my brother."

He takes a pause and looks off, replaying it in his head. "After the first day, I realized I'd already made a mistake by leaving and wanted to come home. But I convinced myself I was a man, and by God, men don't apologize for anything. After the second day, pride got in the way. It took me the full week to see the light. Bless your mom because she was a forgiving woman. When I came back…," he gets choked up and has to stop again.

With tears in his eyes, he explains further, "When I came back, I had those pearl earrings with me. I told her she was the rarest of them all, and no two are alike. When she gave you those earrings before she died, it was because she knew they were special. Love is all about forgiveness, honesty, and recognizing when you've got a rare one, honey."

My dad has no clue how his words resonate with me as I lift a shaky hand to tuck a wayward strand behind my ear and touch the pearl. He's very intuitive, and without even having to voice to him that Wes and I are going through this little rough patch, he somehow understands. We both smile through the waterworks, and I throw my arms around my father in the biggest bear hug I can deliver. My dad has always shown me there are so many important things in life, but we all need a little helpful reminder on occasion.

After I return to the present, I end up tossing the project scope manual resting across my lap onto the side table. Work will have to wait for the moment. My hand automatically goes for my earring, and I realize I need to face this head on. If I feel like there's something off between Wes and me, then I need to say something.

I'm going after my man! He's a rare one, all right, and I'm not willing to let anything get in the way of our future.

Springing from the couch, I frantically search for my shoes. They're usually by the door, but I don't see them. I'm going to go find Wes. I'll drive out to the damn Pines and find him in the woods if I have to—that's how determined I am to make this work.

Ash is running around like he knows something exciting is going on. During my quest for my shoes, which leads me to the kitchen, there's a knock at my front door.

My tummy flips hoping it's Wes. I tuck my hair behind my ears since it's wavy and wild today, hoping I don't look like a crazed person, then practically run for the door. When I yank it open, my face falls.

It's not Wes standing before me.

It's Jarrod.

***

Weston

An hour before…

I'm a giant fucking pussy!

Like a damn caged animal, I'm pacing back and forth in the lounge area of the station. I've been a prick. Olivia must be getting tired of me avoiding her. It's like ever since the dinner with her dad a few weeks ago, I can't shake this self-loathing bullshit. Like I've got my dad in my head telling me *what a piece of shit I am.* Telling me *I'm no good for her.* And *I'll fuck it up, so I better get out before I drag her down with me.*

My head isn't in a good place, and I know that. Grant's been off too. Something's bugging him, and I can't seem to get over my own shit to find out what's wrong. I've barely seen him the last few weeks. When we're not working, he's MIA. Doing what, I have no clue.

149

As I continue to pace, I hear someone approach from behind, so I spin around, almost snarling at the intruder encroaching on my space.

"Hey, man, uh, I need to talk to you for a minute."

The normally cocky Grant is not the person standing a foot away from me. He seems hesitant and unsure. *What the hell?*

"Yeah, what's up?" I say rather obnoxiously to my best friend.

"There hasn't been a good time to talk to you lately so...fuck it," he starts to say and grabs a fistful of hair.

He squares his shoulders, and his jaw locks. The serious look he's giving me is challenging.

"Look, I don't know how to tell you this but, I'm dating Mal."

"What the fuck?" I bellow and get in his face.

Before I know it, I'm shoving him back to the wall with my arm locked against his chest. Somewhere in the distance I hear a door open and close—someone may have looked in and wisely decided not to stick around for the throw-down about to occur.

"Jesus, get a hold of yourself!" Grant growls around the pressure I'm applying to his chest cavity.

He's not even trying to fight me, and that makes me more pissed off. It's like I'm stuck in a hole—that black hole I was in as a teen. The one I couldn't climb out of. The one where the darkness permeated every pore of my being, and no matter how hard I tried, there was no escape.

"I love her, man," he tells me sincerely as he stares into my eyes, trying to get through to me.

That does it for me. As if a hand reaches inside to pull me back, I snap out of it suddenly. Loosening the pressure on my arm and coming down from the hype of the adrenaline rushing through my veins, I step away from the man I consider a brother.

I'm fucked up in the head.

Leaning forward, I grip my knees, trying to breathe. Grant said the words that could pull me from the darkness. *He loves her.*

And I realize I'm just like my father. So easily I could attack my best friend—my brother. Who the fuck does that? A person who's wired wrong does that. A person who's jacked in the head. A person like...me. That's what it comes down to. I was right. These feelings I've had telling me I'm no good for Liv are validated in this moment.

Grant stays against the wall, waiting for me to calm down. We're equally matched in size, so it would've been one hell of a fight if we actually threw down. This is one of those times I have to be grateful it didn't come to blows because that's not who I am, and that's not who I want to be. But yet it's what I almost did. *Liv...* Liv would not want me to be that way.

Then my snarky-ass conscience interjects, *does she even know you? The real you? The "you" she hasn't been told about?*

All this shit in my head is making me sick. I slump down to the floor.

"You okay, man?" Grant rests a hand on my shoulder.

"Yeah, sorry."

"Don't be. I deserve it. But I'm not sorry about your sister. You may not believe it, but I really do love her. I have for years, truth be told. I didn't pursue her sooner outta respect for you. I know you warned me off, and for years I resisted because I didn't want to fuck up our friendship—well, that and she was too young. But now, I just couldn't help it since I can't seem to stay away from her."

And now I know why I haven't seen much of him lately; I should've checked at my sister's. The signs were there. A part of me knew this could happen, yet I chose to ignore it. Even Liv tried to tell me. I want to be mad at him. I want to hate him. It's because I'm a selfish bastard—wanting my cake and to eat it too.

"I'm still pissed, but I get it. I can't seem to stay away from Liv, even though I don't deserve her. Mal's a good girl. I just want what's best for her. She could do worse than you, ya know?" I try to grin up at him, and he removes his hand from my shoulder to shoot me the finger.

We both laugh—my laugh is still somewhat hollow because of my mood. We're not one-hundred percent okay with each other, but it's a start. He holds out his hand to help pull me to my feet, and I brush off the dust from my ass where my uniform is surely dirty.

"Now, quit hiding out. Shift ended thirty minutes ago. Go find your girl. Quit feeling sorry for yourself. Get your head out of your ass like I've told you. You're afraid you're going to lose her, yet you're the one causing it," Grant barks on his way out the door.

I call after him, "I'll try."

Hearing him chuckle, his parting words are, "I'll tell your sister you said *hi*."

Not quite sure if he heard my "fuck you" or not, but I'm sure he knows considering we finish each other's damn sentences sometimes.

The forest fires are under control for the time being. I was using the blazes as an excuse, a crutch, something to hide behind. When I said I was being a pussy, I meant it. Olivia deserves a man. A man who will man-up, which is what I have to do.

With renewed purpose and determination to talk to my girl, I head to my locker and quickly change out of my uniform. Staring at the strap mounted inside my locker, it reminds me I owe Grant so much and that life is too short.

When I step outside the station to make my way to my truck, there's someone leaning against my vehicle. He's got his arms crossed—a stance that immediately puts me on guard—and his ankles casually crossed like he has all the time in the world. I'm already growling.

What the fuck is Jarrod doing here?

***

Olivia

"What're you doing here, Jarrod?" I ask with a little vehemence to my words, laced with an undertone of fear and anxiety.

My hackles are raised. I clutch the knob a little more firmly and brace my right foot behind the bottom of the door in case this goes south, and he does something stupid—like try to push his way in. My cell phone is still on the coffee table, so that'll be no help.

Slamming the door in his face is an option, but I don't want to piss him off. Never before did I think there was even the tiniest part of him that would be capable of the things he's done recently, but now I don't know what he's capable of.

"I'm here because you never responded to my text. And since you won't talk to me, you left me no choice but to come here."

Breathing in through my nose and out through my mouth, I try to get rid of the shakiness that will be noticeable in my speech. "You know that we're over, Jarrod, right?"

"Yes. I'll admit I thought you'd come to your senses on your own and see what trash Wes is. Since you haven't, I'm trying to be a good friend and warn you."

What the hell? First he has a hard time accepting our breakup. Then he's creepy and spies on me. He sends me cryptic texts and potentially punches a wall, and now he's here at my door. I'm not even going to accuse him of punching the wall on the slight chance he does in fact have an aggressive streak.

Being a good friend? That's laughable. And to call my boyfriend trash is unforgiveable.

"And what exactly do you think I need to come to my senses about? Wes is an amazing man. He does so much for the community and for me. What did he do to deserve your ire besides being with me?"

"You really don't know him, do you?" Jarrod arches a brow in challenge and gives me a menacing smile.

Swallowing, I throw back in his face, "I thought I knew *you*, but I don't believe I do at all. So I can say the same."

"Olivia, I've never lied to you. But I guarantee your boyfriend has."

No, he wouldn't.

"You're mistaken. He's never lied to me."

There's no way I'll let him put a kernel of doubt in my mind.

There's determination in his features to break me—to break up Wes and me. I'll stay strong.

"Well, Olivia, omission is a form of deceit. So if he hasn't already told you—which I'm sure he hasn't—then it's still considered a lie."

My patience is wearing thin. "Jarrod, enough with all this. Either say it and be done with it, or please leave," I huff and stomp my left foot like a petulant child for emphasis.

He sighs and comes out with it. "You know your boyfriend's father went to prison?"

No! He would have told me. Jarrod's lying—*he's* the liar.

"I can tell by your face you didn't know. And did he tell you that he himself was in cuffs the night he fought his father and ultimately put him in prison?"

"W-w-what?" *Stay strong, Olivia. Don't let Jarrod win.*

With Wes's reluctance to talk about his dad, I kept wondering if it's because his dad ran off and abandoned the family. I never expected there could be something dark and possibly more sinister regarding his blood relative.

"I told you, I'm trying to be a good friend and warn you about him. I realize you and I don't have a chance together, but you're dating this guy, and he has a past you know nothing about. You said you knew him in high school, but a lot obviously happened since then. You're not being careful and safe. He could hurt you."

He reaches out his hand and places it on my arm. Is this a game? A tactic? A farce? I don't shake off his hand—I'm too stunned to move. The wheels in my head are spinning and burning rubber. Processing all this is making a headache form at my temples.

"I-I-I don't understand." I rub my forehead in confusion.

"If you don't believe me, then why don't you ask him? I just left the fire station where I went to talk to him about this, and guess what? He tried to pummel me. That guy has a nasty temper. I even watched him go after a fellow fireman while I was there. What kind of man does that? Unless he's like his father. Do you really want to be with someone like that, Olivia? What if you had kids together? Think about it!"

Wait, what? He saw Wes at the station? And he tried to fight Jarrod? And fight one of his crew members? None of this sounds like the man I love.

"He's not good enough for you!"

My mind is still trying to catch up to half of what he's saying. The fact that Wes is at the station throws me. "Wes was there at the station? I thought he was fighting the forest fires."

"Didn't you hear on the news they were contained yesterday? It seems he has a lot of explaining to do, wouldn't you say?"

The kernel he was trying to implant is starting to imbed itself in my brain. I want to believe none of this is true. I want to believe Wes would've told me all this. *He wouldn't keep something so important a secret.* He should trust me as much as I trust him.

Doing my best to hold on to the words of wisdom my dad gave me the other night, and with an image of Wes in my mind, I close my eyes, wishing it all away. It's a stupid thing. It's not like I'll wake up, and this will magically all have been a nightmare, but I'm so perplexed. And I can't even come up with a response.

"Olivia," Jarrod squeezes my arm slightly, and my eyes open, "you know I'm moving away next week. If there's ever a chance you'd change your mind about us, come and find me in Detroit."

Not a chance in hell! I shake my head indicating *okay* so he knows I acknowledged his offer.

"Take care of yourself. And if I were you, I'd end things with him immediately. He's not good for you. He'll hurt you."

Jarrod leans in to kiss me on the cheek, but I pull back.

"Goodbye, Jarrod," I say firmly.

His eyes flash with disappointment. He rocks back on his heels and stuffs his hands into his pockets like he's contemplating something. Gripping the knob again and bracing my foot once more is my only defense. I don't know which way is up right now. I'm about to fall. I'm about to shatter.

"Goodbye, Olivia."

He finally turns and walks off to his car. With quick movements, I shut my door and flip the locks in place. Then, I stride to my living room window so I can watch him drive away. Tremors are wracking my body.

Once the car is a mere speck down the road, and I can no longer see it, I lean against the wall and sag to the floor. My heart shrivels up and falls to the floor right beside me. Feeling hurt and betrayed, I bury my face in my hands as tears soak my skin—eventually the tears meet the floor too.

Wes…how could you?

Chapter 23: Back to Black

Weston

Black. It's all black. Not just because I'm sitting in my room with no lights on. Nothing has color. Nothing has purpose anymore.

Taking a drive somewhere to clear my head wasn't an option after Jarrod's visit—I didn't trust myself to stay within the lines and not veer off the road because of my stupidity. I'm feeling fortunate I even made it home.

Staying at the firehouse wouldn't have been good because the team would've demanded details about my current state, which I'm not willing to divulge. I can't talk to Grant or Mal right now. The two people I need the most are off-limits to me. Correction: there's one person I need the most, but she's so off-limits—so far off-limits—that she's not even in my zip code, county, or state, with the wide berth I've put between us.

There's nowhere to go without a reminder of Liv. There's nowhere to run. My apartment is the only place where I can be utterly alone and suffer in silence. While Grant is off being happy and in love with my sister, I get to sit here with my life in shambles.

Realizing I brought this on myself is not helping. This is why I pushed Liv away all those years ago—so things wouldn't turn to shit. Remember that old saying *you always hurt the ones you love the most?*

When I think back to Jarrod's ambush, there is a color that flickers in my vision. Red. Red and black are all I see. He's an asshole of the highest degree, and I sorely underestimated him. Clearly, I wasn't a worthy opponent because otherwise he wouldn't have won.

As Jarrod's leaning against my truck at the firehouse, I crack my knuckles and make fists. I may even break my teeth if I clench them together any tighter. We're in each other's personal space, and I straighten to my full height to show him he doesn't want to go toe to toe with me. I'll eat him for breakfast, lunch, and dinner. I'm already wound up and coiled like a cobra from my encounter with Grant, so this sanctimonious asshole will be sorry he ever came here.

Violence isn't my thing even though I almost went after my best friend; however, I may make an exception where Jarrod's concerned. It's hard to loathe myself over what happened with Grant when today just seems like the perfect shitstorm about to rain down its wrath upon me. First, things have been sour with Olivia, then Grant lays a bomb in my lap, and now this prick shows up. What's next?

In an intimidating tone, I curl my lip and ask the asshole, "What the fuck do you want? Didn't Olivia send you packing twice now?"

He laughs. He fucking laughs in my face. If his goal is to piss me off even more, well, one point for him because a second into this, he's already winning.

"Olivia will eventually come to her senses about me. Especially after I tell her about you."

"What the hell is that supposed to mean?"

"It means, I know about your dirty little family secret. It's interesting because when I asked around about you in this town, no one really seemed to know or remember much. So, I dug deeper and unearthed some skeletons."

He pauses for effect before going in for the kill, "And when I learned you sent your dad to prison like the pussy you are, I knew I had your number. You're a fucking menace to society. You're no good for Olivia. I saw you attack that guy in there. And when I tell Olivia what a piece of shit you are, she'll come back to me."

My blood is boiling. I'm shaking with anger. Snarling like a ferocious beast—there's probably foam dripping from my mouth and chin. God, I have never wanted to hit somebody so badly in my life. Not even my father. This guy is the lowest of the low. A bottom feeder not worthy to take up space in the same universe as someone like Liv. I need to warn her about him.

My fist wants so badly to connect with his face, but what's stopping me is the notion that this is exactly what he wants. Plus, I can't ever set eyes on Liv again knowing I did something so heinous. It's like this guy is goading me so I'll haul off and hit him. Why? So he can press charges? Most likely that's the reason, thinking I'll be out of the picture, and he'll have her to himself.

It's out of the question. Not to mention the fact I'll lose my job. I may not be in uniform, but I'm still on my employer's property, and if anyone sees this, I'll surely never be welcomed back by the community in any capacity. I have to try to beat him at his own game—the right way—with words.

"You're fucking delusional and psychotic!" I lob at him.

He may be right about my family and my past—it stings like a son of a bitch, but the sooner this cocksucker is gone, the sooner I can get to Liv.

"I'm not the one with daddy issues. You're in denial if you think Olivia would want to be with someone like you. You'll ruin her. You ruin everything in your path like a hurricane."

Suddenly I'm seventeen again, and Jarrod morphs into my father. Those words. Those goddamn painful words are what he said to me so many times—over and over again. Words said by the man who raised me. A man who was supposed to protect me and love me forever. A man who failed us all.

Jarrod's right. My father was right. I'll ruin Olivia. It's what I always feared, and it's going to come true. She's too good for me.

Mustering what little mental and physical strength I have left, I take a step back from Jarrod and whisper, "Get the fuck outta here."

He pushes himself off my truck slowly and smiles like the Grim Reaper as he walks toward his car. He is the Grim Reaper because he just stole my soul with the snap of his fingers. Liv is no longer mine, and he fucking knows it. Thoughts of needing to warn her escape me as my world falls apart around me.

I'm sorry, Liv...

Torturing myself somehow feels good. Hitting the replay button in my mind as the conversation with her ex loops through like a shot to the heart each time is all that's holding me together—it's something to focus on.

There's nothing to do but sit here and see black. And red. Can't forget the red.

***

Olivia

After picking myself up and brushing myself off following my crying jag, I was determined to find Wes and have this long overdue conversation. Letting this fester is not healthy for either of us. And I want to hear directly from his mouth his side of things.

The station is the first place I check, but there is no sign of Wes. So now I find myself sitting outside of Wes's sister's house. Grant's truck is here. Maybe Wes is with him.

Wes's truck isn't in the driveway. I should've gone to his apartment first—although, for some reason, I thought he'd be with his family. Knocking on her front door a few times, she greets me with the biggest smile.

"Liv!" she squeals and hugs me fiercely.

Her smile and effervescence is contagious—she's so different from her brother. The thing the two siblings have in common is their big hearts. Wes is so convinced he's no hero and I wish I knew why.

"Hey, Mal. It's good to see you. Sorry to drop in on you like this."

"Nonsense, come on in." As she's closing the door she tells me, "Wes isn't here, though; I imagine he's still sulking, wherever he is."

How would they know about the Jarrod thing? Is that what she means?

With bewilderment in my expression I tell her, "Yeah, I need to talk to him. It's important I find him. I thought he'd be here."

Grant comes around the corner with a sandwich—he's always eating, it appears, and it's a wonder he looks the way he does with the humongous appetite he has.

"Hi, beautiful. What brings you here?"

Seems I could be asking him the same question, but I have no doubt why he's here—it's *who* he's here for. It gives me hope that Wes will one day figure out there's something special between his best friend and his little sister.

"I'm looking for Wes. I thought I'd find him here. It's been a very upsetting morning and afternoon, to say the least." I chew on my lip to keep more tears from forming.

"Oh shit. Does this have anything to do with our fight?" Grant asks around a bite of his food.

"What fight?" I demand to know.

Was Jarrod telling me the truth? Is Jarrod right about everything? Bile rises to my throat.

Breathe!

"Uh, he and I got into a little scuffle, I guess you could call it. Not a big deal. I was asking for it because I finally told him about this one over here." He points at Mal.

Scuffle? Is that just a nice way of putting it?

"Hey!" Mal objects and pouts. "What am I, chopped liver? You make me sound so insignificant."

Grant puts down his sandwich on the nearby table and stalks over to her. Grabbing her in his arms, he lays a scorching kiss on her lips, and she melts at his feet. The way he looks at her is the way Wes looks at me.

"You're not chopped liver, doll. You're not insignificant. You're everything," he tells her as he runs his fingers through her multi-hued hair.

Needing to know more I have to ask, "So was it really a fight?"

"Nah. It didn't come to blows, if that's what you're asking. He got angry, but I'd never hurt him, and he'd never really hurt me. He's my brother."

I'm still confused. "My ex says he saw you two fight. I'm trying to make heads or tails of this."

"I don't know what you're talking about. Wes mentioned you had an ex, but I didn't see anyone at the station who would've seen us. After Wes and I had the disagreement, I left to come here."

Apparently, I was too quick to judge Wes based on my ex's words. Guess I'm learning my lesson the hard way because it's harsh knowing I let doubt creep in. If it wasn't really a fight, then either Jarrod exaggerated, or he was lying. Could he be lying about the family history too?

Both of them look at me in puzzlement. Mal's brows knit together, and she's scowling.

"Forgive me, but I thought you were into my brother? Why on earth would you be with your ex today?" Mal questions with hurt in her tone—on behalf of Wes, I imagine.

"It's a long story. One I should've told Wes to begin with about my ex. There's nothing between Jarrod and me. In fact, he's moving away next week, and that's the best thing that could happen. He's been having a hard time accepting our breakup, and he said he went to talk to Wes today at the station. So, I need to sort this out with him. He won't answer his phone. That's why I need to find him."

Breathing deeply, I turn toward Grant because I need more answers to put this jigsaw puzzle together. "When I came by the station a few weeks ago, you said something about being there *that day*. Were you referring to something involving his father?"

Mal whimpers, and Grant puts his arm around her shoulders. I've touched on a painful subject. However, I can't move forward without understanding what's led to this.

"I made a promise to Wes before we went out on the call when you were there. He made me promise I wouldn't tell his story. It's not mine to tell. I may not agree with him about keeping you in the dark, but I won't betray him," Grant says firmly.

"Well, I didn't make such a promise," Mal says while wiping away some tears. "It may not be Grant's story, but it's our family story. And besides, it's public knowledge, so I'm surprised people still don't talk about it."

"It was so long ago, doll. There's been more salacious stories since," Grant reminds her and tightens his grip around her shoulders.

Whether Wes gets upset with me or not, I'll deal with that when the time comes for going behind his back to get answers. Mal licks her lips and takes a deep breath. Somehow, I know this will cut deep, so I brace myself.

"Did you know my dad used to abuse Wes?"

No! God, no!

My chin trembles. It's already too much, so I close my eyes. Memories flood back like the tide has just come in. All those bruises. All those times. All those chances for me to ask—*I should* have asked. Even weeks ago it was right there in front of me. The scars. Those damn faint white scars I asked about, and he blew it off, citing *occupational hazard*.

Needing to sit down because I feel weak, broken, and hurt so badly for my love, I move to the couch. Mal and Grant join me.

"Dad began beating him after we moved here. We think it was

depression and alcohol. I was too little to know what went on, but it finally came to a head when I was fourteen. My dad tried to attack my mom and me, but Wes fought him off. Grant showed up. It was a mess."

"He was protecting you," I say more than ask because it's clear it's the truth.

Mal nods her head anyway. My voice cracks when I go to talk, so I have to try again. "Was Wes arrested too? From what I was told, your dad went to prison, but I don't know all the details."

"No. Wes was cuffed and detained. Of course, they only charged my dad and convicted him. We haven't seen our father since the trial and plan to keep it that way. He's out now, but we hope never to hear from him again. After the conviction, that's when Mom became how she is."

God, it all makes sense now—the family history.

Since we're sitting side by side, I place a comforting hand on Mal's knee, and shake my head in disbelief at all that's come out from this conversation.

"I'm so sorry, Mal. I had no idea. I'm such a damn fool." I close my eyes once more as a steady flow of tears fall.

She sniffles and conveys, "Don't be sorry—well to me at least. But I imagine Wes won't want pity either. He's a survivor. It happened, and it's over. Although, I have to admit I don't think he ever fully healed. Lately, it seems he's being haunted by the memories, and I don't know why."

Opening my eyes, I look to Grant to see if he'll shed some light. As much as I don't want him to feel like he broke his promise, I need to know how I can help Wes. I need to know how I can help him heal.

"Ah hell!" Grant throws his hands up in the air. "I guess since I didn't reveal the fucking awful parts, technically I kept my promise."

He huffs and runs his hand through his floppy hair. This must be hard on Grant too. He's been a part of this family for so long and has lived through all of it with them. Except Wes was the only one who suffered the physical trauma—it's disgusting his father did that. I'm so blessed to have such a loving, caring, nurturing father. Poor Wes and Mal.

"I think his problem is he's always felt you're too good for him."

I whimper at Grant's answer because it hurts to hear, but my eyes are also wide with shock. At the same time, I can't help but recall the words Jarrod said that are reminiscent of what Grant has just revealed. I missed the signs again. Jarrod told me *he's not good enough for you* and *he's like his father*. I'm angry at myself for so many things now.

"*I'm* the one who's not good enough for him." *My hero. My protector. My life. My love.*

"Don't say that. You two deserve each other. Liv, you're the only one he's ever wanted or will ever want. He had a fucked up youth, but his adult years don't have to suffer because of it. Give yourselves a chance,"

Grant pleads with me.

He's such a good friend to everyone, and I have the greatest respect for him. It's not surprising he and Mal are an item. There's no doubt in my mind I will give Wes and me a chance. I only pray I can fix this between us, and I pray he lets me help him—help us.

"We know you love him," Mal chimes in.

"I do. More than anything. I've loved him for over sixteen years. Not telling him yet was a mistake."

Mal inclines her head and gives me a sympathetic smile. "It's never too late. And I suppose he didn't tell you either. So, go find him and tell him now," she encourages. "Grant finally told me."

She leans into his side and snuggles into his chest. They're a striking couple, and I'm so unbelievably happy for them. I want my happy ending too. As my dad has reminded me, *I have a rare one.*

"I gotta go," I tell them and stand up.

They rise too and follow behind me to the door to give me hugs and say their goodbyes.

"Thanks for everything, guys, and I'm really happy for you two."

"It'll work out with you and my brother. You were meant to be," Mal says wistfully.

When I get into my car, I need to sit here for a few moments to collect myself. The weight of all that unfolded and what was unearthed is so heavy. Blaming myself for things is not the answer. Wes needs a strong woman. Wes needs a woman who will help see him through this. I'm not leaving him. I walked away once, and I'll never do it again.

I'm sorry, Wes. We'll fix it...

Chapter 24: Fireproof

Weston

My phone has been going off all day. It lights up the room each time, and I curse the damn thing because I lose my night vision each time the screen brightens. I should turn the damn thing off, but that would require me moving. It doesn't matter who's on the phone—texting or calling. Olivia has Jarrod. Mal has Grant. So, there's no need to worry about anyone.

Time has no meaning. I could have sat here for hours already, or it could be only minutes. Most likely it's been hours because it was light outside but eventually became dark—it's why I never bothered to turn on a lamp. I don't have the energy to persuade my muscles, joints, and bones to work together for the sake of moving.

Is this what it's like for my mom?

Sitting on the floor of my bedroom, I hear banging on my front door. Sounds like Liv's voice out there. *It couldn't be if she's reuniting with that dick.*

Shit, I don't even remember if I locked the door when I came home. It doesn't matter who it is out there. Fuck it. Fuck it all!

***

Olivia

My hand hurts from banging on Wes's apartment door. The cops will probably show up soon from all the noise I'm making out here. His truck is parked outside, so I can't imagine he went anywhere. Whatever I'm doing isn't working, and now I'm really worried something's wrong.

Should I call Grant? Maybe he has a key. Deciding to try the handle, I'm surprised to find it opens. It's so unlike Wes not to lock it, which further shows me he's not thinking clearly.

Hesitantly, I enter the pitch-black apartment. I don't like it. I could cut the air with a knife, the tension in this place is so thick. I'm also sensing pain—Wes's pain. Being in tune with that part of him is a blessing and a curse, a curse because my body is lanced with the same pain he's feeling.

Making my way to his bedroom, I call out, "Wes… It's me."

No reply.

After locating the switch on the wall when I reach his room, I flick it on. Temporarily blinded by the light, I blink rapidly to dispel the dots in my vision. When I'm able to focus, I see Wes on the floor. He's on the other side of his bed with his back to me.

"Wes…"

Then rushing to his side, I crouch down and discover he's staring ahead but not seeing anything. It reminds me of his mom. He told me once she'd retreat in her mind to protect herself—I witnessed it the day I met her.

This beautiful, broken family has been through so much. My soul aches to help mend the wounds. Placing my hands on each side of my love's face, I'm determined not to cry for him. I said earlier I'd be strong for him, and so I will. He's carried the load long enough—it's my turn to help ease the burden.

"Look at me, Wes."

Still nothing.

It's like he's fireproof—nothing can penetrate the barrier he put up. Nothing can get through. I say the one thing I hope will break down that barrier: "I love you, Weston."

His eyes flash over, and his tempestuous mood strikes like lightning. He shakes his head roughly, effectively freeing my hands from his face, then he looks right at me. "No!" His booming voice reverberates loudly through my chest.

Trying not to show him how his refusal affects me, I repeat myself. "Yes, Weston. I. Love. You."

He abruptly stands up, leaving me kneeling on the floor. Looking up at him, all I can do is watch him further self-destruct. Telling him I love him brought him back, but it also lit something within him I never expected: decisiveness.

He's pacing back and forth across his room.

"Talk to me," I beg him.

He stops momentarily only to glower at me.

"What do you want me to say, Olivia?" he asks, holding out his hands for emphasis.

"Anything. Just don't shut me out."

"It's not going to work with us, Liv."

Somewhat expecting him to push me away, I try to remain tough with nerves of steel. "I understand why you think that, but pushing me away isn't the answer."

He looks at me skeptically. "How could you possibly understand anything?"

Disguising the hurt while sustaining whiplash from the verbal strike of his tongue, I school my features to appear impassive. "I know about your father. And I should've known what was going on with you in high school—all those bruises, God, I should've known. You'll never realize how deeply sorry I am for not seeing what was there. Yet, there's no pity on my end—I won't pity you. Because you're a survivor, Wes."

He's breathing heavily, his shoulders hunched, and he's making fists at his sides. Standing up, I walk over to him to block his pacing.

"Grant told you?" he demands to know while his chin juts out.

"No. It was a combination of Mal, Grant, and…Jarrod. Grant never betrayed you."

He growls, and I'm assuming it's at the mention of my ex.

"What happened between you and Jarrod today? What'd he say?" I question.

He moves away from me to resume his trek. If this gets him talking, then that's all that matters. "Nothing I didn't already know."

"Don't believe anything he says. Please. I can only imagine what he said to you. He has a way of trying to manipulate the situation, and I should've realized it sooner."

Guilt swamps me for not telling Wes about Jarrod's peculiar behavior. I'm responsible for what's happened. By remaining silent, I brought this ache upon us.

"Shouldn't you two be rekindling your love or some shit like that?" he asks with ice in his speech. After he delivers the question, he turns away from me.

"What? No. Why on earth would you ask that?"

Wes's insinuation doesn't make sense. It's appalling to think I could be with a man as despicable as my ex. Shaking my head to clear the cobwebs, I stare at his back, wishing he'd turn around so I could discern where this is coming from.

"We're not going to work, Liv—you and me. We're not good together."

He finally turns around, and what I see when I look in his eyes is defeat.

No, Wes. Fight for me. Fight for us.

He moves to his bed and sits on the edge. I swallow down my fear and agony then slink to the bed to join him. Without giving him a second to move away, I straddle his lap and lock my arms around his neck. He has no choice but to look at me and face this head on.

"Let me help you heal. You're not alone in this. I love you, so please stop fighting me. Instead, start fighting with me—for us."

My lips are hovering just an inch from his. He hasn't pushed me away yet. Closing my eyes so I don't have to witness it if he does reject me, I slant my mouth across his. He doesn't kiss me back at first, but then my tongue darts out to move his lips apart. A slight groan escapes him, and I moan into his mouth. At my sound, he stills and stops reacting. What I taste in his kiss is haunting. It's not love on his tongue; it's anger, hurt, and refusal.

Before I have time to register it, he wrenches back from our kiss, slides me off his lap, and bolts from the bed. My breath stutters. My heart lurches in my chest, and I'm crushed like a soda can stomped under someone's heel. I can even hear the internal breaking within my body.

"I'm not going to say it again, Liv. We're through. Leave and don't come back."

Breathe. Stay strong—it's my only mantra.

"You can't possibly mean it," I beg, plead, and pray as my voice cracks.

It's there in his eyes, though. Those gray eyes I adore more than anything show it. Those gray eyes that complement my violet ones so well—together we create a beautiful night's sky— his eyes are telling me we're over.

"I do."

God, those words somehow cut the deepest—probably because I see my future disappearing before me. Tonight I expected to hear the three little words every woman wants to hear. Instead, the two words he gives me—*I do*—are ones I thought he'd say while I was wearing a white dress.

"I see." What else can I say?

Am I giving up too easily? How can I win this battle when he won't let me in? He won't fight for us. I thought I was strong enough for the both of us. But a person can only take so many cracks before they eventually splinter apart.

"I wish you well, Liv. G-g-goodbye."

The catch in his throat makes me think there's still a chance. So, I try once more. "It doesn't have to be goodbye, Wes."

"You're only embarrassing yourself now. I said goodbye, Liv. Now leave!"

The finality in his tone is my undoing. I'll wait to fall apart until after I exit his apartment. Leaving with some dignity intact is important.

On shaky legs, I get up from the mattress and head toward the bedroom door. Turning around, I give him one last look, a look I hope will stay with him for the rest of his life.

"Just remember, Wes, I didn't walk away from you. You're sending me away, like you did back then. We could've had something special—well, we did have something special. The real deal. The love that only comes around once, but you're throwing it away. Your past doesn't define you...your present does. Goodbye."

Knowing full well he won't come after me, I make a hasty exit from his place and slam his front door. The crying starts immediately, but I don't dare cry loudly—no need to further embarrass myself and publicly perpetuate my demise.

When I get into my SUV, I collapse on my seat and curl into a ball. This family car mocks me now—it'll be the most unpleasant reminder of what I'll never have.

When my mom died, I thought I'd never survive the pain that ripped me apart. Today is the second time I've experienced that level of torment.

Chapter 25: Four Steps

Olivia

December 7, 2018

It's freezing outside. We're expecting snow any day—such a departure from the hot summer and mild fall we had. It's two and a half weeks before Christmas. Almost two months since I've seen or talked to *him*. He hasn't tried to contact me, not even once. Life has moved a little slower. The days drag on. The nights creep by.

When I close my eyes while lying in bed, delusions of grandeur dance across my vision. Needless to say, I don't sleep as well as I used to. My body aches for my lover. My soul yearns for my other half. My heart craves the unity only the perfect mate can provide—I don't have any of it anymore.

My dad has been doing his best to cheer me up over the weeks. Ash has tried to comfort me as well as any dog could. Sammy's been coming over whenever she can—wine, chocolate, and action films have been my lifeline.

Malory texts me every now and then. We don't dare mention her brother. She knows snippets of what happened, and I'm not going to bash him—I still love him too much to put him down. Maybe his painful past was just so great that our love couldn't bear its weight.

As devastating as the breakup was, I can't begrudge him. However, I haven't been brave enough to hang out with Mal and Grant for fear of not being able to cope. Mal on her own, I could probably handle, but those two are inseparable according to her. Therefore, I wouldn't dream of hording her time, especially since it would most likely entail her watching me wallow in my misery. Grant's presence would only serve to torture me. After all, he is an extension of *him*. I miss everyone, though.

Jarrod moved away as he said he would. He hasn't contacted me, and I never plan to open a line of communication between us ever again. He caused turbulence and made the path I was flying on veer off course enough times; he only proved time and time again why we weren't right for one another.

I'm beginning to think Jarrod's final attempt to talk to me wasn't to win me back, but more of a ploy to destroy my relationship with…I can't bring myself to say his name. The disingenuous actions and attitude Jarrod demonstrated signified *If I can't have her, no one will*. Seems like my relationships are better suited for becoming a Lifetime movie—surely I win the award for drama.

Spending more time at the shelter has helped. The more I make a difference, the less pain I'm in. I moved on from *him* once before; I'll learn to do it again. At seventeen, though, I didn't know what it was like to feel his body against mine. Now that I've experienced it, it's like drinking a mug of rich, dark, hot chocolate with a sprig of dill—having to gulp down the sweet and the bitter. It's hard to swallow because the two don't go together.

Needing to get some headspace, I decide to go to Sammy's house for once. Tom's away on a guy's golfing weekend trip in Florida—he left earlier today—so me and my bestie are going to hang out and do one of those paint and sip parties tomorrow.

After arriving at her place, I'm ushered in and we immediately open a bottle of red, pull out a pint of Halo Top ice cream—because if I'm going to be bad, I'll do it the low carb way—and put on an action flick starring The Rock.

With flannel bottoms, a thermal long-sleeved top, and fluffy pink socks, I stretch my legs out on the coffee table and devour my ice cream. She, on the other hand, is wearing a posh sleepwear set, and her makeup still looks fresh. Sammy's one of those women who goes to bed looking that way and wakes up looking like a movie star. With no one to impress on my end, I'm fine with sporting the homely look.

"Did you see the new CAD designer they hired? Holy shit, if I weren't married, I'd jump on that," Sammy admits, purring at the end.

"No."

"Well, I hear he's single, but with the girls in the electrical department strutting their stuff around him, he might not be for long." She arches her finely sculpted brow while tossing around the suggestion.

I bite my lip to squelch the urge to groan. I don't like being a party-pooper. After setting down my spoon and pint, I turn to face her on the couch, tucking my legs under me—fluffy socks and all. "I'm not ready yet.

Who knows when I'll be."

"It could just be sex, ya know. It could just be for fun. You remember what fun is, right?"

"No. It couldn't, Sammy. You know that about me. Honestly, could you move on from Tom?"

"Hell yeah," she jokes.

Of course, there's no way in hell she could. I appreciate her trying to help me move forward—but it's too soon. My hope is wherever *he* is, and whatever he's doing, he's well. His happiness will always be important to me.

Playing with my ponytail and twirling it through my fingers, I'm wishing Ash was on my lap. My dad took him for the weekend for me.

"The offer is still there for me to kick him in the nuts if you're so inclined to finally grant me permission."

Lifting a shoulder and half-smiling at the idea, I sigh thinking I could never wish him harm. For all that pain that was inflicted upon me, I'd never want that for him. He was already in pain. *If only he would've let me help heal him.* At least I got to tell him I love him.

"You're a good friend—the best—but we'll just leave him be."

"And you're sure you don't want to spend Christmas with me and Tom in Hawaii?"

As tempting as it sounds, I'm not encroaching on their romantic getaway. Oh sure, I'd find ways to occupy myself—mainly sunbathing, reading, and taking walks, but it's their trip.

"I'm sure. Just bring me back a lei." She starts laughing at my request, and I giggle realizing what I said.

"By the way, I love the pearl earrings with the fluffy sock look. Such a trendsetter you are."

"I know. It's representative of my life. I'm a hot mess, Sammy. But Mom's pearls go with any outfit, so they're staying."

"That they do. I'm just teasing. You're not a hot mess. And I have a feeling things will get better *very* soon."

Wishing I could believe her, I nod my head. We turn our attention back to the movie, back to the buff hero saving the day.

I had a hero…once upon a time.

***

Weston

Almost two months ago…

Well, I did it. I officially pushed her away and out of my life. Last week after she walked out of my apartment, I knew I'd made a mistake. Here I was thinking I was protecting her from myself, but in reality, it was me being stupid, cowardly, and fucked up.

The letter I received in the mail last night only further proved I made mistakes—many, many mistakes. Expressing contrition for my misdeeds is step one in the process—the healing process. Liv had asked how she could heal me. At first I didn't want her to. I still don't want her to, but what I realized is I have to heal myself—step two.

When the letter came, it was the answer I never knew I needed. It served as closure.

I'm far from healed. However, it's a start and one I relish. Over the next several weeks, I'm going to make sure I'm concentrating on my mental health. When I crawl back to Liv on my hands and knees, begging for forgiveness and pledging my undying love for her, I'm not going to do it as a broken man—I'll come to her whole. The suppliant person before her will be the healthiest version of myself because that's what she deserves, and quite frankly, so do I.

Earlier today I texted Grant to invite him over for a brotherly talk. I'm going to make amends with everyone on my list—step three. I'll start with Grant, then I'll move on to Mal, and finally, saving the hardest for last…Olivia.

My mom may be oblivious to what's going on, but I'm still going to apologize to her too. And before I walk back into Liv's life with my heart on my sleeve like a badge of honor, I'm going to have a long talk with her father and discuss my intentions—the intentions I've had since the day I laid my gray eyes on her amethyst ones.

A knock at the door tells me Grant's arrived. Whether it's a dick move or not, I asked him not to bring Mal. We need to talk man to man. I've been on vacation for the last week. My chief approved my time off in a heartbeat. Anyone around me could see I'd been coming apart at the seams for weeks.

Being the good friend he is, Grant has texted to check on me since the night I sent Liv away. Unfortunately, I haven't wanted to see anyone until now.

When I open the door, I expect to see an angry best friend with pent up animosity. What I see in his eyes floors me—it's relief. Realizing I caused him pain and suffering too hurts like a son of a bitch.

"Shit, man, I'm glad to see you finally got your head out of your ass" His lips twitch, then eventually form a grin.

He gives me a hug, and when we separate, I give him my normal "Fuck you."

As we move to sit on my living room couch, he starts with the round of questions I expected. "How're you doing?"

"Better. I fucked up things with Liv. I fucked up things with you and Mal. I'm going to make it right, though. You'll see."

"I believe ya. And thank fuck for that—you seem back to your normal self. You had me worried you were going loco. What's changed?"

Sighing deeply, I rub at the back of my neck as tension sets into my spine. "The simple answer is I've seen the light." He doesn't realize the significance of me coming out of the darkness, so I'll do my best to clarify.

"Okay," he says and waits for me to elaborate.

"I suppose you know what went down with me and Liv?"

"The short version from Mal, yes. I'm sure there's more to it, but I got the condensed explanation."

Nodding, I have no doubt Liv apprised Mal of a watered-down version of the events. Because that's the kind of woman she is. Even in the worst of times, she still wouldn't make me out to be the bad guy.

"Let's just say I hurt her far worse than that piece of shit ex of hers ever could. She told me she loved me, and I threw her out."

"You did what?" He rears back, and his booming voice echoes through my tiny apartment.

"I said things I shouldn't have. Things I didn't mean. Well, some I did mean at the time. I was angry at her ex, angry at you and Mal, angry with my dad, but most of all, I was angry with myself. She was on the receiving end of it, and I pushed her away."

He expels a breath and tells me, "I was afraid of that. All you had to do was talk to her. That's all she wanted."

"I know. One of my many transgressions. I'm going to fix it."

Sucking in a stuttered breath, I give him my most sincere remorseful look. "I'm sorry for the way I acted. I had no damn right to go after you the way I did. You love my sister, and I couldn't be happier she chose you and you chose her. If you two ever tie the knot, at least it'll finally be official: you'll be my brother."

He starts laughing then throws his head back. Joining in, I match his hearty laugh with my own—it feels good.

"Man, we're a long way off from tying anything. She has dreams I'm only all too happy to encourage. Believe me, I wouldn't mind putting a ring on her finger, but she's young. We've got time."

"And you have my blessing. I owe you so much—still never repaid you for saving me in that house fire."

"Thanks, man, for your blessing, but you don't owe me anything. Consider us even because I get Mal. Shit, you had me worried there for a bit. I thought you were gonna disown your sister and me."

"I thought about it," I say jokingly. "But seriously, I know I was a dick. I'll make it up to Mal. I wanted to talk to you first because she's going to need support when I sit down and talk to her."

He looks at me inquisitively. From the back pocket of my jeans, I produce a folded envelope, well-creased even though I only received it yesterday. I'm still partly in disbelief that it was waiting in my mailbox. Looking down at the envelope, I proceed to pull out the handwritten letter.

"I need to read you this. Then maybe you'll understand why I'm ready to move forward with my life once and for all."

Weston,

I know I'm the last damn person in this world you ever expected to hear from. I've had this letter sitting by my bed for weeks since it's gone through several drafts. I'm finally deciding to send it because it's literally do or die time.

After I got out of prison, I wanted to come find you, your sister, and your mom. I wanted to make peace. My time in jail helped me find my way again. At first, I hated attending the therapy sessions. But after a while, I realized I wanted to be a better man.

I got married again when I got out. She's a good woman. Her name is Marcy. I think you'd like her. She knows what I've done, and she loves me anyway.

Sometimes things happen for a reason. I found out a few months ago I have pancreatic cancer. I'm not responding to treatment. They told me I have a handful of weeks left.

I'm not asking for sympathy. I'm not asking to see you. What I do want you to know before I die is I'm sorry, son. Back then, I was a terrible father. I hated myself so much, and I took it out on you. The drinking was out of control. Don't ever be like me. Don't ever let the ugly and the evil win.

I think I'm getting what I deserve, and I'm okay with that. At one point, I wrote your mom and Malory each a letter, but I ended up throwing them away. So I'm going to leave it up to you. You can choose to tell them or not.

I won't bother you again. If you want to write me back, you've got my return address now. If not, I understand.

Again, I'm sorry. I hope this letter

finds you well, and I hope you found happiness.
Letting you go to fire school was the best thing
that ever happened. I think it was fate or
something because I didn't want you to go, but
your mom talked me into it. Thank God she did.
You were a good kid, and I was so
jealous of that because I knew you'd be more
successful than me. I can admit that now.
Hopefully you found a good woman too.
Take care of yourself. There's no doubt
in my mind you've watched over your mom and
Malory, so I know they're in good hands.
Like I said, don't ever be like me,
Weston.
Regards,
Dallas

"Fuck," is Grant's only response when I finish reading aloud.

"I know. My sentiments exactly. So now you know why I needed to talk to you."

"Yeah, that shit's heavy. Are you gonna respond to him?"

"No. I think the letter was more for him than for me. I said all I needed to years ago. What it made me realize, though, is that if I let Liv go, I *will* be my father. I'll have pissed away the best thing that ever happened to me."

Settling back against the softness of my couch, I know Grant understands more than anyone about fucked up families. "Sure, it sucks ass that he's dying of cancer, but it doesn't change my mind. Potentially opening that door again could do more harm than good, and I think we're better off."

"I get it, man. No one can blame you either way. What do you think this will do to Mal and your mom if you tell them?"

"Honestly, I think it will give them closure. It did for me. Mal's her own person, as you know. If she wants to see or talk to him, then I can't stop her. That's why she'll need you to lean on because I don't know what this will do to her. I can't keep this from her. I've already kept enough secrets from the ones I love."

"I agree. Keeping this from her would destroy your relationship."

Nodding my head, I refold the letter and tuck it back into the envelope. Then, I lay it on the arm of the cushion.

"We'll tell her tomorrow. Together," I assure him.

"Sounds good. What about Olivia? What're you going to do about her?"

"I have a plan. It won't happen overnight, but I'm going to win her back if it's the last thing I do."

"And how do you expect to do that?"

"With a little help from my family." *Step four.*

His look of shock tells me he's not the only one surprised that I'm asking for help, but if I'm going to get back in Liv's good graces and redeem myself, I can't leave anything to chance. She's worth putting all my strength and energy into my redemption because our love transcends time. Besides, she's everything plus infinity.

"So what's the plan? Whatever it is, I'm in."

Smiling at Grant, I'm ready to get back in the game—I just hope I don't lose.

Chapter 26: Rhinestones and Pearls

Weston

Almost two months ago… (continued)

The next day, Grant and I sit down with Mal and my mom. Mom's alert today, and after just reading the letter, she's still quiet but aware of her surroundings.

"I still can't believe it. After all this time, he reaches out to share that news," Mal says, and Grant pulls her into his side for comfort.

"I know, Baby Girl. If you want to see him, it's your choice," I tell her.

"No. What's done is done. Moving on from him was the best thing this family ever did. Let's keep it that way," she says softly.

Grant kisses her sweetly on the lips, and I squeeze her hand, letting her know everything's going to be all right. Mal's a strong woman. But we're making that final turn of the lock in order to close the door and never open it again—something we all needed.

Mom's vacant expression tells me she's affected by this, but not enough to comment. I have to hope she'll still snap out of it one day.

"Now on to the other thing we need to talk about," I start to say, but I'm interrupted.

"Oh, God. There's more? What else are you going to lay on me?" She bites her lip, her eyes looking worried behind her thick-rimmed glasses.

"I need to apologize to you and Mom."

She looks at me like I'm deranged and blinks rapidly—so much so, her eyelashes are hitting her lenses. "Okay…," she says hesitantly.

"I'm sorry for not being supportive of you and Grant as a couple. You have my blessing, and I couldn't be happier for you two. And…I'm sorry I've been absent emotionally for so many years for both you and Mom."

"Thank you for that—for me and Grant. But don't ever apologize for the second thing. You've never been absent in any capacity. Wes, you've always had to carry the load and the burden. You've done a great job holding everything together. Without you, we wouldn't have what we have and be where we are today. I love you for that!"

Mal winces and then adds, "I also have to apologize to you. When you asked me that night we went to dinner if I liked Grant, I told you *no*. Obviously, I kinda lied. At the time, it didn't feel like a lie because I didn't just like him, I loved him. However, it was wrong of me to lead you to believe otherwise."

"Thanks, Baby Girl. I love you, and I just want you to be happy. All is forgiven; it's water under the bridge—hell, we'll start a new bridge."

She hugs me, and a weight has been lifted off my shoulders. I can finally breathe for the first time since the night I found Mal and mom huddled in the corner under my dad's hand.

"There's one more thing I need to tell you, and this is a biggie."

"Uh oh, does it have anything to do with Olivia? And by the way, you're lucky you and I are even on speaking terms right now because I'm devastated you broke up with her. I just didn't want to pour salt in the wound or meddle in your affairs by bringing it up." She purses her lips, and Grant's holding back a grin at the way his woman is acting.

Pressing at the ache in my chest with my fingertips, I feel the burn in my heart over Liv. Then I soldier on for both our sakes.

"I know. I really screwed up, but I have a plan to win her back. So, I need everyone's help. My next stop will be to see her dad, and then I'll get in contact with Sammy and her husband somehow."

"Oh, I have Sammy's number. We really hit it off at the cookout, and she wants me to do her hair sometime. I can take care of Sammy and Tom if you let me in on this so-called plan."

Rubbing my hands together, I tell her what I have in store for the love of my life—another chance and a second *dance* to do this right.

***

Weston

Almost two months ago… (conclusion)

After looping Mal and Grant in on the plan, I find myself sitting at Liv's father's kitchen table. He's a man of few words, but when he speaks, it's with purpose and conviction. The lines in his face are not menacing like my dad's were. His lines show wisdom, tenderness, and loyalty.

He crosses his arms, making the pewter-colored cable knit sweater he's wearing into a barrier—almost like chainmail on a knight. He's not going to be easy to sway, and I wouldn't expect anything less if it were my daughter. It's evident he's hurting with her and doing his best to be civil—it's more than I deserve.

"I love Olivia," I confess—it's the easiest and most important confession of my life.

He taps his teeth together, not budging from the epic stare-down he has me engaged in.

"Robby, I'm sorry I hurt her."

"It's Mr. Watson."

At that, I grin. I respect him all the more for loving his daughter so much and being so protective—qualities I hope I'll be able to live up to.

"I'm sorry I hurt her, Mr. Watson. She's everything to me. There's no excuse for how I acted, but I can tell you it won't happen again."

He steeples his fingers, his elbows propped up on the table as he contemplates my words.

He's still reticent, so I continue on, "You may think I saved her the night of the accident, but it was the other way around. What she couldn't save me from, though, was myself. I wasn't ready to accept help from my family and friends. I thought I wasn't worthy of her love, but I'm ready now! I've always loved her, and I'll never stop loving her—not in this life or in the next."

Clearing his throat, his eyes soften. This is the kind of father I want to be one day. One who listens. One who understands, and one who loves unconditionally.

"Son, I've never seen my daughter so happy like she was when she was with you. When she looks at you, talks to you, or talks about you, it's like seeing Beatrice all over again. It's because Olivia loves with her whole heart and whole self. It's a rare gift. When her mom died, I couldn't help Liv heal either. So as a man and as a father, I understand what it's like to feel like you failed someone. Just don't hurt her again."

"I won't, Mr. Watson."

"It's Robby."

He cracks a smile, and his crooked teeth make him somehow look boyish. This is the kind of man I wish my mom would've met after my dad. With so many things to set in motion before I go after Liv, there's just one more thing I need to know from Robby.

"How do you feel about flying?"

***

Olivia

December 8, 2018

"Okay, where's this wine and painting party again? We've been driving for over an hour, and it looks like we're heading back toward my house. What're you up to?"

Sammy asked if she could drive my SUV, and I figured it's because she knows I hate driving in north Jersey—I can't quite maneuver around like the New York-commuters who mostly inhabit that area. Now I'm suspicious of her request because we left north Jersey a while ago, so clearly that wasn't the reason she wanted to drive.

"Don't worry. You'll see soon enough. It's not so much a wine and painting party, but it is a party of sorts."

My mind is spinning. *Oh, God, a male strip club? A female strip club? What does she have planned?* My imagination is running wild—and dirty, for some reason.

"Please don't tell me we're going to a party where I have to look halfway decent?"

"You look great, doll! But I've taken care of that too."

"Doll? It sounds like you've been hanging around Grant!" I laugh at the absurdity of that even being a possibility.

She doesn't remark. *Weird.* After another ten minutes, we're driving in a very familiar part of town. So familiar, in fact, that we pull up to a place I never expected to visit this soon.

"What're we doing at Mal's house?"

"You'll see."

"Sammy…"

"It'll be okay, Liv. Trust me."

I close my eyes, steeling myself for the inevitable discomfort that will wash over my body. I resign myself to the fact that I would eventually need to deal with seeing the people still in *his* life. Of course, I knew there would be a day when I would run into one of them. I may have managed to not bump into him in the years following college, but that doesn't mean fate wouldn't be cruel and send him, or those close to him, my way.

Sammy gets out of the vehicle then comes around to my side and opens my door.

"I'll have Grant come out and get you if I have to," she threatens.

Expelling an exasperated breath, I swing my legs out of my SUV and trudge into the house muttering obscenities to myself. My poor attitude is thwarted by the bubbly Malory, who comes barreling at me once we walk through the door. Stumbling back at her overzealous hug, I've already forgotten I was in a grumpy mood. Sammy disappears into the kitchen, and I assume she's giving Mal and me a moment to talk in private.

"God, I've missed you," Mal tells me while still clinging to me.

"I've missed you too. Texting is not the same as getting to hang out with you. I've been a crummy friend, and I'm sorry for that."

She pulls back from our hug to look at me, and her face falls at hearing my sorrow. "Please don't apologize. I get it. If I were in your shoes, I'd be in a padded room. You've handled everything beautifully."

"Thank you. I had a few weak moments here and there, but if my mom were here today, she'd want me to be strong, confident, and carry on. Speaking of moms, how's yours? Can I say hi?"

"Well, she's actually not here."

"What?" I ask in shock. "Is she okay?"

"Oh, yes, she's fine. You'll see her a little later."

Puzzled by her response, I shrug and accept it. As I look around her living room at all the makeup, hair products, and dresses strewn about, I'm in awe. "Wow, are you doing hair and makeup for a wedding tonight or something?" My eyes drift over all the material, tulle, and vibrant colors.

"Not exactly."

I'm about to ask her more questions, but in walks Grant. Holy crap! He looks amazing. He's dressed in a classic tuxedo with his hair styled in such a sexy way; I stifle a laugh because I realize he's not eating something, which is so unlike him. Instead, my chin is to the floor, and I can't believe Mal hasn't attacked her man yet. She looks at him dreamily— okay, so she is affected, even after these few months of dating him.

"Hey, doll!" Grant picks me up in a brotherly hug and kisses the top of my head. He's such a great guy. I've missed him just as much as I've missed Mal.

"Hi," I squeak out.

"I hate to run out, but I'm gonna be late if I don't leave now."

"Late for what?"

"You'll see." He grins and winks at me.

"Why does everyone keep saying that?" I look from him to Mal, and when Sammy walks in, I look to her for answers too.

"You'll see," he repeats and laughs until he's out the door.

Spinning around to start in with the questions on Mal and Sammy, they both hold up their hands to halt my inquisitiveness. "We promise you'll find out soon. Tonight's going to be a fun night. So just sit back and relax, and let us work our magic," Mal insists.

Sammy hands me a glass of wine—she knows how to placate me. "Technically, I wasn't lying when I told you we were going to a wine and paint party. Here's the wine, and the painting is the makeup job Mal's going to do."

"That doesn't count," I say in protest.

"Bite me!" she says cheekily then saunters off to fetch a glass for her and Mal.

Over an hour later, I'm exhausted from the priming, primping, buffing, grooming, and dressing. I haven't seen myself. My hair is in some kind of updo, my face is complete with false eyelashes, and the dress is purple. Mal did most of it, but Sammy picked the dress. The two of them should go into business together styling people because I imagine I don't look like myself, which isn't a bad thing. Tonight I've been their very own life-size Barbie doll.

Mal went to her bedroom to retrieve her full-length mirror. When she walks out with it, and I get my first glimpse of myself, I'm stunned by the image. I never thought I'd look like a princess, but here I am.

My mom taught me hair and makeup before she passed, but I never got to do the whole mother-daughter thing during the vital teen years. I didn't go to dances or have a sweet sixteen party because she was sick for so long before her body gave out.

The heels are a deep purple that perfectly match the dress. And the dress, oh my! It's an eggplant shade that is shorter than I'd ever go for—I think of the term *teeny-bopper* when I look at it, but somehow it works. The bodice is done in rhinestones and white beads mimicking pearls. The top is cut into a sweetheart neckline, and it's strapless. Thankfully my boobs can hold it up!

My mom's earrings look spectacular with it, and they left my neck bare. The updo is artistically crafted, an intricate style with braids crisscrossing every which way. Soft tendrils float around my face and tickle my skin. The makeup is stellar with a smoky eye that makes my purple irises pop—although, the dress alone would've had the same effect. Not being able to help myself, I sniffle.

"Don't you dare cry!" Mal admonishes.

At that, I laugh, but tears have collected in my eyes anyway. Sammy is dabbing at hers, then Mal goes for a tissue and runs it under each of her own eyes.

I hadn't noticed until now that Sammy got dressed. She's wearing a little teal number with black strappy heels, and as I'm checking her out, Mal disappears to put her dress on. They both have their hair in updos—not as elaborate as mine, but no less breathtaking. Their makeup is flawless but more subtle than mine. It appears I'm meant to be the star tonight. Of course, I still have no idea why.

"Ready?" Mal asks when she returns in a slinky, sleeveless, short silver dress with silver heels.

"Sure! I have no idea what I'm supposed to be ready for, but at least I'll look good."

We all laugh and head for the door. It's cold outside, so we throw on our coats, and when we step out into the chilly night air, there's a limo waiting at the end of her driveway.

What in the world? Maybe I'm in some alternate universe because I feel like a belle going to a ball. If only I had a Prince Charming to meet me there.

Chapter 27: Walk my Way

Weston

It comes down to moments. Everything has led up to this moment. The plan I've been working on for about two months is about to be put to the test when Liv walks in here any second.

We're at the firehouse. Since the banquet hall is attached to the station, I've rented out the facility for the night and transformed it into a place fit for a king and queen. The event and momentous occasion is prom—it's sixteen years overdue. And the theme is *Time After Time*.

I've enlisted everyone's help to pull this off. Grant, Tom, and I have been decorating all day. Mal took care of dresses, hair and makeup. Grant picked up our tuxes. Sammy's job was to get Liv here under the guise they were attending a different type of party. Tom helped me finish final details and stayed at my apartment last night—Liv thinks he went on a trip.

We got my mom dressed up and out of the house; she's currently sitting at a banquet table looking like how I remember her from when I was a kid. She's alert tonight. Liv's dad is dapper in his tux, and he's keeping my mom company. The two seem to be good companions for one another because it's the first time I've seen a spark in my mom in years. I don't think there'll ever be a romantic relationship between them, but I'm hoping they can be friends.

Liv's friends from work are in attendance, as well as the members of my fire department. As I look around the fire hall at my handiwork, I'm extremely proud and grateful for the friends and family in my life. This night wouldn't have been possible without them.

There are strings of lights hanging from the ceiling, which is covered by gossamer and gives a soft glow, setting the perfect ambience. The color scheme is white, gold, and silver. We hung decorative wall clocks all over to keep with the theme. Gold linens cover the tables and are adorned by replica grandfather clocks, which serve as the centerpieces. The last touch—thanks to Robby's suggestion—are pearl beads scattered on the tables, adding a hint of elegance.

It all came together. I'm standing at the back of the room so I can watch Liv arrive. I'm not sure which dress Mal and Sammy put her in, but I'm hoping it's the purple one. Next to me, are two red-velvet-cushioned, gold painted thrones we borrowed from my former high school. It was generous of the theatre department to loan them out. And the crowning element is the red velvet runner I have leading from the entrance where guests walk under a trellis straight to the thrones.

There's a gift under the queen's chair. Again, something I can't take credit for—this one was Sammy's idea. It's something Liv has always wanted but never purchased for herself. I hope she'll accept my offering. But most of all, I hope she'll accept me. I'm ready to make the biggest apology and plea of my life.

Sweat dots my forehead and beads up above my lip. As I lightly dab at the moisture with my handkerchief, I marvel at the purple square—it represents Liv's eyes. I paired it with a matching bowtie. In my hand is an orchid corsage, and my boutonniere is the same delicate flower letting off a sweet scent.

The speakers crackle while the DJ does a sound check. There are finger foods, punch, and various snacks on the far left table, keeping tradition with typical prom accoutrements. A photo booth is on the other side, and there's also a setup for prom portraits by a professional photographer.

Liv's dad took care of ordering the limo. He insisted upon it because he said it was his duty since he didn't have the opportunity when she was in high school.

Any moment now, Liv will be walking through that door. Wiping my brow once more, I hear a commotion at the entrance. The DJ starts playing Cyndi Lauper's *Time After Time*.

The moment is here.

As Liv walks down the red carpet with her eyes darting around the room in disbelief, my heart beats frantically. She looks breathtaking. I literally feel like I can't breathe. And then I finally notice, she's in the purple dress.

I say aloud, "It's time."

***

Olivia

We pull up to the firehouse. The last time I was here was the day I lost the love of my life. "I can't; it's too much. I can't be here," I tell Mal and Sammy before I close my eyes, fighting the tears threatening to spill over.

Cowardice is not something I wish to portray, but this is the most painful place to visit. Why, of all places, are we here? I've gone along with this evening so far with little objection because I'm trying to be a good sport, but I don't think I can handle whatever's on the inside of the building.

Mal holds my hands and squeezes them. Tucking my lips into my mouth, I clamp down so I don't let out a cry.

"Wes is in there. This night is for you. I can't tell you anything more than that because it's a surprise. But he did all this…for you."

I wince when she says his name. "Did all what?" Still not grasping what's going on, my brows furrow when I add, "And don't tell me *you'll see.*"

She cracks a smile at my attempt to be angry with her. "I wouldn't dream of it. Now get your gorgeous self in there because you're not going to want to miss this—you've waited long enough, from what I hear."

Taking a deep, cleansing breath, I step out of the limo with the help of the driver, and we three girls walk to the entrance of the banquet hall. As we step inside the foyer, an attendant takes our coats and puts them in the cloak room. Sammy spins me around to check my hair and makeup, and that's when I finally hear the music coming from inside the banquet area, easily recognizing Cyndi Lauper's distinctive voice.

While we walk under the trellis and onto a plush red carpet, my eyes finally take in the scene. Scanning the room, everywhere I see are friends and family who have gathered for something special. The place is decorated beautifully with clocks lining the walls. And at the back of the building is a huge banner that reads, *2002 Prom Redo: Time After Time.*

Whimpering as I finally realize what I've walked into, I look down at my shoes because I'm so overwhelmed. My girls flank me, each grabbing one of my arms. Cheers ring out, and boisterous clapping fills my ears upon making my entrance.

When I follow the red carpet with my gaze to where—or I should say *whom*—it leads to, my intake of breath hurts because it's sharp and cutting. It's Wes standing at the end.

Wes.

Even though Mal told me he'd be here, I still wouldn't let my heart hope. I wouldn't let my brain register the possibility.

When I meet his eyes and see the most genuine smile he's ever worn with moisture shimmering in his eyes, I stop walking down the red path, taking a moment to stare and absorb it all. Infused with the very thing I was so afraid to embrace, hope stirs within.

The girls continue to walk me to the end. When we reach Wes, he falls at my feet. I hear him say under his breath, "God, you're so beautiful."

The feeling is mutual with the way he looks in his tux. He's too beautiful for words. Wes is on both knees. Seeing this man at my feet does not give me pleasure. We are supposed to be equals. We are supposed to be partners. So I join him, mirroring his position.

"What're you doing?" he asks me while laughing and shaking his head.

"I should be asking you the same thing."

All eyes are on us, and the music has been lowered to a soft background noise. Wes cups my cheeks in his hands and stares into my soul like he hasn't laid eyes on me in forever—it feels like it's been forever.

"I'm on my knees because I'd crawl through fire for you. I'm on my knees to beg. There's so much I need to say. Mostly things I'd like to discuss in private—I will finally answer all your questions. But publicly, I will tell you in front of everyone that I'm so very sorry for everything." He pauses a moment to take a deep breath.

"Liv, I didn't think I was worthy of your love. You're the light in the darkness. You're the kindest, most loyal, most gorgeous woman I've ever met. I love you more than life itself. Please give me a chance to make it up to you and show you that I can be a man worthy of your love?"

He doesn't need to beg. He doesn't need to ask. The answer is always going to be *yes* when it comes to him.

He said it, he finally said it—*I love you*. That's all that matters.

Without giving a verbal response, I move in and kiss his lips hungrily, starved for him. He kisses me back fiercely. My knees are aching from kneeling on the hardwood, but I don't care. Red knees and scuff marks to my shoes are worth it when I'm in his arms.

When he releases my lips, he rests his forehead against mine. Then the unrelenting cheers begin to echo through the hall. The music is turned up, and the DJ comes across the speakers welcoming everyone to the "2002 Prom Redo."

The DJ opens the dance floor, and bodies start moving to the beat, while some others have migrated to the refreshment and food tables. Wes stands up and offers his hand to help me up; I teeter slightly, still trembling from our kiss. After weeks of being miserable, I feel like I'm in a dream. Suddenly, all the hurt and pain are forgotten when everything I ever wanted is right here in this room—my family, my friends, my love.

I whisper in his ear, "You owe the biggest apology to Ash. I can't imagine that little guy hasn't missed you."

He chuckles and then looks sheepish. "Confession time: I've seen him a lot over the weeks. All those times your dad was watching him at his house, well, I'd stop over and visit both of them."

"What?"

"Liv, not a day has gone by where I haven't been in your life in some way. My presence has been there this whole time; it just wasn't visible. If I was going to win you back, I had to go all out. I've been planning this for almost two months."

A part of me wants to be upset that I've been in agony all this time, and he could've stopped it sooner. Another part is telling me to get over it because I've spent long enough being unhappy, and in the grand scheme of things, I got what I wanted in the end—him.

"You have a lot of making up to do for allowing me to suffer all this time," I tell him, and my eyes become piercing slits so he knows he's in deep trouble.

"I know, baby. My apology list is long. It's not right what I've done, and I promise I'll explain a lot more later. I also needed to be in the right mindset to get you back. Working on myself first was important."

This man amazes me. I wanted to help heal him, but the fact that he was able to recognize this and do it for the sake of himself, his family, and for me, makes me love him even more. I'm so very proud, and I look forward to hearing about it.

"I have one very important question, Miss Watson."

"Oh yeah, what's that?"

"Will you please be my prom date?"

Now I'm crying. I can't help myself as the stream of tears drip down onto the swells of my breasts. He looks at where they've fallen and takes out his pocket square to wipe them away.

"I'll take that as a *yes*."

"Yes. God, yes!"

We kiss again, then he produces a vibrant orchid corsage. After sliding the band on my wrist, I beam. I'm a teenage girl with her first—and only—crush all over again.

"I have two more surprises for you, baby."

"Oh my God. It's not even Christmas."

He reaches under the chair to our left. Well, technically it's a throne, so I imagine this is for the prom king and queen—I have no doubt Wes will at some point announce those titles belong to us. He really pulled out all the stops. My heart is so full right now, knowing I'm loved and knowing we can make it through anything that comes our way. We've already survived the hardest parts.

When he rights himself, he has a black leather-bound jewelry box in his hand, large enough to house a necklace.

"Wes, you know you don't have to buy me anything. All I've ever wanted was you."

"And that's why I love you even more. Believe me, all I want is you too, but this is something you've always wanted. Please let me enjoy treating you whenever I can. I know I don't make a whole lot of money, but I can afford to buy you some nice things once in a while."

Beyond moved by this gift—whatever it is—I take the box from his hands. My fingers run across the decorative silver flower embossed across the top. Gently, I lift the lid, and what awaits me inside is a set of beautiful pearls. Looking up at him and then back down at the necklace, I'm stunned.

"Are these what I think they are?"

"Yes, Olivia. To go with your mother's earrings, here's the saltwater pearls you've always wanted. What'd Sammy call them? Your *power pearls*?"

Now I'm crying all over again. Mal's going to throw a fit when she sees I ruined her makeup.

"I take it you like them?"

"No. I don't just *like* them, I *love* them. Thank you."

Looping my arms around his neck while still holding the box, I pepper him with kisses, and then kiss him more deeply, passionately, showing him all my love and thanks. When we separate, he takes out the necklace and fastens it around my neck—no wonder the girls left my neck bare. This man has thought of every little detail this entire evening, and it's only beginning.

"May I have this dance—the one I've waited a lifetime for?"

"Wes…," I start to say and then my breath hitches. "You never have to ask. I'll forever and always be your dance partner."

He gives me a goofy grin that I swoon over as we head to the dance floor.

After an hour of him spinning and twirling me around, we make our way throughout the room so I can thank everyone for coming. We spy my dad sitting with Wes's mom, and I smile thinking how the two could be good for one another. Dad needs to socialize more, and Judy needs to socialize period.

By the time we work our way around the whole room, grab a snack and a drink, the DJ comes back on the speaker. "Wes, I believe you have an announcement to make? The mic is yours."

He smiles my way as I give him one of those *what are you up to?* looks. Then, he pecks me on the cheek and heads toward the DJ. Once he grabs the mic, he turns toward the crowd to address everyone.

"You all know why we're here tonight. It's because I never got to go to the prom and neither did Liv. I gave her one surprise a little while ago, and now I'm going to give her the second."

Oh my God, I forgot there was a second!

"Liv, how do you feel about Christmas in Hawaii?"

Everyone gasps, and the oohs and ahs are heard in every direction over what he just proposed. Here I thought Sammy and Tom were going by themselves, and they invited me out of pity. Immediately, I seek her out in the crowd and find her clinging to Tom with a knowing grin.

After I mouth "you're in big trouble" to her, she sticks her tongue out at me. Looking back to Wes, he gestures for me to come to him.

"So, is that a *yes* to Hawaii, baby?"

"Yes," I squeak out, and everyone claps.

He hands the mic back to the DJ, who apparently has one more thing to say. "Before we get back to dancing, it's tradition that we crown the Prom King and Queen. The votes are in, and you've selected Mr. Weston Thorpe and Miss Olivia Watson as your royal representatives. Congratulations to the happy couple."

More cheers—it's deafening. In a moment, someone is going to have to pinch me so I finally accept this isn't a dream.

Once we're crowned and seated on our respective thrones, Wes shares more news with me. "Besides Tom and Sammy, we're also bringing Mal, Grant, your dad, and my mom to Hawaii with us."

"Are you serious?"

"Of course."

Squealing, I pepper his face with kisses once more. My enthusiasm knocks his crown off his head, and we laugh at the spectacle. "Wes, this is the most amazing evening. I can't believe you did all this."

"Baby, I'm only sorry I didn't do it sooner. But there's more."

"Oh my God, how could there possibly be more?"

"You'll see at the after party in your bedroom."

Chapter 28: Clam Shell

Olivia

"Yes, just like that. Yes," I tell Wes as he's working his cock into me from behind.

Being on all fours in doggy-style is an otherworldly experience. We've been making love all night, but I'll never tire of it. Never will I tire of these sensations and the flames of ecstasy scorching my body each time he enters me.

"Fuck! Baby, you're so tight. You're so damn wet. That's right. Squeeze my dick with that delicious pussy."

Moaning, his balls slap against the lips of my sex, producing an erotic sound to match his sexy grunts as we're both about to come. There's no greater feeling than knowing he's inside me bare. It's amazing I still have energy after the prom we attended earlier tonight, but for him, I'll muster up the energy each and every time he's willing to work my body over.

"I'm about to come, baby," he rasps in my ear as he licks the shell of it.

"Ahh!" I explode.

Not being able to hold himself back, he releases and ruts into my center like he can't get deep enough, leaving us both trembling with aftershocks. I collapse, and he slumps on my back. He eventually moves us to our sides, adjusting me so I'm more comfortable, then he chuckles at the condition I'm in.

"It's not funny. You're going to kill me," I whine with my face firmly planted in the mattress.

"Death by sex? Not a bad way to go."

"True."

"Shower time?"

"Not on your life, Tiger!"

He laughs heartily, kisses my head, and pulls the covers over us. We'll shower in the morning and have the talk he alluded to earlier.

My eyes are heavy; I'm already slipping under. When I finally drift off, I dream about clocks and how we have all the time in the world to be together.

***

Weston

I'm sipping coffee and sitting at Liv's kitchen table, taking turns petting Ash. Robby dropped the little guy back off before the prom started. The pup moves from chair to chair at our feet, waiting for attention.

"God, Wes. I'm so sorry. I can't believe he wrote you."

With Liv having just learned about my dad's letter, she bites her lip. There's sadness swimming in her eyes for me.

"Honestly, baby, it's okay. The letter was a good thing. I'm finally able to move on."

"I'm so proud of you."

"Thank you, Liv. Believe me, I'm not opposed to seeing a therapist, and that may be a possibility in the future. It's not that I believe I magically healed myself and my demons are slayed. What I do believe is the letter was my salvation."

Taking another sip, I sigh knowing we need to have the next leg of conversation in order to put everything behind us and clear the air. "You ready to talk about what happened the day Jarrod showed up to see me at the station?"

She winces at the reminder and nods *yes*.

"I'll start. That day, he said things that triggered my past. I was already in a bad place at the time, feeling like I wasn't good enough for you. After just finding out about Mal and Grant, it sent me right to the edge of the cliff. What Jarrod said, though, brought it all back to the surface—that's when I went over the edge."

Needing a second to collect myself, I press on, "Regardless of the shitty things he said and how he acted, I should've come to find you because I was fearful he was going to do something. His behavior was strange. But I was too paralyzed and selfish, so I went home to escape. Then when you came over, it was easier to push you away rather than deal with reality and face the truth. I'm sorry. It was fucked up."

She puts her hand on my forearm and looks lovingly into my eyes.

"I understand. We all make mistakes. I made a big one too. I could've saved us a lot of trouble if I'd told you beforehand about Jarrod's...issues."

My grip on my coffee mug handle tightens, then I loosen it, realizing I'll break the damn thing. I have a feeling I'm not going to like what she has to say. "What did he do?"

She swallows and sighs. "There's no proof he did some of this, so I'm only speculating, but he was watching me at times because he'd text me and know you were with me. I think he punched a hole in the wall at work, and then his behavior toward the end was erratic and creepy."

"Damnit, Liv! You should've told me."

She winces. *Shit, I didn't mean to snap at her.*

"Baby, I'm not mad at you. I just can't believe you didn't tell me something so important, and you put yourself in a dangerous situation. But him coming to see me wasn't your fault. If I'd known he had issues, you never would've had to see him again. I would've confronted him."

"See, that's why I didn't tell you. I was so afraid you'd do something you'd regret. And I didn't know what Jarrod was capable of. At times, I was worried he was going to do something to get you fired or mess with you somehow."

What she's saying makes sense. Jarrod tried to bait me that day, and I still believe he wanted me to assault him.

Thinking about her love for me, my shoulders unbunch and my tone softens. *She was protecting me.* It's a case of hypocrisy on my end because I didn't tell her about my dad in order to protect her.

"God, I love you. I can't believe you were trying to protect me, Liv."

"How could I not?"

Standing up, I pull her into my arms and carry her to the countertop—the couch and her bedroom are too far away. Hiking up her long T-shirt, I rip her panties right at her hipbone near her strawberry birthmark I love so much, and yank down my pants. My erection enters her in a split second, and I'm buried to the hilt.

This is what we do. This is how we are. I'm always needing her, always seeking her out. I want to comfort her physically, emotionally, and verbally—she does the same for me. Finally, I tell her the words that have been there for so long unsaid.

"Liv—my everything plus infinity."

***

Olivia

December 29, 2018

We leave tomorrow to go back home. It's hard to say goodbye to paradise. Ten days is all we get on the island of Honolulu.

Christmas was magical. Spending it with my favorite people was nothing short of a miracle. And Wes made it all happen.

Standing on the balcony of our hotel room, watching the sun set as the sheer white curtains billow, I'm in awe of the horizon. The sun meets the land and water, casting perfection upon the earth. Never have I seen anything more glorious than the bright orange of the fiery sun and the aqua of the water.

The hula dancing, swimming, nightly luaus at the hotel, sightseeing, and walks on the beach are more than I could've ever imagined. As sad as I am to be leaving, it doesn't mean the magic will disappear—Wes and I make our own magic. We'll be home in time to ring in the New Year in Jersey, and I'm excited to start 2019 with my man. We're talking about him moving in with me. It makes sense since I have the house, and he can end the lease on his apartment.

We couldn't bring Ash on the trip, so he's being watched by the chief and his wife. Upon our return, Wes will volunteer more at the shelter with me, and we're contemplating adopting another animal. Things may seem to be moving quickly again in our relationship, but it's on our terms and our schedule—so it's what we make of it.

There's no doubt in my mind that our past has been laid to rest. The things holding us back as individuals—and as a couple—are no longer a threat. My hand moves to my throat where I lovingly caress the beautiful pearls he gave me. Then, I rub at my earring, telling my mom up above I'm thinking of her.

Two arms wrap around me from behind, and I lean back against Wes's strong frame. The steady, comforting rhythm of his heart beats at my back. And the calming rise and fall of his chest almost lulls me to sleep. This is home to me—his arms.

His scent enters my nose, and I could get drunk off it. After nuzzling my neck, he kisses it. Smiling, I spin around to meet his eyes.

"Come with me for a moment, baby? I want to show you something."

Nodding, I follow him into the gorgeous bedroom covered in white linens. The walls have a decorative Loulu palm design, which we had the opportunity to learn about from one of the native stories. Sitting on the duvet cover are dozens of fresh flowers—he knows I love fresh flowers as a reminder of my mom. Together, the bouquets form a heart on the bed. In the middle of the heart is a clam shell. *That's strange.*

When we approach the bed, Wes picks up the small object and hands it to me. Sure enough, it is a clam shell with both halves intact.

"Open it," he encourages while smirking.

"Don't I need a knife or something to shuck a clam?" I joke.

"Nah. This one's already been open before. If you notice, it's clean. It even smells like lemons."

"I'll take your word for it. So, if it's already been opened, what do you expect me to find?" I'm just giving him a hard time. It's fun to rib him since Grant's not around at the moment to do it.

"Hopefully, your future."

My smiling face now turns into one of surprise and confusion. *Could this mean what I think it does?* Swallowing, I pull apart the shell and almost drop the halves when I see what's inside.

With all my attention going to the innocuous object in my hand, I failed to realize Wes is down on bended knee.

Sitting on the smooth, white surface on the inside of one half-shell, is a stunning ring with a silver band and a single diamond in the middle, flanked by a pearl on each side. These three beauties in the setting have so much meaning. Not only can it represent my past, present, and future, but it could also represent the three people in my life whom I treasure most— Wes, my mom, and my dad.

Seeing that I'm sobbing and barely able to see through my tears, Wes chuckles and grabs my free hand so I have to look down at him.

"Olivia Kay Watson, you've kept me waiting long enough. You're my Prom Queen, the love of my life, and my everything plus infinity. You'll be loved every second of every day. Please marry me, baby?"

"Yes! A million times yes!"

Tackling him to the floor, we kiss passionately for a good while. When we sit up, he locates my ring, which fell to the floor during my attack on him, and he slides it on my finger. Holding out my hand, I admire the most perfect ring in the history of jewelry. I also cherish the clam shell; he's so thoughtful and adorable. Although, I don't have the heart to tell him most pearls come from oysters.

"So, when can I marry you Miss Watson?"

"God, I'd marry you tonight if I could."

"It's funny you mention it, because it just so happens I have arranged an evening wedding on the beach in the event you wanted to do it before we left."

"What? Are you serious?"

"Always."

By now I should know he's always two steps ahead of me. I shake my head in awe and swipe at the remainder of my tears. "Of course you planned it. You're amazing, Weston Thorpe."

"No, I'm not. I'm just a man in love."

"Now I know why you invited everyone on the trip."

"Well, I wanted to spend Christmas with all of them, but they came for that reason as well."

"What if I would've said *no*?"

"There was no chance of that because I would've carried you down the aisle anyway."

Giggling at his remark, I know he's also serious. Then, my face contorts into a frown.

"Baby, what's wrong?"

"Oh, nothing. It's silly. I just didn't bring anything nice to wear that's fit for our wedding. But it's not important as long as we get to say *I do*."

He's grinning wider than the night of our prom redo. *What's he up to?*

A knock at the door halts my curiosity as Wes goes to answer it. A moment later, Sammy and Mal return with him. Sammy's carrying a garment bag, and Mal has a huge makeup case in hand.

"Oh my God, Wes! You did it again." My girls are here, ready to style me once more.

Wes walks over to me and kisses my lips softly.

"In a few hours, you'll be Mrs. Weston Thorpe, and my life will finally be complete."

Wrapping my arms around his neck, I stare into the gray—the gray I love so much. Raising my eyes to the sky, I thank my mom for sending me this man. He's a rare one, all right, and he makes me feel what my mom always hoped for when she said *"Be the lead in your own movie, not a supporting cast member."* When I walk down the aisle tonight, I'll have everything I've ever wanted and needed.

I'll use Wes's word…our story is *timeless*.

Epilogue

Olivia

Seventeen months later...

My rounded belly still amazes me. As I stare at it in the mirror, I mold my hands around the basketball-sized mound under my silky maternity dress. It's a beautiful May day, and the open windows allow a lovely breeze to blow through my long hair.

"How's our baby doing?" Wes asks as he watches me in the mirror.

"He or she is doing fabulous, Daddy."

He kisses my shoulder and puts his arms around me. He rests his hands on top of mine on my belly. "You ready to find out if it's a he or she, baby?"

"Absolutely."

We're having a gender reveal party today as well as my baby shower. Deciding to do both events at once was my idea. I'm due in six weeks, so it's now or never. We're having the party at our house. We decided to keep my place since we loved its character and charm, and it's perfect for raising a family.

Ash and Cinders both bark at our feet, and we laugh because they always want to be included. Cinders is the newest addition to our family. She's a miniature pinscher mixed with some other small breed. She and Ash are the best of friends.

Everyone's waiting out back on our deck for our appearance. I have no idea what the decorations are since Sammy and Mal took care of everything. Sammy's seven-month-old daughter is no doubt in the arms of

Judy or my dad, who are both preparing for grandparenthood. Judy has really turned her life around and is more or less normal now. She lives with us, and we're happy to have her here.

Grant and Mal moved in together and bought a house down the street from us. They got engaged this past Valentine's Day and will be married sometime next year. Mal, with Grant's help, opened up her own salon, and she and Sammy do styling for weddings and other events on the weekend—it's proving to be a successful side-business.

I'm still with my engineering firm, but I cut back my hours so I could enjoy my pregnancy and upcoming motherhood. Wes and I were worried at first about my family history, so I was tested for cervical cancer. The doctors will keep an eye on things as the years go on, but all is well for now. Knowing my mother is watching over me gives me peace, and I'm sure she'll also watch over my child.

There is someone who won't be here today. Wes's dad did pass away right after we got back from our wedding in Hawaii. I can't say I'm sorry I never met him, but I can say I'm sorry he is gone from this world. Dallas's new wife had informed us through a letter. We've all sort of become pen pals now.

I was surprised Wes did write his dad back before his passing. I'm not really sure what was in the letter; it's private and something Wes will share if and when he's ever ready to do so. Mal was upset with her brother for writing Dallas back after agreeing not to, but she also understood his reasons. My husband is a good man through and through.

We make our way downstairs and onto the deck where we're met by all of our friends and family. Sure enough, Judy is holding the baby, whom Sammy named Lulu since she was conceived on our trip to the island.

After we socialize for a bit, eat, open my gifts, and have cake, it's time for the gender reveal. I'm nervous and excited. Having no idea how we'll be informed of the gender, I look to Wes because I'm sure he has a plan.

He leads me out to the front of the house where one of his firetrucks is sitting on the street. Looking at him in confusion, he motions for me to wait a moment.

Keith and Rick point the fire hose to the sky, while Ethan mans the truck. They count down from ten, and when they turn it on, the spray that comes out rains down pink in my front yard. Everyone starts screaming, and I realize we're having a girl.

"It's a girl?" I ask Wes as he walks back over to where I'm standing—out of the spray, of course.

"Yes, we're having a mini-you, God help us," he jokes.

"Hey, I'm the most amazing woman. You said so yourself."

"That I did." He smiles, then kisses my lips, and finally pecks me on the cheek.

We watch the spray for a few more moments before they turn it off. He explains to me that they filled the tank with a special dye.

Once the firetruck drives away to return to the station, someone in the crowd asks what we're going to name *her*. Wes and I smile at one another as he grabs my hand. Then my handsome husband turns to announce our baby's name:

"Pearl Beatrice Thorpe."

The End

Acknowledgments

Of course, I love *all* my books, but this one has a particular soft spot in my heart. It's such a departure from my normal writing style. Anyone who knows me, expects I always inject some levity into my stories to break up the intensity. And laced throughout my words, you'll always find whimsical elements along with the sweet, tender, and steamy sprinklings. I held back a lot of my raunchy bits for this book, as well as a lot of my puns and typical humor. You're welcome! With this story, I really dug deep to incorporate another level. I hope I delivered a tale that stays with you long after you close your book or turn off your device.

My husband truly is my real-life hero because of his military service and volunteerism as a firefighter and EMT. He's out there each and every day defending our borders or responding to calls. I'm the luckiest woman to have found him at such a young age (we met when we were nine), and we've had so many wonderful years together—I look forward to so many more! I could never produce the stories I do without his patience, support, love, and encouragement.

My two little boys motivate me to go after my dreams. I'll continue to do that for my kiddos. I love them more than life.

Mom (my alpha reader), you championing me is the ultimate sign of who a mother is. I hope I've made you proud and can do the same for my kids one day. "We got a break, hot dog!"

To the rest of my family and friends, thank you for giving me reasons to keep on writing. I know I can be crazy when we're mid-conversation, and suddenly I'm scribbling something down so I can use it in a scene later on for one of my characters; I appreciate you indulging me. But I draw a lot of inspiration from my personal life, and I wouldn't have that without each and every one of you.

To my incredible team of beta readers (Brandy, Alyne, Erica, Carolyn), editor (Krista), cover designer, photographer, models, PR (EJ), and book tribe (KB 101), words can't express my sincerest thanks. You render me speechless because I'm in awe of what each of you brings forth in this process. We did it again!

And I always save the best for last—my readers. I wouldn't exist in the literary world if it weren't for you. Thank you for reading my stories, for believing that love is what guides us in life, and no matter what, we all deserve our very own ever-after. Liv and Wes helped me see—not just anything—but *everything* is possible.

Hearts & Smiles,

Kara Liane

P.S. ~
Again, anyone who knows me, understands my passion for poetry. I couldn't fit this poem in during the story, but I love it, so it's going to be put here, lovingly, at the end.

The Road Calls Me
It's a road that keeps calling,
It's a place that keeps talking,
It's a road that keeps calling, calling my name.
It's a path I keep walking,
It's a face that keeps gawking,
It's a path I keep walking, walking my way.
It's a course I keep stalking,
It's a pace I keep balking.
It's a course I keep stalking, stalking all day.
—K.L.

About the Author

Kara Liane is a lover of all things romance. She holds several degrees, including a master's in management from Wayland Baptist University. Her husband since 2002 proudly serves in the military. The family, which includes twin elementary-age sons and two adult dogs, resides in New Jersey.

Stay connected with Kara Liane by visiting her web site: www.karaliane.com You can also sign up for her newsletter: http://bit.ly/2j8lbjr

www.ingramcontent.com/pod-product-compliance
Lightning Source LLC
Chambersburg PA
CBHW020424180626
46812CB00003B/1131